As light as a feather, she laid her palm against his jaw.

"I do worry about you, Sean. I worry that you don't see the good in yourself. I worry that you take on far too much responsibility for someone who says he doesn't want any at all. I worry that you mistake safe choices for good ones."

Safe choices. Yeah, that was what he'd been making all these years, and where had it gotten him? He couldn't help but think that taking a few risks couldn't have landed him in any more trouble than he was already in and might have been a hell of a lot more fun, too.

But he didn't want to think about any of that. Time was limited, and he had a beautiful, sexy woman waiting to be kissed in a way he hadn't kissed a woman in a long time. She smelled of tequila, Mexican food and something delicate and expensive, and her shoulders were slender beneath his hands as he leaned closer.

Dear Reader,

For a long time now, I've been wanting to write Sophy Marchand's story. She's been in every Copper Lake book, I think, since the series actually began taking place in Copper Lake. (The first two didn't.) I always knew who her hero would be—bad boy Sean Holigan, come home from wherever he escaped to—but I couldn't quite get a handle on their story.

Until I gave Sean a sister in jail and two nieces in need of a family. The rest of it just fell into place.

You know how kids in fiction tend to be better behaved than real-life kids? (It *is* fiction, after all.) Not Daisy and Dahlia. They're hair-raising, patience-testing, tantrum-throwing, scheming, break-your-heart little hooligans who are determined to drive their foster mother—Sophy—right to the edge of Crazy Town. I absolutely fell in love with them. So did Sophy, no surprise. So did Sean.

I read something somewhere that said no matter how big and tough and emotionally guarded a man might be, somewhere there's a small child who can wrap him around her little finger. In this case, the wrapping is mutual: not only do the girls work their way into Sean's heart, but he does the same with them. (And, of course, with Sophy.)

If you need a laugh and maybe a bit of a cry, come visit my favorite town and see how it all works out.

Marilyn Pappano

UNDERCOVER IN COPPER LAKE

—

Marilyn Pappano

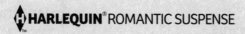
HARLEQUIN®ROMANTIC SUSPENSE

Recycling programs
for this product may
not exist in your area.

ISBN-13: 978-0-373-27886-2

UNDERCOVER IN COPPER LAKE

Copyright © 2014 by Marilyn Pappano

Printed in U.S.A.

Books by Marilyn Pappano

Harlequin Romantic Suspense

Silhouette Romantic Suspense

MARILYN PAPPANO

has spent most of her life growing into the person she was meant to be, but isn't there yet. She's been blessed by family—her husband, their son, his lovely wife and a grandson who is almost certainly the most beautiful and talented baby in the world—and friends, along with a writing career that's made her one of the luckiest people around. Her passions, besides those already listed, include the pack of wild dogs who make their home in her house, fighting the good fight against the weeds that make up her yard, killing the creepy-crawlies that slither out of those weeds and, of course, anything having to do with books.

For the kids in my life, some grown, some still working on it, who gave life to Daisy and Dahlia:
Brandon, Lauren, Kate and Kevin
Kadon, Cameron, Gavin and Declan

Chapter 1

A stiff breeze blew in off the harbor, carrying with it the smells of salt and fish and pollution, along with a chilly hint of fall on its way. Sean Holigan stood in the shadows of two buildings, face to the water, and toyed with the cigarette he held. Though he hadn't had a smoke in six and a half months, the temptation to light it was there, the desire no less than it had been 195 days before.

But the flare of the lighter, the glowing end of the cigarette and the acrid blue-gray smoke would be like a neon sign pointing straight at him. Not the best idea, since the last place anyone expected him to be at 3:00 a.m. on a Sunday was on the docks. If his boss or their buddies found him there, it was a sure bet he would pay the price for it. He just didn't know how big a price that would be.

Maybe, probably, death.

Fog swirled around the two massive warehouses that shielded him and turned the cargo containers stacked between them and the water into islands of dull metal. The damp seeped into his jacket and misted across his skin. It darkened the thin paper of the cigarette wrapper and increased the stiffness in the middle three fingers of his left hand. Ever since he'd gotten them caught between an engine and a car frame three years ago, those fingers had developed an aversion to cold and damp.

He'd been waiting more than ten minutes without bothering to check his watch when he sensed rather than heard someone approaching. Like him, Alexandra Baker was always early to these meetings. Unlike him, she completed a thorough check of the area before appearing before him, tonight from around a corner, like a magician's illusion.

She wore dark clothing, dark shoes, a dark hood covering her white-blond hair and casting her pale face in darkness. She could stand absolutely still on a night like this and blend completely into the background. The way she moved and walked and talked was unnaturally quiet, still. *Illusion* was a good description of her. Since she'd first approached him three months ago, she seemed about as real as a dream.

A bad dream.

"Why do you tempt yourself?" she asked, her voice quiet but not soft, her question personal but lacking curiosity.

He glanced at the cigarette, shrugged and slid it

into his jacket pocket. "Why do you get me up in the middle of the night?"

"Because I know Kolinski's tucked safely in bed."

Craig Kolinski. His boss. His best bud for thirteen years. The man responsible for Sean's relatively comfortable life. The man he was betraying every time he spoke to Baker.

"He's going to ask you to look into something for him tomorrow," she went on. "It'll mean going out of town for a while. You'll agree."

Sean didn't ask how she knew Craig's plans. He figured his boss had more bugs than a Volkswagen plant, thanks to the Drug Enforcement Administration: his house, his cars, his office above the garage, probably even the garage bays themselves. Sean hoped whoever listened to all those hours of tapes got a headache from the constant whine of pneumatic tools.

"Where out of town?"

If it were anyone else, he would have said Baker hesitated, but since she was the calm, collected ice queen, he would call it a pause instead. "Georgia."

A chill passed through him that had nothing to do with the temperature. He'd grown up in Georgia and had left the first chance he'd gotten, swearing he would never return. Nothing, not the family he'd left there, not even the father who'd died there eight years ago, had lured him back.

"Where in Georgia?"

Ice queen or not, this time she flat-out hesitated. She and the DEA knew damn near everything about him, including where he was from, why he'd left and why he'd go hundreds of miles out of his way to avoid the place. They knew Georgia wasn't an acceptable answer. They'd already demanded too much from him and he'd given it, but this…

"Copper Lake," she said with the first hint of emotion he'd ever heard from her, as if her frozen little heart knew what a huge request—order—this was. But it was just a hint. Emotion didn't rule Alexandra Baker. She didn't sympathize, never felt regret, never let feelings get in the way. She was committed 100 percent to her job, and by God, she would do what she had to do.

Which meant everyone around her would do what they had to do.

"No." He never thought of the place if he could avoid it, never considered it home. Home was a place where a person belonged, where he fit in, where people wanted him around. Copper Lake was a nightmare that had taken eighteen years to escape.

Baker didn't say anything.

"I didn't have much of a choice in ratting out Craig." There were limits to what he could overlook, and his boss had stomped all over them. "But I'm not doing this. I'm not going back to Copper Lake."

"Kolinski will ask you to go, and you will. You don't have a choice this time, either."

The calm disinterest in her voice, as if the idea that she wouldn't get her way had never occurred to her, got under his skin. He shoved his hand through his hair, dislodging water. "The hell I don't. I've told you everything I know about Craig's business and his personal life. But there's no freaking way in hell that I'm going to—"

"It's about Maggie."

That sucked the air from his lungs. He hadn't heard his little sister's name in more years than he wanted to count. He tried not to think about her, either, in a situation worse all those years ago than his own. She'd cried when he left and begged him to take her with him, and, bastard that he was, he'd promised to send for her just as soon as he got settled.

Did it make any difference that part of him *had* wanted to take her with him and give her a better life? That he hadn't known he would land in prison, just like every Holigan man before him?

No, no difference. Because from the time he was twelve years old, he'd intended to leave everything behind, including Maggie. He'd wanted a life with no responsibilities but himself. He'd wanted to escape the curse of his family, and how could he have done that dragging his baby sister along?

"What about Maggie?" His voice was rough, harsh, in the night air.

"Did you know she's involved romantically with one of Kolinski's people?" She didn't pause long enough for him to answer. She already knew the answer. "She lived with the guy before his most recent arrest. They trust him to keep his mouth shut about the business. They don't trust her. You know what happens to people they don't trust."

He'd seen it for himself once. Imagining his sister in that position, terrified, on her knees, begging for her life... Bile rose in his throat, and for one moment he thought he was going to puke right there in front of Baker. Nothing like showing weakness to someone who was as cold-blooded and single-minded as Craig was.

"He'll call you into the garage today and tell you to go to Copper Lake. To keep an eye on Maggie. To determine whether she can hurt him. He'll use your information to figure out the best way to deal with her."

"Am I supposed to believe you'll use it to keep her safe?"

Baker nodded, the action practically lost in the folds of the oversize hood.

How the hell had Maggie caught the attention of one of Craig's dealers in the first place? And why in hell had that dealer been in Copper Lake long enough to even meet her?

Leverage, maybe. Sean had been loud in his opposition to Craig's first expansion of the business, to the point that he'd almost walked away from the garage he'd worked his ass off to help save from bankruptcy. Craig had made a few concessions, keeping what he laughingly called his parts supply service separate from the garage and keeping the next expansion to himself.

And maybe sending someone to Copper Lake to find something to hold over Sean if it became necessary.

He shook his head slowly. "I won't do it." But even as he heard his own words, he recognized them for the lie they were. Maggie was the only person in the world who could make him return to the town he'd run away from.

"We'll be in touch with you once you get there." More sure of him than he was of himself, Baker tugged the hood forward another inch, then melted into the darkness. He didn't hear her footsteps as she retreated, couldn't even sense her presence. She stepped around the corner and was gone.

He let his head fall back until it connected with the warehouse wall with a solid thunk. How the hell had he come to this? Was this the payoff for betraying a friend? For abandoning his family as if they'd never existed?

He snorted derisively. Craig was a friend, yeah— one who'd made a fortune in stolen vehicles and drugs. What felt like a betrayal to Sean was really just the regular action any normal person would take. If Craig had dragged Maggie into this to control Sean, *that* was a betrayal.

Sweet damnation, all he'd wanted was a regular life: a job that didn't make him want to shoot himself; enough money to pay his bills and have a little fun on the side; a place to live that wasn't falling down around him. He hadn't wanted any attachments to people, places or things. Drinking buddies, not friends. Hookups, not girlfriends. No obligations, no emotional connections, no having to think of anyone besides himself.

And he'd had that for a lot of years. Until three months ago, when he'd stopped by the garage late one night to pick up the cell phone he'd left behind and walked in on Craig shooting a man in the back of the head.

Everything had gone to hell after that.

Tomorrow he was going to another kind of hell, better known as Copper Lake. He would hate every damn second of it, but he would go and do whatever was necessary to protect Maggie. He'd let her down once before.

He wouldn't do it again.

* * *

For Sophy Marchand's entire life, Sunday morning had meant church, and though she'd missed the past two Sundays, she vowed that stopped today. She stood in the guest room of her second-floor apartment, one hand on her hip, watching the two little girls snuggling together in one of the twin-size beds, eyes closed, lips parted, looking angelic in sleep.

Except they weren't asleep, and God bless them, there was absolutely nothing angelic about them.

"Dahlia, Daisy, this is the last warning. Get up now, or we'll be late to church."

One of them—Dahlia, she thought—made a sound that was more snort than snore, but neither moved. No lashes fluttering, no eyes shifting beneath their lids, no twitch of their mouths.

You are the most incompetent foster mother in the history of the world, Sophy chastised herself, but that didn't stop her from lifting her free hand, fingers wrapped around vivid yellow plastic, and squirting both girls in the face with cool water. It was a trick her grandmother had used when trying to rouse five recalcitrant boys to do their chores, and it proved effective.

Daisy, the younger, slighter child, shrieked and dived under the covers, while Dahlia, older by a year, sprang upright and fixed a mutinous glower on Sophy. She refused to swipe the fine mist from her face but instead folded her thin arms over her chest. "You could've just woke us up."

"I woke you up. Three times." Sophie set the spray bottle on the table just outside the bedroom door, then went to the closet. "You've got just enough time to brush your teeth, comb your hair and get dressed. Hustle, now."

Dahlia grumbled as she pushed back the blanket, exposing Daisy to the sunlight that filtered through the sheer curtains at the windows. Her black hair in a tangle, Daisy scrubbed her fists over her eyes. "What about breakfast? I'm hungry."

"You could have had breakfast if you'd gotten up the first three times I was in here. Now there's no time." Of course, there were protein bars waiting on the counter beside Sophy's purse. She would never send them off without something to eat, though they didn't know that yet. Before they'd come to stay with her nearly three weeks ago, their previous experience hadn't included anything like consistency, stability or being a priority for anyone, not even their mother.

The thought sent an all-too-personal pang through Sophy. She knew how it felt to have a father who didn't want you and a mother who couldn't take care of you, and she wouldn't wish it on anyone.

She pulled a hanger holding a pastel dress from each side of the closet. Daisy's was white with her favorite cartoon characters, while Dahlia's was simple, a pale green shift with a forest-green ribbon that served as a belt and a three-quarter-sleeved sweater in the same shade.

Daisy's natural response on seeing her dress was a smile of pleasure, but after an elbow poke from Dahlia, she wiped it away and scrunched her face into a frown that matched her sister's. "We have to wear that?" Dahlia asked.

"Yes, you do." Sophy hung each dress on hooks on

the closet door, then gestured toward the bathroom. "Teeth, hair, dress. Go."

As they stomped across the hall and into the bathroom, her phone rang from the kitchen counter. Her heels made soft taps on the aged wood floor as she strode to the phone, picking it up on the fourth ring.

"Are you skipping church again today, or did you decide to catch the later service?" her mother asked without a greeting.

"Uh, no, Mom, we're just running a little behind."

"How are the children doing?" Caution seeped through Rae Marchand's voice. It underlaid everything she and Dad had said to Sophy from the moment she'd told them she was becoming a foster parent and that her first kids would be the five- and six-year-old Holigan girls.

"They're getting ready now. They've never been to church before, so they're not eager for the experience. They've been dragging their feet."

I want to give back, Mom, she'd told her. *Someone fostered me when I needed it, and you and Dad adopted me. I just want to pay that along.*

Rae had choked up. *You've got a good heart, and I love you for that. But Maggie Holigan's kids? Honey, that's like going to buy your first kitten and coming home with a Siberian tiger. Jill Montgomery told me they're the hardest kids she's ever had to place. No one wants them.*

That was why Sophy wanted them: no one else did.

"Will you be over for dinner?"

Dinner at her parents' house was another Sunday tradition. Her older sister, Reba, and her family always came, too—four kids who adored their aunt Sophy. Maybe they would be a good influence on Dahlia and Daisy. "I plan to, but it depends on how things go at church." Whether the girls tried to escape, went on a rampage, maybe burned down the sanctuary. They could well be the first kids ever kicked out of Sunday school in Copper Lake and banned from returning. Even the Lord's patience had limits.

Matching stomps sounded in the hallway—amazing how much noise two skinny little girls could create—and Sophy's fingers tightened. "Here they come, Mom. I'll let you know about dinner."

As she laid the phone down, she watched Daisy and Dahlia enter the room. As far as she could see, they'd done as she'd instructed. Their teeth had been brushed, if the toothpaste stains on Daisy's chin were to be trusted. Their hair was combed with zigzag parts and bangs wetted and pasted flat against their foreheads. Their dresses were on, though Dahlia's belt hung untied from two slender loops and her sweater was askew. They even wore shoes—ratty sneakers Dahlia had brought with her and bright yellow flip-flops Daisy had fallen in love with when they went shopping.

The best advice Sophy had been given so far: pick her battles carefully. She wasn't going to argue about shoes.

"Wipe your chin," she said, handing a napkin to Daisy. "You look lovely. Let me grab my stuff and we'll go." She slid her cell into a pocket of her purse, handed each girl a breakfast bar and grabbed her

Bible, then went to the door, undoing multiple locks, ushering them out.

"Why're you taking a book?" Daisy asked. "You plannin' to read while we have to go to Sunday school?"

Sophy blinked. "It's a Bible." Seeing no comprehension cross their faces, she explained, "This is the book we study at church."

Still no understanding. It was hard to imagine the girls having zero exposure to something as common as the Bible. Sophy had received her first one—white leather with her name embossed in gold—her first Christmas with her new family. She still had it.

But Daisy and Dahlia were Holigans. Enough said in this town.

It was entirely possible to live life comfortably in Copper Lake without a car, though naturally Sophy had one. Her apartment was above her quilt shop less than half a block off the downtown square. Her favorite restaurants and the businesses she primarily dealt with were within a few blocks. The house where she'd grown up and the elementary school she'd attended were along the way to church. The grocery store was a nice walk away, and living alone, she didn't have to worry about buying more than she could carry.

But she wasn't alone anymore, she reminded herself as she took Daisy's hand, waited for Dahlia to claim the other one, then headed across Oglethorpe with them. They might be skinny little girls, but they'd increased her shopping list by about 500 percent. Instead of frozen dinners and ice cream, she now had to buy milk, fruit, veggies, snacks, green and yellow and red foods, chicken fingers and hot dogs and hamburger fixings.

It was almost like having a family of her own.

"Why do we have to walk everywhere?" Dahlia asked, scuffing her feet along the pavement.

Sophy kept her voice measured and calm. "I like walking."

"I do, too," Daisy echoed. "It's fun."

"Daisy!"

"Sorry!"

Dahlia's chiding and Daisy's apology were so habitual that their voices overlapped. They were close, not only in age but also in heart. It was a good thing, since they didn't appear to have anyone else.

"Daisy's allowed to have an opinion of her own," Sophy said, earning a scowl from the older sister.

"We don't walk nowhere 'less Mama don't have the money for gas." Daisy hopped over a crack in the sidewalk where a tree root reached for the surface, then swiped a strand of hair from her face with the hand clutching half an oatmeal bar. "When is she comin' home this time?"

Her chest constricting, Sophy avoided looking at either girl. They were young, but they'd experienced things no kids ever should. If she lied, they would recognize it, or at least suspect it. "I don't know."

Truth was, Maggie wasn't coming home from jail this time, not unless she had something substantial to offer the district attorney in exchange for leniency. This was the third time she'd been caught making meth in the house with the girls. With a lengthy list of previous offenses, this one would surely send her to prison.

Before either girl could respond, Sophy gestured to a house fifty feet ahead of them. "Bet you didn't know that's where I lived when I was a little girl."

Dahlia's look and shrug made clear her response: *Bet we don't care.* Daisy, though, stared wide-eyed. "It's got a porch. And a swing. And grass and flowers. And it's yellow. That's my favorite color."

From their time spent together in the quilt shop, Sophy had learned that Daisy's favorite color changed on a whim. Yesterday it had been lime-green. The day before it was red stripes with purple polka dots. "I used to sit on the porch swing and pester my sister while my dad mowed the grass and my mom knitted in that rocker. We had a big ole Irish setter who stretched out across the steps, so we always had to climb over him to get in or out."

Her smile was a little pained. Those had been happy times, doubly precious because of the heartache she'd been through leaving North Carolina and her first family behind. She still loved her birth mother, two sisters and brother, still resented the hell out of her birth father, but she would forever be grateful to her Marchand family.

"What's an Irish setter?" Daisy asked.

"A dog."

The girl sighed longingly. "We had a dog once. She licked my face and slept on my feet and had really stinky breath. Her name was Missy, an' I loved her. But she had babies, and we had to move, and Mama said she couldn't come, so we left her behind."

For the hundredth time in a week, Sophy wondered how the Maggie she'd known in school had turned out to be such a poor excuse for a mother.

Sure, her situation at home had been tough. She'd been born into the world with automatic strikes against her. But people could overcome their upbringings. Sophy's sister, Miri, was a perfect example.

When their father abandoned them to the care of their mentally ill mother, Miri, ten years old at the time, had taken charge. When the state had terminated their mother's rights after a failed inpatient treatment, Miri managed to stay with her, doing whatever it took to survive and keep her safe. When their mother had died, Miri had buried her, mourned her and finally, for the first time ever, begun to live her life.

Now she lived in Dallas with a job she loved and a husband she loved even more. She used her computer skills to locate men who abandoned their children and denied them support, and private investigator Dean did the rest. Just as Miri had looked out for Sophy, Chloe and Oliver when they were little, she was still looking out for kids, making their lives a little easier.

While Maggie used drugs and drank and neglected her babies.

"Is that it?"

Daisy's question was accompanied by a tug on her hand, pulling Sophy from her thoughts. She glanced up and saw her church across the street, the red-brick-and-white-wood structure glowing in the morning sun, looking solid and strong and peaceful. She hoped the girls found a measure of peace inside.

Failing that, she hoped they didn't destroy it.

"Come on, kids, we're just in time. Let's get you to your Sunday school class."

Sean let himself into Kolinski's Auto Repair and Restoration, closed the door and walked to the middle of an empty bay before taking a deep breath. Grease, metal, paint, solvents, leather, sweat—it all smelled like *home* to him. As a kid, he'd spent more hours at Charlie's Custom Rods than in school, learning the basics of car repair and restoration from Charlie himself. It had been the first practical use he'd found for fractions and the first place he'd felt safe, and he'd known then that working on old cars was what he wanted to do.

Craig had given him the chance to do that and make decent money. This was the best garage in three states for turning old rusted heaps of junk back into the classic beauties they were meant to be, and Sean had pretty much free rein.

Over the legal part, at least. He didn't mess with the stolen auto parts, and he stayed hell and gone from the drugs. He was a Holigan. He didn't need cops or pharmaceuticals to screw up his life.

The coated concrete floor softened the sound of Craig's footsteps, along with the running shoes he wore. He never ran, he joked, but he never knew when the sport might be required, so he was always prepared. "Some people start their days with coffee. You start yours with engine grease. You're just not happy without it, are you?"

You used to be the same way. When the old man had died and left the broke-down place as his only inheritance, Craig had worked hard to make a go of it. Like Sean, he'd been tinkering with cars most of his life. The work was in his blood.

Unfortunately, it flowed with a good supply of greed. Keeping the garage in the black, building a reputation as the best, making more money than his dad had ever dreamed of—none of that had been enough for him. Once he had a taste of success, like an addict, he'd wanted more.

He had more now. An expensive condo, a collection of restored cars whose value ran into seven figures, a weekend place near the beach, a different gorgeous woman every week, regular vacations to Atlantic Beach, Las Vegas, New York and Miami… and his own secret squad of DEA agents tracking his every move. Would he learn something when he lost it all, or would he somehow manage to skate on the charges and go on with life as usual, if more discreetly?

"Goober said you wanted to talk." Sean gestured toward the small door in the back that led upstairs to Craig's big fancy office above. He didn't need to see the bodyguard to know he was there in the shadows; one or two beefy brawler types went everywhere with Craig. He didn't bother to see which one it was, either. He called them all Goober to keep from having to learn their names, and Craig kept them from kicking his face in for it.

"I need you to do something for me, man." Craig tore off a length of heavy-duty paper toweling, scrubbed the surface of the chair behind him, then tossed the paper onto its mate before sitting.

Feeling like a puppet with everyone else pulling the strings, Sean obeyed the unspoken order and sat on the second chair. Damned if he'd clean it like a fussy old maid first. Wadding the paper, he tossed it into the nearest trash can, then laced his fingers loosely together, arms resting on his knees, waiting.

"I know we agreed I'd leave you out of the stolen-parts business. That's why I never told you about my other, uh, income source. I wouldn't be telling you now except I've got a big problem and it involves your sister."

Sean had wondered if he'd be able to fake surprise when Craig brought up Maggie, but he didn't have to fake anything. His eyes narrowed, and he felt the blood leaving his face, turning his skin pale. His lips barely moving, he said, "If you've gotten her involved in anything—"

"I wouldn't do that, man. You're my family, and she's your family. I would never have let anything happen. I just didn't know about it in time."

Craig dragged his fingers through his hair. He paid a hundred bucks every few weeks for a haircut that always looked as if he'd just dragged his fingers through it. His shirt cost two hundred, his shoes three, his watch five grand. His jeans, on the other hand, looked a lot like Sean's—old, faded, ragged along the hems. Maybe thirty bucks a lot of years ago.

"Moving auto parts from the South to New York isn't the only thing that turns big profits. I expanded into the drug market a few years back." Craig raised his hand to head off any reaction Sean might have. "Don't preach to me, okay? I knew you wouldn't go for that. That's why I kept it secret, totally separate from the garage. Anyway, my guy in Copper Lake obviously isn't the sharpest knife in the drawer. He hooked up with your sister—did you know she has a meth problem?" He waited long enough for Sean to shake his head grimly. "They started living together—him, her, her kids. Did you know she has kids?"

Sean's gut knotted, and his hands grew sweaty. *That girl's gonna be pregnant before she's sixteen,* their dad always predicted. On her sixteenth birthday, though Sean was locked up, he said his annual prayer. *Don't let her be pregnant.* On her seventeenth, the prayer had been, *Don't let her get arrested.* Every year since then, it had been, *Let her have a better life than all those bastards in Copper Lake thought she deserved.*

A meth head with kids and a drug-dealing boyfriend.

Apparently, God hadn't been listening.

"Yeah, two girls." With two fingers, Craig pulled a photograph from his pocket and handed it across. "Pretty little things, aren't they? Someday I'm gonna have kids. A whole houseful of 'em. I'll join the PTA and we'll go to church on Sunday mornings and have dinner together every evening. You know, they say kids who sit down to dinner with their parents regularly get in less trouble."

Sean took the picture, and his hands began to shake. Two familiar little faces—dark eyes; lank hair awkwardly cut, straight, black. The younger one grinned from ear to ear, while the older scowled, arms folded over her chest, one hip cocked and one bony knee turned out.

They were Maggie twenty-some years ago, happy when she was younger, convinced everyone in the world loved her, sullen and put out when she was older and discovered what a lie that had been. She shone in the little girl's face and lurked in the shadows of the older one's.

Craig knew when to talk and when to be quiet, and he didn't know that Alexandra Baker had already coerced Sean into agreeing to his yet-unasked request. He waited, giving Sean plenty of time to notice every detail in the shot. The house in the background, shabby and well-worn when he'd lived there himself. The yard, mostly bare of grass thanks to the tall pines that covered the ground with their needles. Two rusted lawn chairs, one missing a screw so it tilted drunkenly to one side, the other with a hole punched through it. The carcass of a beat-up pickup, wheels missing, balanced on cinder blocks. Birds had made nests on its dash, and the bed was half-filled with trash.

Trash. That was what the Holigans had been for the past hundred and fifty years. Poor white trash. Drunks, fools and thieves; irresponsible, lazy and worthless, uncaring about the children they brought into the world.

Heat ignited inside Sean, burning outward until his face gleamed with it, until it felt as if it would singe off his ears. It was fueled by anger and resentment and bitterness, but mostly shame. He was so damned ashamed of where he'd come from, who he was, what he was. Yeah, he'd gotten out; he'd escaped the town and his family and made something better for himself, but he'd left Maggie behind to ruin her life just as surely as he would have ruined his.

He'd left her to ruin her babies' lives.

"So." Craig leaned forward, hands together. "The thing is, my guy got arrested a couple weeks ago, along with Maggie. I know he'll keep his mouth shut, but…Maggie isn't exactly known around town for her discretion. If the D.A. offers her some sort of deal, she might tell him everything she knows."

After committing the two faces to his memory, Sean looked up and offered the picture back to his boss, but Craig gestured. *You keep it.* Sean held it carefully in one hand. "So you want me to…"

"Impress on her the importance of staying quiet. She's a doper, Sean, a meth head, and she's locked up. She'd sell her soul for a little comfort. She'd sell her kids' souls. She needs to understand how bad that would be for everyone." Craig waited a moment before adding, "Especially those pretty little girls."

His skin that had been burning a moment ago cooled with the chill that exploded through him. Sean had never been any more violent than was necessary. In Copper Lake, it just wasn't possible for a Holigan to reach eighteen without his share of fistfights, but he'd never let it go beyond self-defense. Even at twelve, fourteen, sixteen, he'd had a plan to get out, and self-control was a part of it.

But right this moment, he wanted to hurt Craig. Wanted to hurt him bad, to smash his face in, to beat the hell out of him for even implying that he or his people might hurt Maggie's kids.

It took a moment to make his voice work, and it came out rough as gravel with sharp, pissed-off edges. "You want me to talk to Maggie. Convince her that going to jail is the best thing for her now. Make her keep her mouth shut or…"

Craig's only response was to pointedly look at the picture.

A muffled sound came from the shadows at the back, Goober shuffling his oversize feet, probably moving to stay limber in case he needed to spring into action. Sean and Craig both glanced that way, and Sean muttered, "Freakin' rat."

It was hard to tell from Craig's grin whether he suspected which of them Sean was referring to.

"I know you left Copper Lake for a reason, man, and like I said, normally I wouldn't ask you to get involved, but when it's family...we gotta make exceptions for family, right? Little sisters, little nieces... Man, I'm sure you wouldn't want me sending anyone else, would you?"

Muscles so taut a few were on the verge of spasm, Sean stood. "Yeah, right." He walked a few paces before turning back. "If she keeps her mouth shut, if she doesn't roll on you..."

"If she stays quiet and still doesn't go to jail, I'll pay for the best rehab around. We'll get her clean. If she does do time, when she gets out, she and the kids will have a new start. I'll set 'em up wherever she wants to go. Either way, I'll take care of her."

"Okay." Without further conversation, Sean crossed the bay to the door, let himself out and strode to his car.

Craig's last words should have been reassuring. *I'll take care of her. I'll see that she's safe and healthy and clean and can be a decent mother to her girls. I'll give her a new life in a new place where no one knows her name or her history. I'll get her counseling and medical care and help her to live the life she deserves to live.*

That was what Sean would have meant by *I'll take care of her.*

But Sean wasn't a cold-blooded killer.

And Craig was.

Chapter 2

As Sophy combed conditioner through Daisy's silky black hair, the little girl peered up at her. "Are me and Dahlia stupid?"

Startled by the question, Sophy lost her balance and slid from her knees to the floor beside the bathtub. "Of course you're not stupid. Why would you think that?"

"We played a game at church, an' the teacher asked a lot of questions. Me and Dahlia didn't know the answer to any of 'em, and this kid named Paulie said we were stupid. I think any boy named Paulie is stupid."

Sophy sighed internally. Paulie Pugliese's father was a deacon, his mother the choir director. They loved their authority in the church and their spoiled brat of a little boy better.

From the far end of the tub, hidden beneath a dress and cap made of fragrant pink bubbles, Dahlia deigned to join the conversation. "Miss Jo said you can't know a subject you ain't been taught. She asked Paulie to count to ten in French, and he couldn't do it. She said he wasn't stupid and we weren't stupid. We just needed to learn."

"Un, deux, trois." Sophy smiled awkwardly when both girls scowled at her. "Counting in French. Miss Jo's right. If you've never been to church or read the Bible, how could you know what's in it?"

"It don't matter." Dahlia stretched one leg up and fashioned a bubble high heel. "Mama'll be home soon, and we won't have to go again."

"I kinda liked it." Daisy anticipated her sister's censure and didn't wait to respond, "Sorry! But they sang songs, and they had pictures to color, and there were doughnuts. I like doughnuts."

Sophy pushed to her feet and dried her hands. "You guys get rinsed and dried off and put your jammies on, and maybe we can have our bedtime snack outside."

Dahlia almost drowned out Daisy's cheer. "Sitting on dirty wooden stairs? Oh, boy."

"It may have escaped your notice each time we've gone into the shop, but there's a lovely porch downstairs with flowers and chairs and everything. Go on, now, and help your sister."

The last wasn't necessary, she acknowledged as she left them in the bathroom. Dahlia was always quick to give Daisy whatever she needed. Maybe part of it was just being the big sister. Probably a larger part was that their mother had rarely been in shape to help the kids herself.

In the kitchen, she pulled out the industrial-size blender that used to make margaritas when she had friends over but now mostly turned out fruit smoothies. Listening to the up-and-down of the girls' voices, the words indistinguishable, she spooned in ice cream, milk, a little vanilla and three crumbled chocolate-chip cookies her mother had sent home from dinner with them.

By the time the girls shuffled in, she'd divided the milk shakes between three tall cups, added straws and long spoons, and placed them with a pile of napkins on a tray painted with sunflowers.

Used to her inspections, Dahlia had brought a towel and the wide-tooth comb. Neither of them minded water dripping down their backs from wet hair, Daisy had earnestly explained to her, and Sophy had just as earnestly explained that *she* did. She gave both heads a quick rub, combed their hair, made sure they wore flip-flops, then picked up the tray of shakes.

After securing the front door behind them, Sophy led the way down the stairs and around to the front porch. With the flip of a switch, two ceiling fans came on, one above each side of the porch. The glass-windowed doors in the center looked in on the dimly lit quilt shop, all bright colors and endless possibilities, and a path led across the tiny yard to the picket fence and the sidewalk.

The evening was relatively quiet. Most church services were over. All the bars were closed. An occasional car passed on Oglethorpe Avenue, and a few couples strolled around the square, their destination A Cuppa Joe or one of the restaurants still serving customers. It was her favorite time of day, a time to reflect, to unwind, to set her worries to rest and consider the next day.

Or to answer questions.

"What is this?" Daisy asked. Dressed in ladybug pajamas, she ignored the rocker and crouched back on her heels, holding the drink in both hands.

"A milk shake."

She jiggled it. "It doesn't shake."

"No, but it can make you shake. It's cold."

"What's in it?"

"Milk, ice cream and a surprise. You have to taste it to find out."

Hesitantly Daisy put her mouth to the straw and sucked until her jaw puckered. "I can't get any."

"It's got to melt a little first. Use the spoon." Sophy took a large bite of hers, savoring the richness of the ice cream and her mom's incredible chocolate-chip cookies.

"Where'd you learn to make it?"

"My sister taught me."

"Miss Reba?"

"That's the one." Sophy used one foot to keep her rocker moving. To Reba's kids, Daisy and Dahlia had just been two more kids to play with after Sunday dinner. Their mother hadn't been so accepting.

You brought Hooligan kids into your house? You'll wake up one morning trussed like a hog with all your money and your car gone.

They're five and six years old. Where do you think they're going to go?

Reba had scowled. *I see TV. I read the news. The little one works the pedals while the big one steers. Besides, my friend Linda is a foster parent, and she said they couldn't pay her enough to take those kids again. Her friend Tara fosters, too, and she said they set her house on fire. They climb out windows, they jump off roofs, they run away, they steal. Neither one of them's ever spent a day in school.*

Sophy had given her a dry look. *Then they'll keep me alert and aware and on my toes.*

Reba had sighed. *Oh, Sophy.*

Sophy knew what that meant: poor, childless, clueless Sophy. Overprotected, overoptimistic, all sunshine and rainbows. Reba had forgotten the Christmas when Sophy had been threatened by two armed killers in the back room of her shop. She wasn't Mary Sunshine. She knew bad things happened in the world, and if she could keep a few from happening to Dahlia and Daisy, she would be happy.

"Miss Reba doesn't like us." Dahlia sat cross-legged in her chair, all skinny limbs, her usual scowl fading only when she took a bite of ice cream. "She called us Hooligans."

Heat flooded through Sophy. She'd thought the kids were occupied in the family room with Reba's kids and her father when her sister had started that conversation. She should have known better. Know-it-all mother-of-four parenting-expert Reba certainly should have.

"She shouldn't have said that," Sophy agreed. "It was rude, and it's not true."

Dahlia shrugged. "'Course it's true. Mama says

most people don't like us, and that's okay because we don't like 'em back."

Sophy didn't know what to say to that, because sadly that was the case. Way back in middle school, when some kids had been giving Maggie a hard time, she'd overheard one teacher ruefully tell another, *Everyone has to have someone to look down on*. Maggie, it seemed, had gone out of her way to give people reasons to look down on her. Where someone else might have taken it as a challenge to prove them wrong, she'd been in their faces, flaunting every bad decision and behavior.

Granted, she'd never been taught anything different. Her brothers, her father, her uncles…Holigans had made an art of reveling in their reputations.

"I like you," Sophy said. "And Mom and Dad, and Mr. Ty and Miss Nev and Miss Anamaria." Lord, it was a short list. It made her heart ache.

Dahlia responded with a disbelieving snort before taking a huge bite of ice cream. On the floor, without lifting her gaze from an ant crawling across the boards, Daisy asked, "What's a hooligan?"

"Remember, Mama told us. It's someone who runs wild and breaks all the rules and misbehaves and acts like a heathen."

"I like running wild and making people shake their heads and say, 'You ain't nothin' but trouble, Daisy Holigan.'" Daisy grinned. "I like being a hooligan."

Wondering which neighbor or irresponsible family member had told her that, Sophy forced a smile. "You like *acting* that way. But the secret is, you and

Dahlia are clever and smart and capable little girls who can be anything you want to be."

Another snort from Dahlia, and she'd lost Daisy's attention completely. The girl had risen to her feet and was avidly staring at the sidewalk—rather, at the dog being walked there.

"Good evening," the man at the other end of the leash called.

Sophy repeated his greeting as Daisy moved to the second step. "What's your dog's name?"

"Daisy! We don't talk to strangers!" Dahlia whispered fiercely.

"But he's got a *dog*."

Sophy made a mental note to talk to the girls about strangers and ruses involving pets.

"Her name is Bitsy," the man said. "You want to meet her? If it's okay with your mom."

The girls' voices drowned each other out: "She's not our mom," from Dahlia and "Please, can I?" from Daisy.

"Sure." Sophy followed Daisy into the yard as Bitsy pulled her owner through the gate. Wiggling from nose to tail, the dog sniffed the girl, making her giggle. The sound almost stopped Sophy's heart. Was that the first time she'd heard Daisy laugh?

The man offered his hand. "Hi. I'm Zeke."

"Sophy." She shook his hand, his fingers long and strong, his palm uncallused. She still thought of Copper Lake as a small town, but he was one of the twenty thousand or so residents who weren't a regular part of her life. He was fair skinned with auburn hair, blue eyes and a grin that had surely charmed more than his share of women. Though only a few inches taller than her, he was powerfully built—broad shoulders, hard muscles, not lean but solid. First impression: he was the sort of guy who could make a woman feel safe.

Though she knew better than to rely on first impressions.

"You picked a perfect evening for sitting on the porch with milk shakes."

She glanced at the glass in her left hand. "The day's not over until we've had ice cream."

"A woman after our own hearts. Bitsy loves the ice-cream shop, but we've got to be careful. Her vet caught us there once and wasn't happy."

A glance at the short distance between the dog's rounded belly and the ground made that easy to believe. "Cute name," Sophy said while thinking the opposite. All of the dogs she knew had solid names— that they lived up to—Frank, Misha, Scooter, Elizabeth, Bear. Bitsy sounded so fussy for a grown man's dog.

Zeke winced. "My daughter named her. Bitsy has a digging fixation, and my ex is a big-time gardener, so Bitsy came to live with me."

So he was handsome, friendly, liked dogs and was single. Sophy was beginning to wonder how their paths hadn't crossed before tonight. She thought she'd dated every friendly single guy in town.

Every one of whom had wound up married or engaged. To someone else.

Oh, Sophy. Reba's sigh echoed in her head. It wasn't a good time to meet anyone new, particularly anyone handsome with a quick grin. She'd taken on a huge responsibility when she'd volunteered to keep Daisy and Dahlia, and that meant putting her social life on hold.

"Your daughter and Bitsy are lucky you were able to take her."

"There's not much I wouldn't do to make my kid happy…besides get back together with her mom. And I've kind of grown attached to the mutt, too."

A car turned onto Oglethorpe at the nearest cross street, and they both glanced in that direction. The engine made a low growl, one that spoke of power tightly reined in. Sophy wasn't much of a car person, but she could tell the vehicle was older than she was, was meticulously maintained and pretty much defined the phrase *muscle car*.

And it was painted a gorgeous deep metallic red. Her favorite color.

The air shimmered and the ground vibrated as the car slowly passed. Okay, maybe that was a little fanciful, but it *felt* that way. When it was gone and she turned back to Zeke, he was crouching on the ground beside Bitsy, head ducked, coaxing her to offer Daisy her paw for a handshake.

When the dog finally obeyed, he stood. "We'd better head home. She always wants a treat when she shakes, and I didn't bring any. It's been nice meeting you, Miss Daisy, Miss Dahlia…Miss Sophy."

"Nice meeting you, too. Maybe we'll see you again."

Zeke grinned as he and the dog headed toward the gate. "You can bet on it."

Monday was the kind of late-summer day that helped keep Sean in the South. The temperature was in the low eighties, the humidity down for a change, and occasionally when the wind blew across the Gullah River, he could smell the coming of fall, cooler weather, changing leaves, shorter days.

He'd driven around Copper Lake the night before, noticing how much things had changed and how much they'd stayed the same. New businesses and old ones, new people and old ones, familiar places, even a good memory or two. Charlie's Custom Rods on Carolina Avenue looked as if the only turnover had been in merchandise. The front plate-glass window that Sean and his buddies had cracked late one Saturday night a lot of years ago was still there, the crack still covered with duct tape grown ragged.

The SnoCap Drive-In was still open, too, though it had had an update on its paint from neon turquoise to a subtler shade, and the same old guy who'd run it fourteen years ago was behind the counter.

The Heart of Copper Lake Motel still stood on Carolina, too, seriously renovated, but he would have recognized it. That was where he'd checked in, taking a parking space on the back side of the building even though his room was on the front.

After a restless night's sleep, Sean knew the first thing he had to do today was talk to Maggie. He'd left the motel with that in mind but decided to have breakfast first. An hour had passed, and he still sat in the coffee shop on the downtown square, a couple blocks from the jail, nursing his third cup of regular sugar-and-cream coffee, reluctant to confront two blasts from the past at once: the sister he'd let down and the jail where he'd spent more than a few nights himself.

The bell above the door rang every few minutes with customers arriving and departing. Most of them were in a hurry to get to work and paid little attention to anyone besides the couple filling orders. They were named Joe and Liz, husband and wife, he'd picked up eavesdropping, and they were strangers to Sean. He'd seen a few older faces that were vaguely familiar—lawyers, maybe, or probation officers or social workers—but none that he could put a name to.

The knot in his gut knew his good luck wouldn't last.

Liz was topping off his coffee when the doorbell sounded again. "Morning, Sophy," she called, then asked him, "Can I get you anything else?"

"No, thanks." Without glancing her way, Sean stirred sugar and cream into his cup. He'd been concentrating on the scene outside the window—square, gazebo, flowers, war memorials, traffic, pedestrians—for so long that he'd memorized it, but it was better than actually making eye contact with someone.

It beat the hell out of making eye contact with someone who might recognize him.

A young and unhappy voice came from the vicinity of the door. "I. Want. To. Go. To. School."

"I know you do. You've made that perfectly clear. But you're not old enough," a woman, presumably her mother, replied. She sounded tired, as if they'd been having this conversation for a while.

"That's not fair! I'm not a baby!"

"I didn't say you were. You'll start next year."

"I want to go this year!"

Sean had never had conversations like that when

he was a kid. For starters, his mother had left them when he was about five, and they'd all been born knowing not to tempt their father with tantrums. Patrick Holigan hadn't been a talkative lad to start with, but he'd had loads of things to say about what happened to children who disrespected their dear old pop.

"You want your usual for here or to go, Soph?" Liz asked, and Sean detected hopefulness for the second option in her voice. The coffee shop was too peaceful a place for a small child who excelled at whining.

"We'll take them to go," Sophy said. Hopefulness in her voice, too, as if the kid might suddenly become sweet and sunny when they walked back outside.

Good luck with that, lady.

He shifted his head enough to see Sophy, her back to him, wearing a red dress that clung to a sleek body—muscular arms, narrow waist, well-toned butt, great legs. She wore her blond hair in a pony-tail falling halfway down her back and shoes that seemed a compromise between looking good and feeling good. It was a great backside. Did the front side live up to its hype?

Standing beside her, also with her back to Sean, was the girl with the voice pitched to cut glass. Her red shorts skimmed her knees, her top was red with purple stripes, and on her feet were yellow flip-flops decorated with fuzzy, sparkly blue-and-green butter-flies. Too much color for this early in the morning.

Her hair was straight, too, pulled into a pony-tail that was falling loose, but unlike her mother, hers was jet-black. Her arms were folded mutinously across her middle, and she was tapping one foot as if planning how to break into school and stay there.

Pushing them out of his mind, he rubbed one hand over his jaw, two days' worth of beard scratching even over the calluses years of mechanic work had built on both his hands. He'd called the jail when he got in last night and found out that they were generous in their visiting hours, taking breaks only for meals. In double the time it would take him to drive over and find a parking space, he could be sitting in a room with Maggie.

Telling her *Don't talk to anybody. Don't cooperate. This is worth going to jail for.*

Most of Craig's employees in his other businesses knew that from the start. Don't snitch; don't inform; take the heat and the time from any trouble they got into, and they'd get along just fine with the boss.

Maggie hadn't known, probably hadn't cared. Hell, she'd gotten herself and her kids on Craig's radar without the benefit of even one paycheck.

If there's a bit of trouble around, you kids will find it, Grandpa Holigan used to say. Apparently it was still true.

Sophy and the girl left, taking drinks in paper cups with them. He waited a minute to give them time to walk away, left a decent tip for table rental, and walked out to find Sophy standing at one of the outdoor tables and chairs that had been in his blind spot, talking to an older woman, and the girl stealthily making her way to the corner of the building.

Sean passed her, turned the corner and, totally surprising himself, stopped, waiting for the little girl to slide around the corner to freedom. It came in about five seconds, ending in a sudden halt as she realized she wasn't alone. Her gaze traveled up from his work boots, over his legs, on up across his black shirt and finally reaching his face.

If his shaggy hair and unshaven face scared her, it didn't show. She still looked as bold as could be. But the sight of her put fear into him. The dark skin and black hair he'd seen in the shop, but the delicate features of her face: the shape of her nose, the deep dark eyes with long lashes, the mouth, the jaw, the fragile, vulnerable, tough air about her…

This was his niece. Maggie's baby. The threat Craig was using over both him and Maggie.

"Who are you?" She had the sense to whisper so her voice wouldn't draw Sophy's attention.

"The one who's gonna drag your butt back to your foster mother if you don't go on your own."

A scowl transformed her pretty little face into a pretty little unhappy face, and she folded her arms over her chest. "You're not my boss."

Matching the scowl was easy. He'd perfected it sometime between crawling and learning to walk. No five-year-old could do it better.

After a stare-off, she backed up a few steps, curving around the corner until she was out of sight. Her voice whispered back, though. "I don't like you."

"Good for you."

A moment later, Sophy called, "Come on, Daisy. It's time to get to work."

Leaning one shoulder against the warm brick wall, Sean imagined just being with Daisy all day was work in itself, especially for a pretty blonde who hadn't been raised in the Holigan ways. Apparently, it was too hard for Maggie when she *had* been raised in the family.

He watched Daisy dance away as Sophy tried to claim her hand to cross the street. Sophy won that round. The kid dragged her feet, but Sophy kept her moving. Daisy deliberately walked on the wrong side of the light pole at the next intersection, forcing Sophy to release, then quickly reclaim her hand. His gaze followed them all the way to their destination, an old house with a shop on the first floor and living quarters upstairs, just down the street, then he spun around and headed for his car.

He'd seen the younger of his nieces. Now it was time to see Maggie.

The county jail was located behind the Copper Lake Police Department. Back in the day, most of the cells had been in the basement with only small, barred windows high on the outside walls. The only thing a prisoner could see, depending on his position, was the sky or the feet of people walking by. The glass, inlaid with wire between the layers, had been thick, making conversation tough though not impossible. Being loud and disruptive was one of the Holigan family qualities.

Sean parked his car, shut off the engine and stared at the squat brick building ahead. He could think of about a hundred things he'd rather be doing—even wrangling the youngest Holigan had to be easier than this—and he seriously considered putting it off for an hour or two or five. He hadn't talked himself into action either way when abruptly the driver's door was jerked open.

Sean flinched, leaned away, drew one leg onto the door frame for a quick kick, but a flash of images stopped him: eyes he'd once known as well as his own, an ear-to-ear grin, a gold badge, a holstered weapon. That was all he had the chance to notice before strong hands pulled him from the car and into a bone-jarring hug.

"I'll be damned," Ty Gadney said, letting him go, then giving his shoulder a punch that made him fall back against the car. "Granddad always said you'd be back someday, and here you are. Hell, Sean. You could keep in touch with the people who tolerated your smart mouth at least once every fifteen years."

Ty, all grown up, shaved head, a detective, just like he'd always wanted to be. How many nights had Sean shared his room, dimly lit, the box fan in the window drawing in the damp night smells, talking about what they were going to do someday?

Sean had to force his voice to work. "How is Mr. Obadiah?"

From behind Ty came the answer in a distinctly sultry, sweet Southern woman's voice. "Feisty and sassy as ever." She stepped into view, pretty, womanly, and maternal and sexy all at once.

Ty's grin widened as he slid his arm around her waist. "My old buddy Sean. My fiancée, Nev Wilson."

She offered her hand, and Sean took it after a moment. She held on longer than he expected. "So you're Daisy and Dahlia's uncle. Heartbreakers, all of you."

Saying that he'd only learned of his nieces' existence yesterday, that he'd caught his first glimpse of

Daisy this morning, didn't seem the way to ingratiate himself with Nev, so he pulled his hand back. "Don't blame them. You can't choose your family."

"Oh, don't I know it," she said.

There was a story behind that fervent agreement, but he wasn't here to learn anyone's story but Maggie's.

Letting his hold on Nev slide free, Ty circled to the front of the car, hands on hips, an admiring look on his face. "So you got The Car. Babe, from the time he was thirteen, this was all he ever talked about— *this* car. A 1970 Chevelle SS 454. Oh, man, she's a beauty."

When Nev made a dismissive sound, he gave her a chastising look. "Don't be making fun of my appreciation for a fine vehicle. You practically cried when your car burned up at the Heart of Copper Lake, and it had nothing on this one."

"That car was my baby."

"This car is his baby." Like a cloud passing over the sun, Ty went serious. "You here to see Maggie?"

"If she'll see me."

"Of course she'll see you. Why wouldn't she?"

Sean could think of fourteen years' worth of reasons.

"Hold on, and I'll go in with you."

Taking Nev's hand, Ty walked with her to a big old Mercury a few spaces away, half a block long and two lanes wide, hell on gas but with enough room for a party inside, all done up in baby-blue. Sean had worked on that car plenty of times when he was living with the Gadneys—and plenty of times when he wasn't. It was the only way he'd had to repay Mr. Obadiah for giving him a place to stay when he needed it.

Another thing he would have to do: go see Mr. Obadiah, knowing that he'd let him down, too. This trip was going to be all kinds of fun.

After kissing his fiancée and helping her into the car, Ty stood back and watched as she drove away. Sean watched, too—his old friend, not Nev—then quietly said, "She's a beauty, too."

"Ain't that the truth." Ty grinned. "I'm a lucky man." He slapped Sean on the back and turned him toward the jail entrance. "So what have you been doing all these years, and where have you been doing it?"

What have you been doing? Patrick used to ask Declan and Ian, among other relatives, when they showed up after an absence. *Time* was the answer so often that it became a family joke.

One fifteen-month stint in prison had taken all the humor from it for Sean.

"Working on cars." Being able to give a respectable answer sent a kind of relief through him. "Mostly for people who buy cars like mine and don't have the time or the skills to restore them." Honest work, even if his boss wasn't.

"I'm not surprised. You've always had the magic touch. And where?"

Sean walked through the glass door Ty held open. "Norfolk." Just inside, he stopped. An air-conditioning vent in the ceiling nearby blew cold air onto the back of his neck—the reason a shiver was doing its damnedest to break loose. Not nerves. "Tell me, Ty. How much trouble is Maggie in?"

As Ty's face went somber again, Sean could see traces of his grandfather in him. "A lot. This is the third time she's been caught making meth at home with the kids. You know she's got kids?"

Sean nodded.

"She loves Dahlia and Daisy as much as she can, but…she's an addict, Sean, and a bad one. She's got to get straight before she kills herself, for the kids' sake if nothing else."

His gut knotting, Sean stared at the wall behind the check-in desk. He figured pretty much his entire generation of Holigans had experimented with at least marijuana, but he didn't know of any who'd gotten addicted. Like their father and grandfather and *their* fathers before them, most Holigans preferred a good Irish whiskey to feed the soul, enliven an evening and dull the pain.

"You ready?"

Though he wanted to run away like a scared kid, he nodded and followed Ty to the desk. Within ten minutes, he was in a communal visiting room filled with round fiberglass tables with four stools of matching orange attached. They reminded him of playground seating, somewhere between child- and comfortable adult-size, with no back support to lean against. They were bolted to the floor so they couldn't be used as a weapon and seemed pretty indestructible. A box of ragged toys occupied one corner, and signs warning against physical contact of any sort hung on the institutional-green walls.

It was depressing as hell.

He was standing at one of the barred windows overlooking the alley when the door opened and

Maggie shuffled in. The fact that she was here, finally in a room with him after so many years, shocked him. Her appearance *really* shocked him.

Her hair had been bleached blond at some point in the recent past and hung, greasy and tangled, to her shoulders, the strands about equal parts blue-black and dingy yellowish-white. She was fourteen years older, a few inches taller and thin, emaciated, looking more like a scarecrow than the girl he remembered. She didn't lift her feet when she walked, and she had a bad case of the shakes, like a kid on a major caffeine high—or a meth head on an involuntary withdrawal.

People who knew him, other than maybe Craig and Ty, would scoff at the thought, but his heart broke just looking at her.

Her gaze darted around the otherwise-empty room, skimming across him a couple of times before finally settling. "Look at this." She turned to include the guard standing impassively at the door in her words. "My big brother, Sean, finally come home. You know, me and Declan's kids had bets going for a while that you were dead somewhere. Guess I win."

Part of him wanted to step forward and wrap his arms around her and cuddle her the way he used to when bad dreams woke her in the night. The other part of him recoiled from the idea. "Hey, Maggie."

"What brings you back here?"

"You."

"Took you long enough. I've been here more than three weeks."

"I just found out yesterday."

She shuffled to the nearest table and plopped

down on one stool, making the entire thing tilt. "Well, if you hadn't run off and pretended the rest of us didn't exist, you would've known sooner." Picking at a sore on her arm, she asked, "You gonna get me out of here?"

"I—" Sean was at a loss for words. Craig hadn't said anything about bailing her out, and he hadn't given it a thought. If he did pay her bond, he could take her home, talk to her in private, have unlimited time to persuade her of the best action to take.

Or maybe run away with her.

Though if he took her home, Craig and his thugs would know where to find her. They could *take care of her* at their convenience, and him, too, and maybe Daisy and Dahlia. Surely she was safer in jail. Yeah, they could reach her there, but it would have to be harder inside than out.

And if he took her home, he would have to duct tape her wrist to his. She'd been an expert at sneaking out when she was thirteen. Twenty-eight and in need of a high, she would disappear the first chance she got. He'd be on the hook for the money *and* for her escape.

"I don't have that kind of money," he lied. "Sorry, Maggie."

Anger knotted her thin little face. "What the hell you been doing all these years?"

"I work on cars."

"Of course." She rolled her eyes. "You always did love them stupid cars more than any of us. So if you're not gonna bail me out, what the hell are you doing here?"

"I—I want to help you." *Help you get out of this*

life, help you stay alive, help you clean up... Though she didn't look much interested in getting clean at the moment.

For a time she stared at him, then a ghost of the grin he remembered so well touched her mouth. "If you want to help me, go to Marian at Triple A Bonds and buy her goodwill with ten thousand bucks. That's ten percent of my bail. Otherwise, I'll take care of myself, Johnny boy, like I've been doing ever since you took off."

Johnny. Only family had ever called him by the American version of his Irish name. Hearing it stung.

As she stood, hitching up her too-big pants, and walked away, he blurted out, "Maggie, I saw Daisy this morning."

That stopped her a foot or so from the door. Slowly she turned, gave him a flat look, then said, "Yeah. Well. She's five years old. If you hadn't run off, you could've seen her a lot of times." Dismissing him, she turned back to the guard. "Come on, bubba, get me outta here."

After the door closed behind him, Sean exhaled heavily. "That went well."

Oh, yeah, this trip to Hell was going to be all kinds of fun.

Chapter 3

Hanging by a Thread, Sophy's quilt shop, opened at 10:00 a.m. six days a week. Business was good enough that she could hire Saturday help—Rachel, just graduated from high school last spring—but weekdays were generally hers alone.

Hers and Daisy's.

Sophy turned the Closed sign to Open, switched on lights all around the shop, stowed her purse in the storeroom and booted up the computer before giving her attention to Daisy. If only she were the older of the two girls, the morning would have gone so much more easily. Daisy thought school was a grand adventure: other kids, toys, books, play, classroom pets. She *wanted* to go.

Dahlia didn't.

She'd never been away from her sister. She was so

much more suspicious of strangers and so much more aware of her family's place. She didn't trust anyone but her mother and Daisy—and Sophy wasn't sure about Maggie. Her job had always been to look out for Daisy, to make sure she didn't talk to anyone or say anything she shouldn't. She was the protector, and how could she protect when she was locked up in a stupid school with stupid people?

Daisy was walking in circles around the work-table Sophy had made available for her and Dahlia, the rubber soles of her shoes squeaking every other step. Her ponytail had failed completely, the band hanging from a small clump of strands, ready to fall any moment. Pink from her strawberry milk rimmed her upper lip, while her lower lip was stuck out in major pout mode.

"What do you want to do this morning?" Sophy asked with a cheer that was mostly phony.

Daisy gave her a look that was mostly stony. "I want to go to school with Dahlia."

"Besides that?"

"Nothing." She gave her foot a little twist, intensifying the squeak against the wooden floor, then did it again.

"Stop that, please."

Defiantly, she did it again.

Jaw clenched, Sophy turned to her own work area. In addition to selling fabrics and quilting supplies, she offered her own quilts for sale, taught classes, made custom pieces and machine-quilted tops for customers interested only in the piecing aspect. She always had a dozen or more projects in the works, and as Daisy continued the noise-making, she pulled out a plastic tub that contained one.

The piece was a twin-size quilt, creamy-hued pieces of fabric, plain or with tone-on-tone patterns so subtle she had to look twice at some to see them. It was a simple quilt, twelve-inch blocks with a scalloped edge. The beauty of this one was in the quilting, a meandering maze that led to a small outline-stitched heart. Though the long-arm quilting machine stood a few yards away, Sophy was finishing this one by hand because it was special.

It was for Dahlia, and maybe it would be with her when she someday found her heart's desire. *Please, God, let it be more worthy than her mother's.*

Daisy continued to wander, but the shop was a reasonably safe place to let her do that. The back door required a key to open the dead bolt. The stairs that had once led to the second floor ended at a blank wall and were used for display. There was a bell at the front door that chimed the instant anyone stepped on the floor mat, before they'd had a chance to even touch the door, and the windows were secured with extra locks.

As Sophy settled in, a sense of peace seeped through her. She loved every aspect of quilting, from choosing a pattern to assembling fabrics, cutting and piecing and quilting. To make her parents happy, she'd tried to major in business in college, dutifully attending classes at Clemson, stuffing dull facts she cared nothing about into her brain, giving up her social life and spending all her time studying. Quilting was the only other thing she made time for, and when one of her quilts won a major competition, she'd thrown in the business-major towel. Though there had been some lean times the first years the shop was open, she'd never regretted it.

Thanks to a Christmas gift from her sister, Miri, she wouldn't have to worry about money for a long time.

When the bell dinged, she secured the needle in the fabric, then set the quilt on the worktable. Neither Daisy, too short to be seen over the stands of fabric bolts between them, nor the customer was visible from Sophy's location, but clearly they could see each other as Daisy greeted the newcomer.

In a particularly Holigan sort of way.

"What are *you* doing here?"

Giving her chair a hip bump to slide it into place, Sophy hurried down the wide center aisle.

"Maybe I came to make a quilt."

Sophy blinked. The voice was low and gravelly and definitely male, definitely not anyone she knew. It was the kind of voice that belonged on the radio in the middle of the night with a half-moon casting slivers of light across the bedroom floor while the half-open windows provided brief drafts of air cool enough to dry the skin. She would have recognized it if she'd heard it before. She would have dated this voice without caring a damn about the rest of him.

She saw Sophy first, head tilted back, hands on her hips, then another couple steps brought the man into view on the other side of a sampler hanging from the ceiling. She stopped suddenly.

She was wrong. She'd heard this voice before, a long time ago, and it had been Reba dating him. Her rebellious stage, Reba had later called it, designed to drive Mom and Dad insane. But Sophy had always thought her sister's laugh when she said that seemed a tad wistful.

"Men don't make quilts," Daisy announced as if she actually knew.

Sean Holigan. Sophy had spent maybe a total of twenty minutes in his presence in all the time he and Reba had dated. She'd practically lived on the front porch swing back then, and he'd never been invited in while her parents tried to dissuade Reba from leaving the house with him. He had always leaned against the porch railing, smelling of cigarette smoke and heat and essence of bad boy, and he'd usually ignored her with her nose buried in a book.

Naive and just turned fourteen, she'd pretended to ignore him back, but deep inside, she'd been intrigued by him. It had broken her innocent little heart when he and Reba broke it off after less than a month. Soon after, he'd left Copper Lake, followed in the family tradition of going to jail, then disappeared from the radar.

And now he was back.

Not yet noticing her, he gazed down at Daisy, the resemblance so strong that anyone could see they were family. "Men can make quilts if they want to."

"Nuh-uh. I've been here a long time, and I never seen one man makin' a quilt." Daisy's vigorous head-shake was the final straw for the band holding her hair. It flew loose, landing on the floor right between Sean's scuffed boots. He bent to pick it up and, somewhere in the process, became aware of Sophy's presence.

Slowly he stood, his gaze rising with the same

easy fluidity. Her feminine ego wished she'd chosen prettier shoes, was glad she wore a dress that showed a lot of leg and hugged all her curves, and couldn't help but shiver inside as he reached her face and his dark eyes turned smoky.

She'd bet her eyes were smoky, too. In fact, she was pretty sure steam was escaping wherever it could—her ears, the strands of her hair, the pores of her arms. The handsome teenage bad boy was all grown up, sinfully and wickedly, heart-stoppingly gorgeous. His black hair was a little too long, his jaw unshaven for a few days, his mouth quirked in a way that was part smile and part sardonic curl and totally sexy.

As he finished straightening, he stretched the hair band over the second and fourth fingers on his left hand. She couldn't help but look at his hand, noticing the absence of a wedding ring first, the scars and crooked joints of the fingers second. He'd been one of the guys who'd hung out at Charlie's Custom Rods back then, always messing with cars. That could be dangerous work. So could being a Holigan.

It finally penetrated her dazed brain that she should say something, but before she could find even one word, he spoke.

"If it isn't little Sophy Marchand. You grew up."

Heat bloomed in her cheeks, and her heart fluttered. Her fourteen-year-old self was dancing in circles: *He noticed me! He remembered me! He knows my name!* She was searching for the woman sharing space with the girl—she didn't want to act like a flustered kid—and thought she managed a reasonable substitute. "Sean Holigan. I didn't know you were back in town."

A blur somewhere on her left, Daisy said, "Hey, that's me and Dahlia's name, too. We're hooligans. We like to run wild and break rules. Do you run wild, too?"

Aw, Sean Holigan embodied wild and rule breaking.

That quirk touched his mouth again. "Me? Do I look wild?"

Daisy's gaze narrowed as she studied him. "Yup," she concluded. "You got long hair and a beard."

"Nah, anyone can grow hair and a beard. It takes more than that to be a Holigan. Your mama doesn't have a beard yet, does she?" He pretended to scrutinize Daisy's jaw. "Though it looks like yours is about to come in. There's a tiny hair here and another over there."

With a squeal, Daisy ran off to find the nearest mirror.

Smiling, Sophy drew him away from the door and deeper into the store. "How did you remember my name?"

"I waited on the porch at least three times a week for nearly a month, with you in your prissy little dress and your prissy little ponytail and your prissy little books. You're the only one in the family who didn't routinely close doors in my face."

Though he said it lightly, shame stabbed at Sophy. When Sean had shown up for his and Reba's first date, Mom and Dad had been arguing upstairs with her, so Sophy had answered the door. She'd invited him inside, and he'd taken maybe two steps across the threshold when her father had rushed down the stairs, ushered him back out, then closed the door. A quick peek out the window had shown that his features were bronzed, but they'd been nowhere as hot as her face was now.

After Reba had ridden off with the bad boy destined to lead her straight into hell, Sophy and her father had had a rather heated conversation about manners and being polite and standing behind the *welcome* they symbolically issued to everyone. The conversation had run in Dad's favor, and that was why she'd made the point of being on the porch every time Sean came over. Waiting outside with her, she'd figured, would seem less a slap in the face than being told to wait out there alone.

"I'm glad you stuck with the dresses. Legs like those should be seen, not covered."

The warmth of a pure flush touched her cheeks. "I remember hearing about this in middle school. Blarney, isn't it? Pleasant flattery, charm, not to be trusted?"

"So young to be so cynical. All those books you were reading on the porch swing…what were they? Dry, dull stories by people who didn't get their share of flattery and charm growing up?"

His description might describe the outside of the books, but she'd usually had one of her mother's romance novels hidden inside. She would admit—only to herself—that despite the characters on the covers, all the heroines resembled her as she'd imagined herself in ten years, and a fair number of the heroes had had black hair, beard stubble, tight jeans and tighter T-shirts.

Interesting to know that fourteen years later, he was still prime romance-novel cover material.

Corralling those thoughts, she gestured toward the work space. "Come on back. We've got coffee and snacks." She patted an empty table as she passed and felt when he stopped following her there. It was a combination of heat and cold, comfort and risk and danger. Giving herself a mental shake, she continued to the corner, started the coffee, and carried napkins, forks, paper plates and her usual box of pastries from A Cuppa Joe to the table.

"Daisy, are you going to join us?" *Please don't,* Sophy thought. *No, please do.* Pint-size safety was better than none.

Daisy skipped over to kneel on the chair across from Sean's. "You fibbed. I don't have any hair growing there." Her pout made clear she was disappointed. She would have had some fun with whiskers.

"You will before long," Sophy murmured back in the corner, putting coffee mugs, cream and sweetener on a tray. She didn't intend for Sean to hear her, but his grin when she turned around suggested he had.

She carefully set the tray down, then took the chair beside Daisy. "I don't believe you two have actually met, have you?" she asked as she took her coffee, holding the cup in both hands to steady it.

Daisy looked up over her apple juice, poured into a coffee cup so she didn't feel left out and earnestly replied, "We *just* met. He's a hooligan, and I'm a hooligan. Didn't you hear?"

Sophy smiled for the girl but kept her gaze on Sean. After a sip of coffee, he grimaced, shifted his attention to his niece and asked, "Do you know your mom's brothers?"

"Yup." She held up one hand to count them off. "There's Declan and Ian and Sean. They're all gone. That means they're in jail." Conspiratorially she whispered, "Mama's in jail, too, so she's gone—"

As understanding dawned on Daisy's face, Sophy realized that gripping the cup wasn't enough to keep her hands from shaking. She set it down and clasped them together in her lap.

"My mama's got a brother named Sean, and your name is Sean, too. Isn't that funny?"

Maybe it was premature to say *understanding*.

"Not really." Sean took a breath. "I'm your mom's brother. I'm your uncle, Daisy."

Sean had never imagined himself saying those words to anyone. Hell, he'd never planned on having family in his life again. He'd had enough of Holigans to last three lifetimes, and he had no intention of taking on a wife, her family, maybe kids. Too much responsibility.

But he'd said them, and here he was, holding his damn breath waiting for them to sink in. He had no idea what to expect, but it wasn't the reaction he got.

Daisy stared at him a long time, her head tilted to one side, then put her cup down, got to her feet and slid her chair under the table. "Mama says she don't need her worthless brothers, so we don't, neither."

Picking up the cup again, she walked away with a fair amount of dignity for a five-year-old.

Maggie's words were no surprise. Neither was the fact that she'd said them to her daughters. She'd always been one to speak first and consider the consequences—well, usually not at all. The surprise was that hearing them in Daisy's little girlie voice added an extra sting to them. He hadn't even known she existed before yesterday, and she knew just as little about him. Of course she would repeat what she'd heard Maggie say.

"I'd love to be able to say something wise here, but the truth is, I'm pretty new at this fostering business. I've only had the girls a few weeks, and we're still getting to know each other." Sophy smiled ruefully. "They have a lot of personality."

That was a polite way to put it. He'd usually heard words like *unruly, undisciplined, out of control, disreputable* when people described Holigans. "I wasn't expecting a warm and fuzzy reunion." He shouldn't have met the kids at all. There was no need. He was here to deal with Maggie.

But when he'd left the jail, he'd walked out to his car, then kept on walking. Before he'd known it, the sign for Hanging by a Thread—looking like a tabletop holding scissors, needles, thimbles and a big spool of thread, with a slender pony-tailed blonde climbing up its dangling tail—was ahead of him. He'd turned automatically through the gate, climbed the steps, walked through the door…and there had been one of the Maggies he remembered: young, inquisitive, bold and innocent.

Innocence being relative, he thought, recalling her casual words: *Gone means they're in jail.*

Five-year-old girls with big eyes shouldn't know what jail was.

"So..." Sophy fiddled with her cup. "What brings you back to Copper Lake?"

"I heard about Maggie."

Concern crossed her face, making her brown eyes shadowy. "You came for the girls?"

"You mean to take them?" He'd faced a lot of scary things—hell, he'd been in prison—but the idea of taking custody of a five- and a six-year-old girl made him quake. "What would I do with them?"

Relief washed over her, and she tried to cover it by breaking off a piece of cookie from the box in the middle of the table. "Mostly answer questions. Repeat things to them. Try to teach them a few manners here and there. Chase them down."

"Are they escape artists?"

"The best."

Sounded familiar. "Our father used to tell us about when Declan started school. He ran away and made it all the way back home by himself three of the first five days. Ian did it four."

"And did you make it five?"

He shrugged modestly.

"They haven't succeeded in getting away from me yet, except for the day Ty and the social worker brought them. Since Ty was still here, I share the blame with him." She rapped her knuckles on the wood tabletop for luck. "The only reason they haven't escaped yet is because this place and my apartment—" she gestured toward the second floor— "are pretty secure. They've tried when we're out, but I'm fast and I know my way around better than they do."

The minds of kids baffled him. He had a pretty good idea what life was like for Daisy and Dahlia with their mom—a shabby house, probably never cleaned, dirty secondhand clothes, no regular or healthy meals, baths only when they couldn't be avoided, men in and out, always a little drama going on. Sophy's apartment was surely as clean as her shop; it was probably quiet, homey, with a room of their own, clean sheets, clean clothes that fit, good food, a healthy environment.

Gazing at her, he wondered if there was a man in her life. Probably. She'd fulfilled the promise of beauty he remembered in her fourteen-year-old self. Golden skin, a pink Cupid's-bow mouth, a smile that could make a man think about forever, and who didn't love a brown-eyed blonde?

If he were a different sort of man, he could. But he wasn't. No attachments, no obligations, no emotional ties—those were his goals.

How's that working for you, buddy?

"Where are you living these days?"

"Norfolk."

"Still crazy about cars?"

"How do you know that?"

She rolled her eyes. "Please. Everyone knew the Holigan boys and the Calloway boys practically lived at Charlie's." Then she grinned. "When my friends and I walked over to SnoCap for cherry limeades, my mom always told us not to talk to any of you. She had us half-convinced that something awful would happen if we did, that we'd go straight to hell or grow horns and a tail or something."

Of course she did. Mrs. Marchand had had very strong ideas about who was suitable company for her daughters and hadn't been shy about expressing them. "A Marchand and a Calloway seems like a good match."

Her mouth pursed slightly, Sophy shook her head. "They're all married and so settled you wouldn't recognize them."

"Even Robbie?" He'd been the youngest of the Calloway brothers, the one least likely to do anything of merit with his life.

"Loving husband, adoring father of two, lawyer, goes to church, does volunteer work and everything."

"I'm impressed." Not that it was hard for a Calloway to amount to something when the family owned half the damn county.

Jeez, even to himself, Sean sounded bitter.

"Why Virginia?"

Before he could answer, Daisy came scuffing back around. She glared at him, then at Sophy. "What time will Dahlia be out of school?"

"About three-fifteen."

"How long is that?"

"Four hours."

"How long is *that*?"

"Halfway between lunch and dinner."

Daisy's face wrinkled with impatience, then she cocked her head Sean's way. "He'd better be gone when Dahlia gets here."

Sean would have let her wander off again, but Sophy turned to face her. "Remember when we talked about being rude? What did I tell you?"

Her ducked-down head muffled Daisy's voice. "Not to, or I'll get a time-out."

"And that would mean no class for you today. Why don't you get your bin out and start setting up?"

While the girl shuffled off, Sean got to his feet. He'd seen the sign in the front window about this month's classes but couldn't imagine one that could hold Daisy's interest for more than five minutes. "I should get going."

Leaving Daisy settling in at another worktable, Sophy walked with him toward the front door. "Have you seen Maggie yet?" she asked in a low voice.

"Yeah, for a few minutes. She wasn't happy, so she didn't stick around long."

"Did she ask about the girls?"

It hadn't occurred to him until now that she hadn't. Even when he said, *I saw Daisy this morning,* she hadn't wanted to know how she looked, if she was okay, if she missed her mama. All she'd done was turn it into an opportunity to criticize him.

He shook his head, part embarrassed, part annoyed with his sister and part of him just plain sad.

Sophy's expression was resigned, as if this wasn't the first time she'd asked the question and gotten the same answer.

They were just feet from the door when it swung open and two white-haired women started inside before freezing in their tracks. One was a stranger to him, but the other had been the queen bitch of Copper Lake fourteen years ago and probably still was. Louise Wetherby had never liked anyone, but especially anyone she considered beneath her. The Holigans hadn't had the money to eat in her pricey restaurant or the right, in her mind, to live in her town or breathe her air. Even now, her nose was twitching as if she smelled something unwelcome.

Though her icy gaze was locked on him—as if

he might grab her purse and run if she looked away for a moment—her words weren't directed to him. "What is that man doing here, Sophy?"

"The same thing you are, Mrs. Wetherby. He came to see about making a quilt."

The tautness of Sean's muscles eased slightly.

The Queen sniffed haughtily while her minion twittered. "Don't be ridiculous. We thought we'd seen the last of him when we ran him out of town all those years ago."

"You must be confusing him with someone else, Mrs. Wetherby," Sophy said with scorn camouflaged by sweet Southern politeness. "As I recall, he graduated from high school one day and climbed on the back of his motorcycle and left town the next. He was gone long before anyone in town even knew. Now, just head on back to the work area. If you ask nicely, Daisy will be happy to help you get your supplies."

Another sniff as the two women began walking again. "A five-year-old has no place in a quilting class," Louise huffed, but her friend hesitantly argued.

"Now, Louise, she *is* learning to piece a quilt top, and that's exactly what the class is for. My grandmother learned to quilt when she was six, so it's not…"

As the old women's conversation faded, silence vibrated between Sean and Sophy. This time she hadn't turned red, the way she had when he'd mentioned the lack of welcome for him at her house, but rather looked more irritated than embarrassed. She opened the door, the bell ringing, then stepped outside onto the porch with him.

He broke the quiet when the door was closed behind them. "I see Louise is still her sunny, smiling self."

"Lucky us. You know, I've always wondered just what is so bad about that woman's life that she has to treat people the way she does. She's had every privilege money can buy."

"Some people are just that way."

She drew a deep breath, and in the late-morning light, he appreciated the fit of the red dress and its contrast against her skin and hair all over again. Out here, away from all the fabric, he could smell her perfume, sweet, teasing, there with one breath, gone with the next. Her eyes were browner, her skin warmer, her presence magnified, her smile twice as dazzling.

"Here I felt honored that you remembered my name, and then you pull Louise's name out of the thin air of your memory."

"Different reasons for remembering. She tried to have me arrested for hanging outside her restaurant. Said we were scaring customers away. And she tried to get us taken away from my dad a couple of times. She didn't think he was a fit father." After a moment, he added, "She was right about that. He was a lousy father, but he was ours. He was what we knew."

"Is that why you didn't come back for Mr. Patrick's funeral?" Sophy asked quietly.

He walked to the top of the steps and stared across the street. On the left was River's Edge, one of Copper Lake's grand old mansions, and on the right, a much-smaller, less genteel place that advertised itself as a bed-and-breakfast.

Probably a more comfortable place than the motel.

Definitely better situated for keeping an eye on Daisy and Dahlia.

As well as their foster mother.

Are you freaking crazy? The kids don't want you around; you need to keep your distance from Sophy; and what the hell does comfort matter to a Holigan?

"It's complicated," he replied at last, the answer as well suited to his thoughts as her question.

She came to stand a few feet away, making the warm day hotter. "Would you like to come over for dinner tonight so you can meet Dahlia?"

His gaze shot to her. A Marchand not only inviting him inside her home but to pull up a chair to the table and eat with them. Was *she* freaking crazy? There would be hell to pay with her parents, maybe even with the social worker. He doubted *hanging out with disreputable uncle* was on the social worker's list of acceptable activities for the kids.

"You can't meet one and not the other. Daisy would lord it over Dahlia to make up for not getting to go to school, and you don't want to see Daisy lording anything over Dahlia. About six? We eat early so they can have a little downtime before I have to wrestle them into the bathtub and pajamas and bed." She made a wry face. "They never had a regular bedtime before, and they're not loving it."

If he said yes, it would be one more stupid, dangerous agreement he'd made in the past day and a half. He hadn't had much chance at saying no to Special Agent Baker or Craig, but he could turn down Sophy. He could suggest coming after school to meet Dahlia, who wasn't likely to be any more welcoming than Daisy. He could even suggest they go out to dinner instead—somewhere about twenty miles away from town. He had a reputation to live down. She had one to protect.

But he didn't try to get the words *no, thanks* out of his mouth. He knew a losing battle when he saw it. All he could do was be on guard. "Okay," he agreed. "I'll see you at six."

Chapter 4

Sophy and Daisy were waiting on the porch when the school bus rumbled to a stop out front and Dahlia climbed off. Bouncing in place, Daisy waited until her sister had come through the gate, then raced to her. "Guess who I saw, Dahlia? Mama's brother Sean."

Shifting her backpack to the other shoulder, Dahlia scowled at her. "No, you didn't."

"Yes, I did. I saw him at Cuppa Joe, and then he come here. His name is Sean, and he's Mama's brother."

Leaning against the post at the top of the steps, Sophy wondered how she could have missed Sean at the coffee shop that morning. Oh, yes, because she'd had a whiny five-year-old in meltdown mode.

"No, you didn't. You're just makin' that up. He's locked up somewhere, just like Declan and Ian."

The set of her mouth smug, Daisy shook her head. "Ask her. She'll tell you."

Dahlia's gaze flickered to Sophy, then away again before she sullenly climbed the steps and went inside the shop.

"How was school?" Sophy asked as she and Daisy followed.

Dahlia shrugged her thin shoulders, continuing to the back, the refrigerator and the treats. Her uniform of khaki shorts and blue polo shirt was surprisingly clean and neat—Daisy wore milk, juice, grime and the *oops* of lunch on her clothes—and her ponytail was still in good shape. Because she hadn't met anyone to play with?

"I wanted to go to school, too," Daisy said, dogging her footsteps, "but I'm glad she didn't let me because then I wouldn't have met Sean. Mama's brother. Our uncle."

After getting a bottle of milk from the refrigerator, Dahlia dropped her backpack on the table, turned to Sophy and gave up resisting. "Really?"

"Really. He's coming to dinner tonight to meet you."

She considered that a moment, then shrugged again. "I don't care. Mama says he's bad and we don't need him."

"That's what I told her!" Daisy exclaimed.

Mama says. Sophy wished Maggie had kept at least a few thoughts to herself. Who was she, anyway, to judge anyone else? Given the life she'd chosen, odds were good that her daughters might have to turn to one of their uncles one day, but loving-mom Maggie had tried to poison the girls against them.

"He's not bad, Dahlia, and he hasn't been locked up somewhere." Belatedly, Sophy hoped that was true. "He lives in Virginia. He just found out your mom was in trouble yesterday, and he came straight here."

"Is he gonna get her out of jail?"

"Um, I don't know." Ty had told Sophy that Maggie wasn't likely to get out on her hundred-thousand-dollar bond. She didn't have money like that, her boyfriend wouldn't spend it on her if he did and her local family—a couple of teenage nephews and two ex-sisters-in-law—couldn't afford it. Could Sean? If he could, would he?

Sophy wouldn't. She loved her sisters and her brother, but she wouldn't risk ten thousand dollars to get them out of jail, especially if they had a track record like Maggie's. But then, her sisters and brother wouldn't be in jail in the first place...well, except for Miri's one arrest. But Miri hadn't been selfish enough to get involved with drugs. She'd tracked down their birth father, gotten a job with his company and, um, *relieved* him only of the child support he'd failed to pay for all those years after abandoning them with their mentally ill mother.

Miri also hadn't expected to slide on it. She'd pleaded guilty, gone to prison and served her sentence...then delivered a share of the money to each of her siblings—Sophy, Chloe and Oliver. The payback was nice. Knowing how hard Miri had worked to recover what their bastard father had hidden from them was precious. Reconnecting with the siblings she'd been separated from more than twenty years ago had been priceless.

"If he's not gettin' Mama out of jail, I don't wanna meet him."

Dahlia got her work bin and settled at the table. She had a great eye for putting fabric colors and patterns together. That had been the hardest part about quilting for Sophy, something she hadn't mastered until she'd been in business a year or two. Even now, she sometimes questioned her choices until she cut out the shapes and laid them out together, but it came naturally to the six-year-old.

"You have an artist's soul," she murmured.

Though she pretended not to hear, the tips of Dahlia's ears turned red.

Sophy spent the next few hours waiting on customers and working on a baby quilt due next week. She'd already completed the rest of the order, all in light blue and tan and featuring a pudgy smiling elephant: a wall hanging, curtains, pillows, linens and, for future use, a tooth-fairy pillow, bearing the same elephant with a pouch beneath his back to hold the tooth and the money the fairy left behind. She planned to do something similar for her own babies' nurseries. She didn't have a dream wedding in mind, but she had already designed a couple of fairy-tale nurseries.

The girls' conversation flowed behind her: *Did you learn to read? Can you do times now? Was there a dog or a goldfish or a hamster? Did you make any friends?*

"There's a girl named Baylee. And one named Kayleigh. And one named Railey."

Daisy snorted. "Them's silly names."

Sophy wasn't sure someone named Daisy got to snicker at anyone else's name. Someone named Sophy definitely didn't.

"Were they nice?"

Hands stilling, Sophy waited for Dahlia's response. It was a long time coming, given softly. "Yeah. They were. We had lunch together and played at recess."

The muscles in her stomach eased, and Sophy was able to breathe again. *Thank you, God—and the "lee" girls.*

Obviously unaware of the importance of Dahlia's answer, Daisy asked wistfully, "Did you learn how to write? Maybe we could write a letter to Mama."

Sighing inside, Sophy added another item to her to-do list. She might not think much of Maggie's parenting skills, but the girls loved her. To paraphrase Sean, she might be a lousy mother, but she was theirs, and she was all they knew.

When five o'clock came—*Dahlia, did you learn how to tell time?*—Sophy laid her project aside and got the sweeper. Daisy liked running it, with *run* being the operative word, and Dahlia had taken well to the job of straightening the work areas. Sophy closed out the register and was about to shut off the lights when a newcomer arrived: Zeke, charming owner of Bitsy the pudgy dog. She'd met two handsome men in two days. She should mark this day on the calendar.

Daisy propped her hands on her hips. "You didn't come to make a quilt, too, did you?"

Feeling like propping her hands on her own hips,

Sophy shook her head. "Daisy, remember what a proper greeting is?"

After thinking about it a moment, Daisy said, "G'd afternoon. Can I help you?" Then, running the words together, she added, "You didn't come to make a quilt, did you?"

Zeke crouched to her level and grinned. "I never thought about it. Do you think I could?"

"I dunno. I never made one, either. Prob'ly not. Where's Bitsy?"

"She's at home." Standing again, he turned his attention to Sophy. "I was wondering if I could take you three lovely ladies to dinner this evening."

"We're havin' dinner with our uncle Sean—"

Forcing her smile to remain steady, Sophy clamped her hand over Daisy's mouth. "Thank you for the invitation, but we've already got plans."

Dahlia, standing out of Sophy's reach, hugged her backpack to her chest. "With our uncle," she repeated. "He'll be here soon."

Zeke's smile faltered, disappointment flashing through his eyes before the smile returned full wattage. "A day late and a dollar short. The story of my life. Well, I won't keep you. Got to have everything perfect for uncle Sean, right?"

Daisy nodded emphatically, dislodging Sophy's hand. "Right. 'Cause he's our mama's brother and he's meeting Dahlia for the first time ever."

"First time ever? That's an important date, isn't it?" He met Sophy's gaze. "I'll have to try again."

She watched him leave with a bit of regret. He was cute, a nice guy who loved his daughter's ugly dog. She knew a half dozen women, including herself, who would like to get to know him better based on nothing else.

Don't complain. You're having dinner with the hottest, sexiest, baddest boy you've ever met.

Was she the luckiest single woman in town tonight?

Or was she courting disaster?

The smell of fall-apart-tender pork ribs basted with teriyaki sauce greeted Sophy and the girls when they went inside the apartment. She'd taken advantage of her lunch break to get the ribs started in the slow cooker and to prep everything else: garden salad, green beans and sweet corn cooked with cream cheese. She was still operating in the dark when it came to most of the girls' tastes, but she figured there had to be something on the menu they would eat, even if it was only the tomatoes in the salad.

She sent the kids to change clothes, then went to her own room to do the same. It was at the front of the house, overlooking the street, with an excellent view of River's Edge from one window and Breakfast in Bed from the other. Though the street was busy during the day, at night there was little traffic, and she was a sound sleeper. She'd spent plenty of peaceful nights there.

Stripped down to her underwear, she stood in front of the closet. She would like to think it wasn't vanity that kept her there so long, but she wouldn't deny the truth: she wanted to look good for Sean. Even though he'd never been her type, even though the only thing between them was the girls. Even though bad boys like him reformed for good girls like her only in the romance novels she'd read. Even though cute, friendly and dog-happy was so much more her speed than gorgeous, brooding and wicked.

Finally she settled on an outfit she would wear any evening—shorts, a sleeveless shirt, sandals— and went into the living room, the keys in her pocket clinking together. When she turned the corner from the hallway, she found Daisy at the door, trying to pick the lock with a paper clip, and Dahlia rummaging through her purse.

"You looking for these?" She dangled the keys, put them back in her pocket and circled the island into the kitchen.

"We thought we heard a knock," Dahlia said sullenly.

"Well, next time that happens, you come get me, okay? I don't want you guys answering the door by yourselves."

"Prob'ly he won't come." Dahlia climbed onto the bar stool at the island so she could spin herself side to side.

Daisy climbed onto the next stool to mimic her as Sophy slid a loaf of bread from Ellie's Deli into the oven. She wanted to say, *Of course he'll come,* but what did she know? The girls had grown up in a family of disappointments, and she couldn't say how or even if Sean was different from the others.

"If he doesn't, we'll have barbecue sammies for lunch tomorrow, and someone else will have to eat his share of the veggies."

The girls were in the middle of a collective groan when footsteps thudded on the stoop, followed by a knock. They stared at each other wide-eyed while

Sophy whisked off another silent prayer. She'd always been a churchgoing girl, but it seemed the number and intensity of her prayers had increased tenfold the past few weeks. She set the corn on one burner, turned to medium, and the green beans on another, then headed toward the door.

Though she hardly felt the need—the butterflies in her stomach were all the confirmation she needed—she lifted the edge of the curtain just enough to catch a glimpse of Sean, then unlocked the door.

He'd changed clothes, too, to a pair of jeans less faded but just as tight as he'd worn that morning and a dove-gray T-shirt that fitted mouthwateringly snug. His hair had been recently combed, his beard shaved. The small changes made him less wicked and more gorgeous, if either was possible.

He approved of her clothes, too, if she was reading the quirk of his mouth correctly. His gaze left heat where it slid over her arms and legs, then back up over her body, all the way to the hair hanging loose around her shoulders. *Wow,* she thought.

Hellfire and brimstone, she could hear her mother warning.

"Come on in." After he took a few steps, she secured the dead bolt and put the keys away.

"Did you just lock me in?"

"No, I just locked the girls in and anyone else out." She made a dismissive gesture, not wanting to explain the overkill of security she needed to feel safe in her own home. "While I was changing, they were looking for my keys."

"Do you sleep with them, too?"

She smiled and shrugged as she faced the kids. "Dahlia, this is your mama's older brother, Sean."

Still swinging her legs, Dahlia studied him the same way Louise Wetherby had. "Are you getting Mama out of jail?" Where did such a young girl learn such a sour attitude? *On the wrong side of town.*

Sean shook his head.

"Then why are you here?"

"There are other ways to help—"

She rolled her eyes and spun until her back was to him. After a moment, Daisy did the same thing.

"Wrong answer, I guess," he murmured to Sophy.

"I've learned that sometimes there is no right answer." She stirred the corn in the melting cream cheese, sugar and milk, gave the green beans a shake, then checked the timer on the bread. "Girls, you've got about fifteen minutes until dinner's ready. You can watch TV if you want. No fighting, no blasting my eardrums."

The kids pushed past Sean as if he were invisible, heading to the television and sofa at the far end of the room. He slid onto the stool Dahlia had vacated. "I guess the rules have changed since I lived in town. If we got arrested, we stayed there until we'd done our time or they got tired of us. No one ever bailed out anyone, and no one expected them to."

It was a hard life he'd lived, one Sophy didn't even want to understand. She felt cosseted and spoiled in comparison, even in the time her birth mother had cared for them. "Mr. Patrick's been gone a long time, so the girls never even knew him. They live by Maggie's rules, and she's…"

"I think the word you're looking for is *self-centered.*"

He gazed at the girls, the backs of their heads identical and so much like their mom's. "Maggie was always spoiled—the only girl in a family of males, our mother running out before she even started walking. She got used to special treatment, and when there was no one else to give it to her, it looks like she gave it to herself."

"I always wondered why your mother left."

He grinned. "Wherever she went was definitely a step up from Patrick Holigan and his four hooligans."

"But you were *her* hooligans, too."

"Maggie and I were. Ian and Declan had a different mom. She took off, too. Women who marry into the Holigan family tend to do that."

"In my family, it was my father." She removed a platter from the cabinet, then spooned the ribs and sauce onto it. She glanced up to see Sean's puzzled look. "I'm adopted. My birth father didn't think it was good for his career when my mother's schizophrenia got out of control, so he left. My older sister, Miri, took care of us and Mom as long as she could, but eventually Mom lost custody and I wound up here."

His gaze moved over her slowly, measuringly. If she hadn't already been warm from the heat drifting out of the slow cooker, just his look would have made her that way. "So that's why you look like the fair-haired stepchild."

She smiled faintly. She'd been old enough to remember her first family when she was adopted. She'd more or less understood the concept, but she could remember looking at early Marchand family portraits, fixated on everyone else's dark hair and blue eyes. To her child's mind, her coloring had screamed *outsider* when she wanted very much to belong. "Yup, my other family are the brown-eyed blonds."

The timer went off, and she turned to remove the bread from the oven, inhaling deeply of the savory yeasty loaf. She tore the foil away, put the bread in a towel-lined basket, then automatically held it out, balanced in both hands. "Doesn't that smell incredible?"

Sean leaned forward, touching his hand to hers to bring the basket nearer, and the butterfly ballet in her stomach started again. Her mouth watered, not for fresh bread, not even for the tantalizing fragrance of his cologne, and she knew the answer to her earlier question.

She was a lucky woman. And she was most definitely courting disaster.

There had been a sad shortage of home-cooked meals in Sean's life. At the Holigan house, they'd thrived on cereal, canned soup and sandwiches. Once he got out of prison, he'd eaten the same things broken up by fast-food meals. Even now, the kitchen back in Norfolk was the least used room in the apartment.

This—eating a regular meal with a nice woman at a cozy table for four, even with the kids—was something he could get used to. Maybe. Five, ten, twenty years in the future.

The conversation wasn't as enticing as the food and the general sense of companionship. Neither Daisy nor Dahlia were showing any signs of warming up to him, and after an hour, he could see that they weren't exactly warm to Sophy, either. It was no big surprise, but his nieces were brats.

After picking at and over their food, they were finally dismissed from the table and allowed to return to the television until bath time. Daisy pushed her chair in hard enough to bump the table and glowered at him. "Do you have a TV?"

"Yes, I do." One that was really too big for his living room with a sound system that could vibrate the downstairs neighbors out of their beds.

"We only get to watch TV *one hour a day.* Isn't that mean?"

Given the way they behaved, he thought they were lucky to get to watch commercials for three minutes. "That's the rule of the house."

Dahlia stopped beside Daisy, one foot pressed against the other calf and rotating side to side courtesy of the socks she wore. "What's that mean?"

"Every house has rules. You obey them or you go live somewhere else."

Her features wide with extreme irritation, Daisy gestured toward the door. "We can't get out to go someplace else. We're pris-ners."

He shrugged. "Prison has rules, too. Lots of them. There, you obey them or you get locked in your cell. You only get to come out for fifteen minutes a day."

"Which is about how much TV time you're going to have left if you don't quit complaining and start watching." Sophy gave them a stern look, and both girls heaved and dragged their scrawny butts over to the sofa.

Sean watched until they settled in, then turned back to Sophy. "I didn't realize you had a masochistic streak. Why aren't you married and raising two or three cute little blonds of your own? What are you doing trying to shape Maggie's kids into something that resembles human children?"

"I was a foster kid myself before Mom and Dad adopted me. I know how important the system is, and they're always needing volunteers, so—" she shrugged self-deprecatingly "—I wanted to give back. To help frightened kids in difficult situations get through them."

"There's the first mistake—Holigans are never frightened," Sean said. He lied. He was scared about what would happen to Maggie and the kids if she opened her mouth. "And their 'difficult situation' is pretty much life as normal for them."

"But it shouldn't be. They deserve a chance to have a better life than their mother has. Maybe they'll learn something here. Maybe something will sink in and help them make a decision down the road that will save their lives."

Nature versus nurture. Could the attitudes and beliefs given a child by his birth family be overcome by a loving environment? Though Daisy and Dahlia were young, they'd already learned a lot from Maggie that could be hard to undo.

He didn't have a lot of faith, but he hoped Sophy was right.

"What about the other question?"

She toyed with her utensils a moment, then abruptly stood and began gathering dishes to carry into the kitchen. After three trips, the only thing left on the table besides their drinks were the salt and pepper shakers and a small bouquet of flowers in a blue pitcher. He knew the yellow ones were daisies and guessed the others were dahlias.

With nothing left to do, she sat down again, far enough away from the table to cross her legs and fold her arms over her middle. "Marriage and babies, huh? It's in my ten-year plan. First I had to get the shop up and running."

"It looks successful enough. So…"

"There are only so many single men in town, and I think I've dated all of them." She corrected herself. "Almost all of them."

"And not one of them was suitable for marriage?"

"Oh, they all were. AJ married Masiela. Tommy married Ellie. Joe married Liz. Robbie married Anamaria. Pete married Libby. Ty's marrying Nev. It's gotten to the point that when my girlfriends meet a guy they're seriously interested in, they ask me to go out with him for a while. It increases the odds in their favor." She smiled ruefully, then turned the question on him. "Why aren't you married and raising a garage full of little mechanics?"

Marriage had never been in his plans, not even when he was twenty-two and half in love with Sara Moultrie. She'd been exotic, with a killer body, a satin-against-his-skin touch and a way of making a man forget everything in life but her. She was the only woman he'd broken his one-month rule for, but not even she had tempted him to consider marriage, though she'd made it abundantly clear in every tantalizing way she'd known that she was willing to consider it.

"Not everyone wants to get married."

Sophy smiled, far from exotic but just as tempting in a wholesome, innocent sort of way. "You don't want to be tied down."

"I like not having responsibility." He really did like it, and she needed to know just in case he forgot. He didn't normally forget things like lifelong beliefs, but he was in Copper Lake now. Having dinner with someone from his past. Dealing with Maggie and her kids. Not exactly feeling himself.

"If you're so averse to responsibility, what are you doing here?" Her tone was pleasant, disguising the pointed question as simple conversation. "As soon as you heard about Maggie's arrest, you took time off from your job, came straight here, made a point of meeting your nieces...."

He couldn't tell her the truth: that he wouldn't have come if not for the threat against Maggie and the girls. That he'd been ordered to come by his drug-dealing, chop-shop-owning, murdering boss, whom he was informing on for the DEA. That he would rather be anyplace else in the world than here.

When he didn't respond, Sophy said, "I think you're deluding yourself, Sean." A slow smile spread across her face, giving her a tender, serene, satisfied look that reminded him of all the softness he'd never had in his life—all the little intimacies a boy shared with his mother, a teenager with his girlfriend, a man with his wife. How in hell had Dahlia and Daisy managed not to melt under its warmth? She *looked* like love and caring and concern and hope and faith and comfort and security.

How much damage had Maggie done to her daughters that they could resist Sophy?

As giggles came from the couch, he glanced at his watch. "It's been twenty minutes."

Sophy gazed at the girls, her expression sad. "They seldom smile, and they rarely laugh. They don't have any friends. The only people they know outside the family are police officers, social workers and drug users and/or dealers. The only medical care they get is when Maggie gets arrested for making meth and they're automatically checked out at the hospital."

It shamed Sean that this was his blood she was talking about, that his baby sister could have so little care for the lives she'd brought into the world. How much of that was his fault? If he'd sent for her when he got out of prison, would things have turned out differently? Would she have finished school? Gone to college? Held a job, learned responsibility, thought twice about having babies?

Or would she have lived the same life, just in a new place? Had it already been too late for her?

"Why hasn't she lost them permanently before now?"

"Overtaxed systems and sympathetic judges. She's always very sorry, always swears it'll never happen again. She voluntarily enters rehab, then checks herself out again after a few weeks. She gets a job and quits within a day or two. She has good intentions, but they never last."

Would prison give Maggie time to strengthen those intentions? Would the threat of death be enough to force her to change the way she lived?

The silence grew between them until finally Sophy smiled weakly and called, "Girls, it's time for your bath."

Daisy's head jerked around. "But we took a bath last night!"

Sophy feigned shock. "I *know.* You've taken one every night you've been here, and you'll keep taking them every night. That's the rule of the house."

Dahlia shut off the television, then tossed the remote on the sofa, her narrowed gaze zeroing in on Sean. "Thanks a lot."

How had a kid that scrawny mastered such snideness?

He smiled back. "You're welcome."

"I didn't mean—" Rolling her eyes, she headed toward the hall.

Without thinking, he said, "Hey, come back here and tell me goodbye…unless you want me to stick around and tuck you in and kiss you good-night."

He'd never used the word *flounce* in his life, but that was exactly what they did, stopping just outside his reach, standing stiff and oozing disdain. Daisy, of course, spoke first. "G'bye. Nice to meet you. Don't let the door hit you on the ass—"

"Daisy," Sophy warned.

"That's what Mama says."

Yeah, this was a pint-size version of the sarcastic Maggie that Sean remembered.

Dahlia stepped in before Daisy could add more. "G'bye. If you don't get Mama out of jail, we don't need to see you again."

Still moving rigidly, they disappeared down the hall. A moment later, the sound of running water filtered back.

Had Sophy known Daisy's and Dahlia's silky

black hair hid devilish horns when she'd agreed to foster them?

He stood, and so did she. They walked the few feet to the door, where she undid the lock for him before sliding the keys back into her pocket.

"Thank you for dinner."

"Thank you for not running out screaming. They have that effect on a lot of people."

"I'm a grown-up Holigan. I can run wilder than those kids ever dreamed of." Her perfume drifted on the still air, sweet and girlie and tempting. Filling a deep breath with it, he blindly located the doorknob, opened the door and lost the scent as warm night air drifted in. "Despite their polite request, I'll see them again if it's okay with you."

"Of course. They need all the people on their side they can get."

With a nod of acknowledgment that she automatically returned, he headed down the stairs and toward the Chevelle parked on the street. Seeing Daisy and Dahlia again meant also seeing Sophy. As ideas went, that one was monumentally bad, but the part of him that had been alone pretty much forever was already looking forward to it.

He was pretty sure that made it officially the worst idea he'd ever had.

Thankfully, the shop was busy Tuesday morning, or Sophy was convinced Daisy would have gone insane and taken her along for the ride. Why had she thought the second day of school would be easier for poor, left-behind Daisy? Oh, no—now that she knew what wonderful things went on inside those brick

walls, she wanted more than ever to put on a uniform, take her lunch and ride the bus. She wanted to
meet Baylee and Kayleigh and Railey—*hey, maybe
we could change our names to Daily and Dahlee!*—
and to have recess and learn everything.

With a nice little staccato drumbeat pounding in
her head, Sophy flipped the old-fashioned out-to-
lunch sign over and turned out the front lights. "It's
lunchtime, Daisy. Are you hungry?"

"No" came the mopey answer from the back of
the shop.

"Want to have a picnic?" For late August, it was a
nice day, and the thought of sunshine, warm weather
and the sounds of nature soothed the ache in her
temples a little.

"No."

Sophy walked through the shadows to the work
area, where Daisy half sat, half sprawled across a
table. The French braid she'd been proud of this
morning had come loose, bobby pins still holding a
few strands of hair, the rest of it falling free. A half
dozen scribbled drawings in clashing colors were
scattered around her head, and her pretty little face
was drooped into the best example of dejection ever.

"Do you feel okay?" Sophy pulled out the chair
across from her.

"Yeah."

"Are you a little blue?"

"Yeah." A sigh, followed by "I don't know what
that means."

"It means you're sad."

"I'm a lot sad." She lifted her head. "Is Mama
ever comin' home?"

Sophy quavered inside. How was she supposed to answer that? Was it her job to tell the kids that this time Maggie was probably going to be gone a lot longer than ever before? Was it the right time to prepare them for the fact that they might be living with her, or other foster parents, not for weeks or even months but for years?

"She'll be home, sweetie, when she's better. But it might take a while."

"How long is a while?"

"No one knows exactly."

"Then why does everyone say it when they don't know what it means?" Daisy jumped to her feet so quickly that her chair fell over backward, one leg scraping her own leg. She yelped, then shoved the chair away. "Stupid chair! Stupid pictures! Stupid place! I hate this place! I hate it! I wanna go home!"

After swiping the drawings and markers onto the floor, Daisy took off down the center aisle, grabbing the display ends of fabric bolts, yanking them to the floor. Signs fell in her wake, and freestanding displays of thread went flying, all accompanied by her unhappy wails.

"Daisy!" Sophy chased after her, sidestepping merchandise, narrowly missing her when Daisy darted beneath a display onto the next aisle, then continued her rampage.

"I hate this place, I hate it, I hate it!" Helped along by her little hand, a shelf full of how-to books hit the floor with thuds, then she yanked the Halloween banners from the thin wires that hung them from the ceiling.

As she rounded a corner, Sophy's foot slid on the

wood floor, and she grabbed to catch her balance. While it was still touch-and-go, Daisy's shrieks and tears and tearing about abruptly stopped. Steadying herself, Sophy saw the girl first, dangling in midair, and then the person who held her.

Relief rushed through Sophy. There were only a handful of people who could have walked in in the middle of Daisy's meltdown without mortifying her—Nev, Ty, Liz, all of whom had had their own experiences with Daisy…and Sean.

And he was such a gorgeous addition to any day.

His dark gaze checked her out before sliding to Daisy. "Do you like cleaning up messes?"

Her eyes that were so like his were puffy, her cheeks red, her breath coming in little hiccups. The defiance wasn't gone, though. "Yes, I do."

"Good." He set her down, turned her around and swatted her butt. "Get started."

She puffed up in shock, staring at him. "You *hit* me! Nobody hits me!"

"I can tell, because if they did, you wouldn't mistake that pat for actually getting hit."

Whirling around, she stomped away, picking up a book here, a spool of thread there. She shook out a banner, folded it in a jumble—but at least she tried—and laid it on a shelf before turning to the next.

Sophy took a deep breath. "It's like herding monkeys one-handed with your ankles tied together."

Again his cool dark gaze moved over her, this time with more intensity than before, and she resisted the urge to make sure her hair was in place, her shirt covering what it should. It was tough enough to display her incompetence as a mother figure for him to see, but thank heavens, she hadn't fallen on her butt in front of him.

"Have you had a break since you took them in?"

She smiled ruefully and finally let herself comb her fingers through her hair. "You mean, like get a babysitter?" The idea hadn't occurred to her before, though she was sure it would have soon. "I can't imagine who would agree to watch them. Maybe if there's an empty cell at the jail…"

The thought gave her pause. "I bet Nev and Ty would keep them for a few hours. Ty's seen them at their worst, and they weren't far off that for Nev."

"Go call them. I'll help here."

Sophy hesitated only a moment. Though she hated the idea of having to ask for help, she really did need a little time off. Just a few precious hours not worrying about what the girls were doing, thinking, feeling, plotting. She climbed halfway up the stairs along the north wall, sat and dialed Nev's number, watching bemused as Sean straightened each bolt of fabric and returned it to its place and Daisy actually seemed to find pleasure in bringing order to the disorder.

"How can I help you, sweet pea?" Nev answered cheerfully.

"What makes you think I need help?"

"The sun went dark, the air turned cold and an otherworldly voice boomed, 'I want to go to school!'"

"She wants to go to school, she wants to go home, she hates the shop, she hates me…. You're right. I'm suffering from caregiver fatigue. I need a break, any time you and Ty are free, just for a couple hours."

"Will you promise to make good use of these hours?"

"If curling up in a catatonic ball somewhere quiet and peaceful counts." Sophy was surprised when strong dark fingers took the phone from her.

"How about dinner in some adults-only spot, complete with wine and chocolate?" Sean asked.

Even from a distance, Sophy heard Nev's deep, full laughter. "Sean, sweetheart, you are clearly my kind of man. Tell Sophy of course we'll do it. In fact, I'll come over around four so she can take her time getting ready, and Ty will come when he gets off. That means you two will be free to leave by five-thirty."

"Thanks, Nev. You're a sweetheart. See you then."

When he returned the phone to Sophy, she wrapped her fingers around it. "How do you know Nev?"

"I ran into Ty at the jail yesterday, and she was with him. Your reprieve will begin at five-thirty."

She gazed at him, on eye level thanks to the steps she sat on. "I didn't know there *was* an adults-only place in Copper Lake, other than clubs and bars."

"That's because you go out with the wrong guys."

He was right. In one way or another, they'd all been wrong for her.

"And if you still need to curl up in a catatonic ball, that's okay, too."

She smiled. "Thank you. What brings you out today?"

His mouth quirked. "I went to see Maggie, but she wasn't accepting visitors."

"She didn't get her share of swatting when she was a kid, either, did she?"

"Nope. For us guys, everything was more physical—

affection, encouragement, discipline. Maggie was 'too delicate for the likes of us,' the old man used to say." He smoothed another couple bolts of fabric, squeezing them in between coordinated swatches, then picked up a handful of spools of thread.

Feeling calmer, less frustrated and less incompetent by half, Sophy joined him on the floor, righted the thread display, then began sorting them into the right color slots.

He lowered his voice. "I'm going to the house to pick up a few things. Maggie wouldn't see me, but she left me a shopping list." He pulled a piece of paper from his pocket, written in a barely legible hand, and held it between two crooked fingers. "Do the girls need anything?"

Sophy considered it. Daisy had her stuffed monkey that she slept with, and Dahlia had her favorite shoes and a tiny pillow. Other than that, all they'd brought with them was a paper sack of clothes, worn and ill-fitting. No much-loved books, according to the social worker, because their mom didn't read to them. No favorite movies because they didn't own any. No special toys because all their toys were second- or thirdhand and mostly broken.

"Can I go with you?"

The whispered words surprised both of them into turning, where Daisy stood, her eyes filled with tears again. "I want a picture of Mama, and Dahlia wants her necklace. Please? I'll be good, I promise." With a sniffle, she dumped two handfuls of thread into Sophy's hands, then retrieved four more spools from her pockets.

Sean looked to Sophy to respond. She looked to

him and shrugged. "Okay." She dumped the thread into a basket nearby. "We can finish this later, can't we, Daisy? Let's go get your stuff."

She locked up, and they walked together to the Chevelle parked right out front. Sophy remembered seeing the car drive past Sunday night and admiring the deep red color and the *rrrumble* of the engine. "Why am I not surprised?" she asked with a laugh as he opened the passenger door, then moved the front seat so Daisy could climb in back.

"Just like I wasn't surprised to find you running a home-and-heart sort of business."

"We are what we've always been—a car guy and a homey, old-fashioned girl." She settled into the soft leather seat, fastened her seat belt, then turned what seemed an enormous crank to roll down the window. The Chevelle was in much better shape than her five-year-old Nissan, but her car was strictly transportation. The Chevelle was talent, skill, commitment, a lifelong love.

It didn't take long to get anywhere in Copper Lake. The closer they got to the Holigan house, the quieter it became inside the vehicle.

Sophy had been there once before, back in fifth grade. She and Maggie had stayed after school to work on a project, and by the time they finished, it was pouring rain. Her mom had insisted on giving Maggie a ride. They'd left the paved road, then followed the rutted dirt road to its end, where several houses clustered together, all belonging to various Holigans.

Maggie's house had been shabby, hardly livable, with trash piled high outside: discarded vehicles, broken toys, garbage. Rae Marchand had looked sad, Maggie ashamed. The place had been a painful reminder of the last place Sophy had lived with Miri, their mom and the younger two, leaving her misty-eyed.

But today was different. The sun was shining. She was better prepared now than ten-year-old Sophy had been. And Sean was here, stoic, unwavering.

There would be no crying today.

Chapter 5

There'd been a time, three or four generations ago, when Holigans had owned all the land they could see from the original home site: up the broad lazy creek that bore their name, down to the banks of the Gullah River. They'd been land-rich but cash-poor and far too fond of whiskey and poker. With each generation, the family holdings got smaller until all that was left was a few acres and three houses that would cost more to demolish than they were worth.

Sean parked at the side of the road, and they got out of the car and met at the front. Daisy skipped ahead, and Sophy waited while he stared at eighteen years of bad memories. When he'd left fourteen years ago, he'd been convinced he would never see this place again. He hadn't imagined Maggie living here, raising her daughters here. He sure as hell hadn't imagined coming here with Sophy Marchand. Back then, his pride couldn't have borne it.

It wasn't a whole lot easier today. He wanted to tell her he would never live like this again, to describe his apartment, relatively new, neat, spotlessly clean. He put things away as soon as he finished with them, he dusted and vacuumed every other day, he made his bed first thing in the morning, he kept even the memory of this mess far, far at bay.

Yellow-and-black crime-scene tape dangled from either side of the door. The screen door lay broken on the ground beside the stoop, and plywood sheets covered several of the windows. He would like to think that was because of the most recent police raid, but weeds were growing through the screen, and the plywood was weathered, the nails holding it rusty. The door was locked, but he knew which brick to remove to find the spare key. When he opened the door, out rolled the smell of general lack of cleanliness, along with the staleness of being closed up for weeks.

Daisy went inside first and straight to a bookcase that had stood against the front-room wall for as long as Sean could remember. Its finish was scarred and stained, its shelves tilted crookedly, and it held everything except books—a pile of ragged socks, empty beer cans, crumpled paper plates, stacks of junk mail. She picked up a picture frame knocked over on the bottom shelf and clutched it tightly as she headed down the hall.

Sean and Sophy followed her into Declan's old room. A mattress and box springs sat on the floor, the sheets a mess. Toys were scattered around, and clothes, empty juice boxes and candy wrappers, shoes, a handful of pinecones and rocks. Daisy plowed through it, heading straight for the wall where a couple of nails pounded into the drywall held necklaces of cheap beads.

"This is Dahlia's necklace. It b'longed to our great-great-great-grandma. She's been dead a long time. We never met her." She held up a short piece of red string, knotted around polished chunks of stone. Sean could remember their father letting Maggie wear it a few times, saying it would be hers when she was grown, that it would be worth something to her someday.

Worth so much she'd given it to her little girl.

He didn't look at Sophy, didn't want to see the pity or disgust or shock on her face. Flushed and edgy, he pulled Maggie's list from his pocket. "I'll get this stuff so we can go—"

They caught the scent at the same time, her nose wrinkling delicately. It was coming from the back of the house, strong enough to overpower years of living and dirt and neglect. His first thought was stupid: *Smoke? In a house that's been empty three weeks?*

The second made his chest tight and his blood pump cold: *They made meth in this house.* He didn't know much about illegal drugs in general, but he damn well knew that the products used to make meth were volatile as hell, and the explosions they caused…

Scooping Daisy up, holding her tight when she wiggled, he grabbed Sophy's arm and pulled them into the hall. "Let's get out of here!"

They made it maybe six feet before the kitchen exploded into flames. The blast threw him against the wall, shook Sophy off her feet, too. Daisy screamed, first clapping her hands over her ears, then wrapping her arms tightly around his neck. They withdrew from the searing heat, past the kids' room, into the bedroom at the end of the hall. No plywood on the windows in there, thank God.

"Take Daisy," he commanded even as Sophy held out her arms, saying, "Give her to me," but the girl refused to let go.

"Hell," Sophy muttered. She shoved the door shut, grabbed something from the floor—part of a long-unused vacuum cleaner—and slammed it against the front window, shattering the glass. Yanking an armful of sheets and blankets from the bed, she knocked out the remaining glass, then laid them over the frame.

Her hair whipped around as she looked for something to stand on to boost herself out the window. With smoke pouring under the door, Sean grabbed her arm. His muscles straining, he lifted her with his free arm until she could slide out the window, then shoved Daisy into her arms, jerking her hands loose from their fierce hold on him.

As he placed his hands on the sill, another explosion rocked the house, blowing the door open, a violent burst of flame shooting six feet into the room. He fell against the wall, his arm stinging, then regained his balance and vaulted through the window, landing hard on the packed dirt outside.

His ears were ringing, the sting in his arm turning to pain. Daisy's tears echoed distantly as soft, tender hands pulled at him. "Get up, get up, get up," Sophy chanted, her voice little more than a whisper. He stumbled to his feet with her help, and they backed off to the creek bank at the far side of the road, where Daisy waited. Immediately she grabbed on to him again, tears running down her face as she stared at the flames.

"Our house! Our stuff! What happened?"

Your mother is criminally stupid.

Sean took a step back, leaning against the pine tree there, then slowly sank to the ground. Sirens sounded in the distance, and every dog within a mile was barking. Sophy searched her pockets, for a tissue, he guessed, and came up with a neatly folded wad of paper towels.

"Tissues are on the shopping list," she murmured as she crouched beside him.

His left arm stung sharply, and he jerked away, but she anticipated the move and held tightly. "You're bleeding," she said, and he looked down to see a long cut along his biceps. The cut and the blood didn't affect him. He'd had far worse of both. But the sight of Sophy's hands on him…

Small, delicate hands. No polish on the nails; when would she have time? Soft, but callused on the tips of her fingers. Skin much lighter than his, warm, gold, a perfect match to her blond hair and brown eyes. A little oval scar between her thumb and index finger.

"I must not have gotten all the glass out of the window." Regret tinged her voice, and a strand of hair fell across her face as she held pressure to the cut. Even the pores on his fingers wanted to brush it back, but with Daisy still clinging to him, he didn't have a free hand to do anything.

"Hey, you got us out of there. What's a little scrape compared to being burned alive?"

"If I weighed ten pounds more, I'm not sure you could have lifted me out the window."

"Nah, I had strength to spare."

Her smile was shaky, and her hands began to tremble. She half sat, half fell to the ground and scooted up beside him, so close he could feel the tremors ricocheting through her body. "Oh, my God, Sean, we could have died in there," she whispered.

Grimly he settled his arm around her shoulders and stared at the house. What were the odds that the house just happened to spontaneously combust when they were there, as opposed to a deliberate act—a message from Craig or one of Maggie's partners in crime destroying any evidence that might remain? It had been stupid to come here, stupid to bring Sophy and insane to bring Daisy.

Thank God they were all right.

And, damn, did she have to feel so good up next to him?

The first vehicle to arrive on the scene was a fire engine, its siren loud enough to make Daisy grab her ears again. Another followed, along with paramedics and a dark Charger. Ty parked behind the ambulance, then strode over and extended his hand. "Give me your keys."

With a grunt, Sean pushed to his feet and maneuvered free of Daisy again, handing her off to Sophy. He dug his keys from his pocket and held them out. "You're just moving it, right?"

Grinning, Ty bounced the keys on his palm before

catching them. "I might take it around the neighborhood a few times."

As he headed for the Chevelle, Sophy sniffed. "I could have moved the car. Or are women not allowed to drive your baby?"

She looked remarkably good for someone who'd just been through a near-death experience. There was some dirt on her clothes, and her hair was messed up a little, but other than that, she was freaking beautiful.

"I've had that car six years, and no one's ever driven it but me." Then, without thought, he added, "Though I might make an exception for you. Depends on what I get in return."

He expected another sniff, a laugh or a dismissal. Instead, she got very serious, leaned close to him and whispered, "I'll keep that in mind."

Well, damn. Now she'd guaranteed that so would he.

Maggie shuffled into the visitors' room, the shadows under her eyes darker and her scowl so like their father's that Sean could practically see the old man there in her place. She went as far as the table with its stools, then cocked one hip and braced her fists on her waist. "Why the hell is Ty Gadney telling me I have to see you? I don't have to see anyone but my lawyer, and you ain't him."

"Because somebody needs to tell you what to do. You don't have the sense to figure it out for yourself."

She shoved her two-toned hair from her face, her bottom lip stuck out the way Daisy's did when she was pissed. "Where's the stuff I asked you to bring?"

Sean smacked his phone on the table harder than he should have. "With everything else you own."

After giving him a distrustful look, she picked up the phone and stared blankly for the time it took her to recognize the scene in the photo. "Oh, my God. Oh, my God, my house— My things— Oh, my God, what happened? What am I gonna do? Where am I gonna live when I get out of here?"

Reclaiming the phone, Sean put it in his pocket, then leaned against the concrete-block wall. "I went there to pick up your stuff. I took Daisy and her foster mother with me so Daisy could get a photo of you and Great-Grandma's necklace for Dahlia. We were there, Maggie, in the hall outside the girls' room when the kitchen exploded. We could have been killed!"

Maggie hugged her thin self, pivoting from side to side. "You say that like it's my fault. I wasn't there! I didn't do anything!"

Sean had a routine physical every spring, and every year he heard the same thing: *you're in good shape, your blood pressure's perfect, your cholesterol, your heart.* At the moment, he was pretty sure his head was about to explode. "You and your worthless friends made meth there how many damn times? And did it never occur to you to clean the place once in a freaking while? My God, you raised your babies there! You let them play on that floor, put things in their mouths, live with criminals and drugs. You raised them like animals, Maggie!"

Her head jerked up, her face pale. "You know what it was like. It was old and shabby and never taken care of, and after Daddy died, it was all I had. What was I supposed to do?"

"Clean it. Put your trash in the trash can, and when it's full, haul it out to the curb. Wash dishes when you're done with them. Sweep the floor every day. Put a fresh coat of paint on the walls. Scrub the bathroom and yourself and the girls and your clothes. Just because the place is shabby doesn't mean you have to revel in it like a pig in a pen."

She drew her shoulders back and raised her chin to look down at him, no matter that he was four inches taller. "Easy for you to criticize when you got a nice place of your own far away and you got plenty of money. Cleanin' that old place is pointless. It's old and ugly and stinking, it's always been old and ugly and stinking, and it'll always be—"

She broke off with a hiccup, no doubt remembering that it was now a soggy pile of ash, debris and brick—and probably smelled better than it had in years. Fifteen hundred degrees of searing heat could clean away a lot of filth. All she had left now was Daisy, Dahlia and herself.

Sean wanted desperately to believe that she valued the girls most, but the unlikelihood of that made his gut knot. He'd told her Daisy had been in the house, and she hadn't even asked if she was all right. All her concern was for herself—*her* house, *her* things, where *she* would live. Not even a halfhearted thought left over for her kids.

"Sit down, Maggie. We need to talk."

She looked about to refuse, then sank onto one of the orange stools. He took the one next to her, turning sideways to face her. "Your arraignment's coming up next week. What is your lawyer telling you to do about these charges?"

Lacing her fingers together, she began popping her knuckles. "That's privileged information." A good fierce scowl made her look away, then heave a sigh and lean close. "The district attorney wants to make a deal. She wants me to tell her everything I know about Davey—that's my boyfriend—and she says maybe I can get a lighter sentence." She scoffed, "Lighter, my ass. I ain't going to jail for what Davey did. I'm waitin' for a better offer. No jail time. A new start someplace better, since we ain't got a house anymore."

As Sean stared at her, old memories flashed through his mind: Maggie at six and eight and ten, young and sweet and still innocent, still hopeful. She looked twice her age now, bony and unhealthy, easily agitated, in denial about her life. Did she really believe the D.A. would offer a new start? That she could turn on a major drug dealer and happily start over in a new place? That she would waltz away from these charges, from Copper Lake, Davey and Craig with no consequences?

Somewhere inside she had to know none of that was going to happen. Dreams didn't come true for Holigans—look at him, back in hell after a fourteen-year reprieve—but Maggie had learned young that pretending was easier than facing reality.

Grimly, he refocused on the conversation. "Ty says they *caught* you and him both, Maggie, in the act. What do you know that could make that go away for you?"

She picked at her nails, swiped one palm on her

loose uniform pants, then leaned even closer. A whiff of odor—sweat, need, despair—wafted on the air between them. "Davey's not just a meth cook," she whispered. "The police don't know that yet. He works for some hotshot dealer back east that the cops have been trying to get for ages, and he told me a lot of stuff."

Not the sharpest knife in the drawer, Craig had said about Davey. He'd been right—and right to worry about Maggie talking. How the hell was Sean supposed to convince her to keep her mouth shut?

She shifted awkwardly. "Come on, Johnny. People make deals all the time. They get off on all kinds of crimes, and it's not like what I did was so bad. I wasn't *making* the meth. I just helped get some of the supplies and let him do it at the house and—and helped him out a little when he needed it."

"And used the finished product. And endangered your daughters' lives, to say nothing of your own and mine and Sophy's. Maggie, you've committed God knows how many felonies, and now you're spouting off about informing on your boyfriend's boss. Do you have any idea how dangerous that is?"

"It's no big deal. It beats going to prison." She shook her head stubbornly. "I done all this before, and I never went. I won't go this time, either."

God, was her brain too fried to realize how lucky she'd been before? The judge had cut her a break every time, and she'd just kept proving she couldn't learn from it. Now the breaks had run out. Prison was the least of her worries, and she didn't have a clue.

"You need to forget about rolling on Davey and his boss. You'll get yourself killed that way. Just accept responsibility, Maggie. Plead guilty. Take whatever sentence they give you and be grateful for it."

Her stare was disbelieving. "Plead guilty? Are you crazy? They'll lock me up for ten or fifteen years! Do you know how long that is?"

Yeah, he knew. It was more than a lifetime. In the beginning, it was impossible to even imagine that *this* was your world now: concrete walls, armed guards, thieves and rapists and murderers. Nothing to wear but a uniform, nothing to do but count the minutes, then the hours, then the days, until you realized you were driving yourself crazy. Losing hope and faith, a little bit of your sanity, a little bit of your humanity.

"It's better than being dead," he said flatly.

Though, in the beginning, not by much.

She shook her head, hair swinging, reminding him of Daisy and Dahlia. "No one's gonna kill me, not when I get my deal. I'll be out of here, Johnny—out of this damn cell, out of this damn town and state. No one will ever find me."

Rising, he walked to the window. He smelled of smoke and pine and dirt, and the dried trickle of blood pulled at the gash when he moved his left arm. He just wanted to take a shower or three, sleep a few hours and wake up to a smarter, more realistic sister who could see past her desire for drugs to the gravity of the situation she was in and the worse one she intended to set into motion.

Since the odds of that happening were somewhere between zero and none...

She came to stand beside him, bumping his arm with her shoulder. He winced but didn't complain.

"Maybe if you'd gotten yourself in trouble more often, you'd understand how the game is played." It was the cheeriest he'd heard her. "When I get off this time, I'm gonna clean up, Johnny, I swear. I'll go to rehab, do counseling, get a piss test every week. I'll get healthy and get a job, and I'll even start taking the girls to church. Dahlia started school, you know. I'll join the PTO and maybe volunteer there. I'll be a good mom and a good sister and a good person. It'll all turn out just fine. You'll see."

Finally, some mention of Daisy and Dahlia. It was too little, too late to impress him, but at least she didn't plan to abandon them permanently.

Which was probably the best thing she could do for them.

He gazed down at her sadly, tiredly. "Here's the thing, Maggie—hotshot drug dealers don't get to be hotshots by being nice guys. They're dangerous, and if the cops can't get this guy, that means he's smart, too, and he keeps an eye on his people. He knows Davey's been seeing you. He knows Davey told you too much. Do you think he would hesitate to kill you if he thought for one second that you might be a threat to his business?"

He hesitated, his voice going deeper, quieter. "Do you think he would hesitate to kill Daisy and Dahlia?"

She swiped her nose on her shirtsleeve, then laughed unsteadily. "You watch too much TV. My lawyer says if my information is as good as I say, the D.A. will deal. I'll get a whole new life. I'll be living the good life, Johnny. Don't I deserve that? Don't my kids deserve that?" She laid her hand on his. "I don't blame you. I understand now that you couldn't take me with you back then. You were too young. But now I can get it for myself. For my kids."

Aw, jeez. *I don't blame you for letting me down, but now don't stand in my way. Let me go on my way, living in my own world, always taking the easy way out, even if it means getting myself killed.*

Bitterly Sean faced her. "Keep your mouth shut, Maggie. Don't talk to anyone, not the cops, not your lawyer, not your cell mate. Even if you don't give a damn about anyone in this life except yourself, for God's sake, keep your mouth *shut*."

Sophy thought she would never get the smell of smoke from her hair, her clothes, her pores, but finally, once the shower water started turning cool, she shut it off and toweled dry. Cheery voices came from down the hall—Daisy, Dahlia, Nev—and she let them wash over her soothingly as she dressed in a denim skirt and plain white shirt. She dried her hair, braided it and put on makeup with a light hand.

She and Sean had decided to skip foster-mom's night out after the incident at the Holigan house, but Nev would have none of it. Sophy needed a break now more than ever, and she and Ty would watch out for the girls with their lives. Since Sean had seemed more than willing, Sophy had gone along for one simple reason.

She wanted time alone with him. She wanted to be a woman, not a foster mom. She wanted to have no bigger concerns than was he going to kiss her and if he tried, was she going to let him?

The second answer was easy. Neither of her mothers had raised any fools.

The timbre of the voices changed, two males adding to the mix. With a spray of perfume, she left the bedroom and walked down the hall. Both men glanced at her, with Sean's gaze lingering, warm and heavy, long after Ty's had moved on.

"—talked to the arson investigator before I left the office," Ty was saying. "She found an accelerant in the kitchen and into the hallway. All it needed was a start, then age and residue from the meth operation took care of the rest. None of the neighbors saw anyone on the street who didn't belong, though there was a call from a guy over on Radcliff Street who reported a man coming out of the woods behind his house and cutting across his yard to the street."

Radcliff Street was the equivalent of three, maybe four blocks from the Holigan house, nothing between them but pine thickets and overgrown honeysuckle and jasmine growing wild.

"Did he get a look at him?" Sean asked.

Ty shrugged. "Average height, jeans and shirt, kept his head down, wore a ball cap, moved quickly."

Sophy hated to ask the question, so she avoided looking at Sean as she did. "Could it have been Gavin or Kevin?" They were his brother's youngest boys, barely into their teens and already started down the troublemaking path. They were at that dumb-boy age when practically anything could sound like a good idea.

"No," Ty replied. "They were doing their weekly community service shoveling the kennels at the animal shelter. Nev was supervising them."

Nev grinned. "You vandalize my car, you'd best be prepared to pay the price."

The drumbeat was starting in Sophy's head again. She didn't know if it showed, or if Nev just wanted her and Sean out of the apartment before things got any more serious, but she shooed them toward the door. "You two go out and have some nice, quiet grown-up time, and don't worry about these children one bit. We'll make sure they're in as fine shape when you return as they are now." To the girls, she explained, "That means we won't be beating you."

Daisy harrumphed. "You wouldn't beat us."

"If you did," Dahlia joined in, "*he* would have to arrest you."

"So maybe cops aren't so bad after all." Ty winked at the girls, then walked to the door with Sophy and Sean. "Seriously, don't worry. I've got my pistol, my Taser and my handcuffs. Things'll be fine here. You guys have fun."

As the door closed behind them, Sophy asked, "Do you think he brought all that to protect the kids or to protect him and Nev *from* the kids?"

"I can't imagine him needing anything more than a stern voice and a look. That was all it ever took for his granddad to control any of us."

"Yeah, well, you haven't seen Ty chasing Daisy down the street. He was looking and sounding stern, but who knows if he would have caught her if Nev hadn't grabbed her first?"

Sophy followed Sean down the stairs, always a nice position to be in with a handsome guy with a great body and the sense to not cover it with ill-fitting clothes. His jeans were snug and faded, and his shirt…ah, T-shirts were made for shoulders and chests and muscles like his.

As they walked along the sidewalk that ran from her porch to the street, she breathed deeply and was grateful to identify nothing more than clean clothes, shampoo, colognes and typical evening smells: coffee and pastries from A Cuppa Joe's, fried foods from various downtown restaurants and the savory-sweet aromas of handcrafted pizzas as a Luigi's delivery car drove past.

The Chevelle was parked on the street side of River's Edge, so they walked to the corner, meeting a few pedestrians, passed by a half dozen cars. It was when they were standing on the corner, waiting for the green light, that the sense of being watched crept between her shoulder blades and down her spine. She cast a long look over her shoulder, sweeping the sidewalks, the square, the businesses along the blocks. She didn't see anyone she knew, but there were a lot of buildings, a lot of vehicles, looking back at her.

She was a little antsy, and she told herself that was okay, mentally shaking it off. She was entitled to be wary, given that she was walking down the street with Sean of the much-gossiped-about Holigans. Without even trying, she could list twenty people who would immediately be on the phone to her parents if they saw her now. To say nothing of the fact that she'd almost been blown up in a meth house. She'd be grounded for months—and, the whole age and independent thing notwithstanding, her mother would do her best to make it happen.

When Sean gave her a tilted look, she realized she'd

chuckled out loud. "Sorry. I was just thinking… When Reba and I were growing up, our mother warned us about everything you could possibly imagine, but the only dangers I've ever faced—getting blown up in a meth house and taken hostage at gunpoint in my own shop—never even crossed her mind."

An electronic bird tweeted to signal the light had changed, and together they stepped off the curb. They were barely to the midpoint when tires screeched down the block. With Sean's hand on her arm, they jogged to the other curb. As they stepped up, a white car cut the corner so close Sophy felt the heat from its exhaust on her bare legs.

"Pay attention, moron!" she called, then frowned. "Oh, my God, either I'm a little giddy from the whole day or the girls are rubbing off on me."

Sean gave her a cynical, sexy look. "Just try not to say anything that I'm gonna get my ass kicked for."

Her gaze roamed over him, finding every little detail perfect and sexy and compelling and *hot-damn*. "I bet you could hold your own against most guys in town."

"Only because I learned Grandpa Holigan's first rule of survival in the crib—always fight dirty."

"Makes sense to me." She waited while he opened the Chevelle door for her, and she slid in as gracefully as her short skirt would allow. Her legs were her best feature, so her motto was show them off whenever she could.

The heat inside was oppressive, but rolling the windows down allowed a cooling breeze. Sean settled in the driver's seat, did this revving thing with the engine that probably put every male within a four-block radius on alert, then pulled from the curb. "Okay, tell me about getting taken hostage at gun-point in your own shop."

The look he gave her was pretty intense, so she assured him, "Oh, they weren't after me. I mean, no criminal deliberately winds up in a quilt shop, right? I would have just been…what do they call it? Collateral damage."

He didn't appear comforted by the words, so she launched into the story. "Did I mention my father never paid a dime of child support? After our mother's death, Miri went looking for dear old dad. John Smith had made a fortune in business and was making another one in politics. She embezzled the money he owed us, went to prison, served her time. When she got out, he didn't want his precious reputation sullied *and* he wanted the money back, so he sent a couple guys after her. They followed her and her boyfriend from Dallas to here, had us in the storeroom at gunpoint, and she pulled a knife and cut the one guy pretty badly. It was enough of a distraction for Dean to disarm the other guy, and they all got arrested, including dear dad."

He gave an admiring shake of his head. "You Smith girls are good to have in a bad situation. She saved you from gunmen. You saved us from the fire."

Her face warmed with pleasure. "I did my part, didn't I? I'm a self-rescuing princess."

"The best kind to be."

She glanced out the window and realized they'd reached the outskirts of town. There was nothing in the direction they were headed but country roads, occasional farmhouses and, three miles out, the lake for which the town was named. It wasn't unheard-of around here to find a restaurant in the middle of nowhere, but she couldn't recall one out this way.

"Where are we going?"

"About the only child-free place I know outside of the jail."

She considered how she felt about eating at a place so far out of town that no one she knew would see her, and she wasn't proud to admit that there was relief mixed in with the anticipation and curiosity. Just the tiniest relief that this time, at least, she wouldn't have to field calls from Mom, Dad and Reba, along with who knew how many others.

Her life had always been so public, and people had always felt justified in giving her the full benefit of their advice. Nev said it was because she never dreamed of telling them to mind their own business. She'd already been on the receiving end of the are-you-crazy calls for taking in Dahlia and Daisy. She didn't want to hear it again, and in less than flattering terms, about Sean.

Watching the breeze ruffle his hair, the way his dark glasses covered his eyes but left her just a glimpse of the corner of his eye and long, lush lashes, she asked, "How did you end up in Virginia?"

"I wanted to see the ocean."

"Why did you stay?"

"Because it wasn't here." After a moment, he slowed, turned onto a narrower road, then glanced at her. "I went to prison not long after I left home. You knew that, didn't you?"

She nodded. Bad news about Holigans, no matter how familiar, always made the rounds. And with

Sean, it hadn't been so familiar. Sure, he'd spent a few nights in jail here and there, but he'd stayed away from the more serious crimes. Some people had thought he would escape the family curse and make a good life for himself. Some had hoped he wouldn't.

"Were you guilty?"

"Of criminal stupidity, among other things. A guy I knew loaned me his car, asked me to pick him up at the store where he worked. He met me in the parking lot and said, 'Drive,' and I did, for the couple miles it took the police to spot us."

"He robbed the place?" Sophy asked quietly.

"Yeah. And the car was stolen. We both went to prison, and when I got out, I headed east. I was thinking maybe Charleston or Myrtle Beach, but I hitched a ride with a guy heading to Norfolk, so I went along. He got me a job at his father's garage, and I stayed. He owns the place now, the pay is good and the city's got a lot going for it."

He'd gotten what he wanted: a new life far from home where no one knew him. A place with no ties to the past he'd been running from. Had he made new ties? Had he put down roots, made a real home for himself, or was he just passing time there?

Before she could ask, he slowed and turned once again. The road wound through trees, giving an occasional glimpse of the lake, before opening into a clearing. She breathed deeply of the fresh-mown-grass smell that drifted on the air. "The only downside of living above the shop is the tiny yard. When I mow, I get one good breath of cut-grass perfume, then it's gone."

"Beats the hell out of smoke, doesn't it?" He

parked twenty feet from the water's edge, shutting off the engine. In that first moment, there was silence, then birdsong, crickets, the lapping of the water. Peace.

Sophy got out and walked closer to the shore. The sun cast her shadow, long and rippling, across the water. A boat motor sounded off to the east, while closer the trunk of the car was opened, then closed again. Eyes closed, she listened to the rustle of Sean's footsteps, the *flap-flap* of a blanket shaken out, the crinkle of paper.

Just this morning, she'd tried to entice Daisy with a picnic, thinking the sunshine, warm weather and exposure to nature would be good for both of them. How had he known she needed this?

Now the footsteps came toward her. Smiling, she turned to face him. His black hair gleamed in the sun. His jaw was shaved smooth, and the bandage on his arm contrasted starkly against his dark, warm skin.

He looked incredibly sexy and intense and dangerous, and being this close to him, close enough to smell his cologne, to feel the heat and the strength radiating from him, sent a delicious little shiver through her.

"I wouldn't have pegged you for a picnic sort of guy."

"Picnicking is underrated."

So was he.

"Look around. The perfect time and place for a picnic, and we're the only ones here."

She did look around: acres of grass, some shaded by tall oaks, the rest in full sun; the water; the serenity; the perfection of it all. The smile that curved her mouth was carefree, contented and full of pleasure. "Let's hope it stays that way."

Chapter 6

Sean had borrowed the quilt from Nev, bought an ice chest at the grocery store and picked up the food from Ellie's Deli on the square—slices of real turkey breast on slabs of homemade bread with lettuce and tomatoes fresh from the restaurant garden, dishes of coleslaw and creamy potato salad, wedges of dill pickle and a dozen cookies.

Not a bad picnic for a first-timer.

Now the sun was barely topping the trees to the west, the food mostly gone, the evening almost unbearably comfortable. He'd dated a lot of women, deliberately limiting his time and emotional involvement with all of them. Even with Sara Moultrie, he hadn't let things get to this point, where being with her was not just easy but satisfying. For damn sure risky.

But after the fire, for the girls' safety, for Sophy's, keeping his distance wasn't an option.

They'd cleared away the food, and now she lay on her back, a brown bottle of his favorite root beer balanced in both hands on her stomach. She looked younger, less stressed, more innocent and serene. Who'd ever thought serene could draw a man in?

"Ellie's staff outdid themselves on the dinner," she remarked. "So did you."

"Is she a friend of yours?"

She considered it a moment. "We're friendly acquaintances. I don't think she ever forgave me for dating Tommy when they were broken up."

"Tommy Maricci?" Tommy had been Robbie Calloway's best buddy, one of the guys Sean hung out with at Charlie's garage.

"Yup. We dated. He married Ellie. The story of my life."

"Someday you should date someone and marry him. Might be a refreshing change." Though the thought of some other guy having a claim on her time and attention and affection sent an uneasy feeling through him, something that felt too damn much like jealousy.

Sean Holigan had never been jealous over a woman in his entire life. Situations, circumstances, material possessions, sure, but never a woman.

Shifting her gaze to the right, she studied him. "That's my hope. To get married and have babies and live happily ever after like my mom and dad. Of course, first I have to fall in love, and I haven't really done that yet. I start every new relationship with high hopes—otherwise, why bother?—but while I loved most of the guys I've dated, I haven't really been *in* love with any of them."

He rolled until he was on his side facing her, head resting on his fist. "Their loss."

"Considering they're all happily married, I don't think they'd agree with you." Using the bottle, she pointed to a cloud drifting slowly. "That one looks like a rabbit."

He didn't look up. He'd found throughout dinner that the clouds she chose rarely looked the way she envisioned them. She gave them more credit for substance than they deserved. She was giving *him* more credit than he deserved. "Have you noticed that all your clouds look like warm, fuzzy animals?"

This time she pointed the bottle at him. "You can never have too much warm and fuzzy in your life. Besides, yours all look like cars or car parts."

Slowly she rolled onto her side so she could drink the root beer instead of gesturing with it. "Are you happy in Norfolk?"

There were pros and cons. He liked the city. His apartment felt more like home than any place he'd ever known...though he feared Sophy's cozy little place above the quilt shop could beat it. He knew his way around town, where to shop, where to eat, where to go to party. He had friends. He liked his job. He'd invested a lot of himself in the garage, in the restoration business.

And the cons? Sometimes the city was too crowded. He'd witnessed his buddy committing murder, and now there was Craig's nasty little threat against the female Holigans.

"It's good," he said. But he wouldn't be staying

there once the DEA arrested Craig. No reason to tempt fate, or the goobers who worked for Craig. He would take his mechanic skills and move someplace else. Someplace new.

Not Copper Lake.

For the first time in his life, he felt a twinge of regret at the thought of leaving again.

"Have you ever been in love?"

The question surprised him. He didn't normally discuss things like love and marriage on a first date—not even on a twentieth date. If this could be considered a date.

He slanted her a wry look. "Are you still feeling giddy from this morning?"

"Maybe a little giddy. I'm happy to be alive, this place has restored my balance and right now I'm pretty sure I can do *anything*. Including recognizing when you're avoiding a question."

"Nope, never have." He grinned. "Never wanted to be. I watched my old man go through that with my mother, Declan and Ian with their wives. I don't need the trouble."

"But what about the joy?"

Sitting up, he faced her, his knees drawn up so he could rest his arms on them. "*Joy* isn't a word used on our side of town unless it's some unfortunate kid's name."

"Okay, then happiness."

"By the time I came along, the only thing between my parents was fights."

Again she mimicked his position. "Don't you get lonely? Don't you wonder what could have been?

Doesn't it give you hope to think that there's someone out there waiting just for you?"

He didn't point out that having someone around was no guarantee of not being lonely. And what was the use of wondering what might have been? Marriage, kids, a good life—maybe. Divorce, child support for kids the ex poisoned against him and trouble—more likely.

As far as someone special out there just for him… hell, he was thirty-three, not thirteen. He'd never believed that fairy tale.

"You may have noticed with Daisy and Dahlia that I'm not exactly warm and fuzzy with kids."

Sophy snorted. "If you get warm and fuzzy with them, they'll bite. They kick, too, and punch and pull hair. If there's one thing no one has to teach them, it's how to defend themselves."

He smiled a little at the image. It was a good thing they were tough. They had to be with Maggie for a mother and who the hell knew who for fathers. Then his thoughts returned to the conversation, and he somberly said, "I'm not father or husband material, Sophy. I've lived with responsibility, and I've lived without it, and it's a lot easier without. You've always known what your life would be, and I've always known what mine would be, and obligation to anybody isn't included." Wasn't he proving that now by helping the DEA build a case against Craig?

"But you can have more than you want."

"I've got what I want. Why would I want more?"

She fell silent, but her gaze never left his face. What was she searching for? Some indication that he was

B.S.-ing her? That on rare occasions he did find himself thinking about—just thinking, not wanting—more?

He held her gaze as long as he could, then turned his head to look across the lake. He'd camped a lot of nights on its shores, when the summer weather was too hot and muggy to stay inside, when somebody old enough to buy beer had invited him along, when Patrick was on the warpath and all the boys thought it best to stay gone. No matter the reason, they'd always had a good time.

Sometimes he forgot that he'd had good times.

"If Maggie goes to prison, what about the girls?"

His gaze narrowed until all he saw was a small section of choppy water. Asked that question a few days ago, his answer would have been easy: let the state terminate her parental rights and put the kids up for adoption. Now that he'd met them, felt Dahlia's scorn and Daisy's fear and tears, it didn't seem so easy.

"You're the only law-abiding, dependable member of their family."

His laugh was sharp. It was a sad family when he was the best of the bunch. "What would happen if I hadn't come to town?" He'd spent the afternoon urging Maggie to plead guilty and go to prison, but he hadn't given much thought to the girls. He just automatically figured any home was better than Maggie's home.

"I don't know. I'm still new to this stuff. I guess they would stay in foster care, whether it was with me or someone else." A regretful look crossed her face that he understood immediately.

"You didn't take them to raise." Weeks, months, maybe even a year, but ten years? Fifteen? She was a single woman looking for love, marriage and babies of her own. Having Maggie's kids that long wasn't fostering; it was raising to adulthood, providing a home, food, education, guidance, love, discipline. Teaching morals and manners and honesty and strength and trustworthiness.

"Maggie's always been lucky—a few weeks here, maybe a month there. But this time…" Sophy's face flushed pink in the setting sun. "Don't get me wrong. They're welcome in my home as long as they need a place. I just wonder if at some point they'd be better off with family. With you."

Could he do that? Change his life to accommodate his nieces? Get a little house, settle down, join the PTO and go to church? Be the one to do the teaching and the loving and the guiding and instilling the strength, all in the hope that they could have the chance at life that he'd denied their mother?

Could he even convince a court to give him the chance?

"I think that's one of those wait-and-see things."

Before Sophy could point out what a lame answer that was, his cell phone rang. Ordinarily, he would let it go to voice mail, but these weren't ordinary times. It could be Ty saying the kids had handcuffed him and Nev and made their escape, or Special Agent Baker wanting an update, or Craig wanting the same.

He pulled it from his pocket, glanced at the screen, then eased to his feet. "Sorry, I've got to…" After Sophy nodded, he walked to the water. "Hey, Craig."

"Is it true what they say—that you can't go home again?" His boss was in a good mood. Music played in the background, along with the usual restaurant noises. Tuesday night, he was probably at his favorite place, where a lobster dinner for two cost more than average people made in a week.

"I don't know yet. I haven't been here long enough to decide."

"How is Maggie?"

"About how you'd expect anyone who's unwillingly detoxing." He glanced over his shoulder at Sophy, lying on her back again, gazing at the darkening sky. She'd removed her shoes and crossed her ankles, and her hands were clasped across her flat middle. Thanks to gravity, her shirt clung close to her breasts. The look on her face… God help him, he'd be seeing her face in his dreams tonight.

"You talked to her about pleading guilty?"

"I've talked. I'm not sure she's listening."

"That's why you're there, buddy, to persuade her. I've heard she's leaning toward making a deal."

Aw, jeez. Who was on his payroll? One of the jailers, another inmate, maybe even her lawyer? And why couldn't she keep her mouth freaking shut? Did she think Sean was kidding about the danger?

Maggie believed what she wanted to believe. It was as simple as that.

"How much does she know, Sean?"

"I don't know," he lied. Grimly, he turned back to the water, scuffing through the grass, putting distance between him and Sophy. "She's messed up, Craig, you know that. I just need time to get through to her. Right now she's just thinking about getting out—"

"And getting a fix."

"Yeah." It made Sean's head throb to agree. "She

hasn't faced the reality of the situation. I'm going to keep seeing her, keep talking to her."

"I would have thought losing her house would help her see clearly."

His fingers tightened on the phone, and he swallowed hard. "Yeah. The timing sucked, though. I was in the house when it blew up. A little warning would have been nice."

"Wouldn't you have tried to stop it?"

Yep, it had been a deliberate act—both a message from Craig and making certain no evidence remained. "Are you kidding? I would have blown up that place a long time ago if I'd had the chance. But I wouldn't have been inside when it happened."

"But you got out, with nothing more than a scratch. And Daisy and the foster mother were fine, too." Craig laughed. "And I mean *fine* in the best possible way with Sophy. Man, she's damn near everything I want when I settle down and become respectable. Compassionate, generous, churchgoing, responsible, beautiful, naive…"

Sean felt like his grandfather's old coonhound, bristling all over when anyone dared violate his territory. The thought of Sophy exposed to Craig in any way made his gut churn. Craig shouldn't even know she existed, much less what she looked like, where she lived, how she lived.

Damn Maggie for bringing Craig into Sophy's and the kids' lives, even peripherally, and damn Craig for being a greedy, heartless bastard.

"You'd have to give up all the bad things for a woman like that." Sean's voice was hoarse, forced through the tightness in his throat.

"Nah, you give a woman enough luxury and gifts, she doesn't care where the money comes from."

Sean didn't disagree. Craig was like Maggie in that way: he believed what he wanted to believe.

"Back to Maggie...her hearing's next week. You're on a tight schedule, buddy. Don't let me down on this one."

Don't let him *down?* Did he think Sean didn't care if his sister was murdered, that he wasn't going to do his damnedest to keep that from happening? "I'm doing my best," he said tightly.

"I hope it's good enough."

The sky was mostly dark by the time they repacked the car, with only faint streaks of pink and purple in the west. The temperature had dropped to almost cool, at least relative to the middle of the day, and Sophy felt languid and limp and lethargic as she slid into the passenger seat. As long as the girls didn't wind her up like a top before bedtime, she would sleep like a rock tonight with so many feel-good endorphins running through her.

Sean's phone call had been the only awkward moment in the entire evening. He'd returned to the quilt, his shoulders stiff, his jaw clenched, and it had taken a while to draw him back into talking. Was his boss wanting him back at work? His girlfriend complaining that she missed him?

He hadn't offered any details, and she hadn't asked. But, darn, she was pretty sure the interruption cost her the kiss she'd been planning to take if he didn't move first.

But they weren't home yet, and the thought spread a smile across her face.

He closed the trunk, then got in across from her, glancing her way. "That smile looks dangerous."

She shook her head. "Just thinking how incredible this evening has been." And the goodbyes, when they came, held such promise.

A satisfied look flashed across his face. He'd done well with his choice.

The headlights cut a wide swath across the grass as he circled back to the road. Around the first curve, they passed a vehicle, pulled between trees, lights off, windows steamy.

Sophy sighed. "Just about every girl I knew came out here with their high-school boyfriends to watch the boat races. I think I was the only one who didn't."

"They still do that, huh?"

"If it works, why change?" Of course, the only boat races on Copper Lake were between old buddies hustling to be the first ones at their favorite fishing spots early in the morning. But as long as teenage boys dropped the lines and teenage girls took the bait, the legend of the boat races would live on.

"Hey, do you know who Maggie's lawyer is?"

"No, but I'm sure Ty does, if she won't tell you." She remembered from school that Maggie could be secretive, but usually about the wrong things. Personal stuff, she shared with the world. Stuff that didn't matter much, she held close to the vest.

"Do you know who the D.A. is?"

"Oh, sure. Masiela Leal."

"Why does that name sound familiar?"

"Maybe because I dated her husband before they

got married. AJ Decker. They both came here from Dallas. He's the chief of police. Mas used to be a cop, then a defense attorney and now a prosecutor." Seeing his scowl, she quickly reassured him. "There's no conflict of interest. AJ has zero influence on her professional decisions. She's proven that. Plus, she nearly got killed back in Texas getting an innocent man out of jail and putting a handful of corrupt cops in. Her loyalty is to the office."

He nodded, and after a moment, his hands eased their grip on the steering wheel. "So you dated the chief of police. And Ty—he's a detective. And Tommy Maricci. He always intended to be a cop."

"Chief of detectives. And Pete Petrovski was a patrol officer when we dated."

"So you like a man with a badge."

"I like honorable men."

In the dim light, his expression turned sardonic. "There's a word no one's ever applied to a Holigan."

"You're honorable," she said quietly, "or you wouldn't be here." She laid her hand lightly on his arm, all muscle and sinew and radiating heat. She could curl up next to him and never be cold, never be afraid. No matter how anti marriage or long-term relationships he insisted he was.

Slowly he removed his right hand from the wheel, slid his arm away until his fingers were wrapped around hers, then rested both their hands on the center console. He didn't say anything, and she couldn't think of anything worth interrupting the pure satisfaction of the moment.

I'm not father or husband material, Sophy. I've lived with responsibility...and it's a lot easier with-

out. Obligation to anybody isn't included. How many times had he offered that warning to other women? More than she would probably want to know.

It was disheartening that life had taught him he was better off alone, but it was sweet, too, that he felt the need to warn her ahead of time not to expect too much from him. She got it: he didn't want to live in Copper Lake, to surround himself with people who'd always treated him badly. He'd never wanted marriage and kids. All he offered any woman was a short-term affair: great sex, a share of his time, even his affection, but nothing more. She understood why he'd put those limitations on himself.

Just as she understood that if they continued the path they were on, he was probably going to break her heart. But a broken heart wouldn't kill her. Unlike him, she put her whole self into every relationship. Some endings hurt more than others, but the hurt always healed. If she and Daisy and Dahlia and time couldn't change Sean's mind, sad as it would be for them all, they would survive.

They were halfway to town when headlights appeared behind them, closing in quickly. It was such a lovely evening for taking one's time and enjoying the night drive, but obviously the other driver didn't share her sentiment. He pulled into the other lane—it was the white car that had been parked at the lake—then passed them in a flash, his taillights disappearing into the darkness ahead.

"Kids," she murmured with a shake of her head.

"Nothing like going ninety miles an hour with the wind in your hair."

"You should know."

"But it's definitely more fun in this car than the family car he probably borrowed from his mom."

Her braid was coming loose in the breeze, so she tugged the band out and combed her fingers through it. "I bet you have a long history of tickets for speeding."

He scratched his jaw thoughtfully. "Not as many as you'd expect. Most cops appreciate a great restoration on a baby like this. Even women cops."

She snorted. "It's not the car the women are appreciating."

It was hard to tell, but she thought he flushed. Could he possibly be unaware that he was the star of a lot of erotic dreams?

When they got home, he parked in the driveway behind her unimpressive family car, and they climbed the stairs together. Ty and Nev were snuggled on the couch, the TV on, when they went inside, but there was no sign of the girls.

Sophy glanced toward their bedroom door, left open a crack with their night-light casting a sliver of light on the hall floor, then faked wiping sweat from her forehead. "Whew. Everyone's in one piece? No bites, no bruises, no tantrums?"

Nev shut off the TV, then rose. "They were perfect little angels. Their halos are just a little askew."

"If they had halos, they would be playing Frisbee with them," Ty retorted.

"Tossing them into trees," Sean added.

"Trying to knock birds out of the sky."

"Aiming for the antennas on passing cars."

Nev elbowed Ty, and he slid his arms around her.

"You got them bathed and in bed and everything? Wow."

"And read them a bedtime story. Granted, Daisy tried to stand on her head the whole time, and Dahlia scowled so hard, her little face probably froze like that. But no permanent trauma was done to either children or sitters." Nev gave her and Sean long, examining looks. "You both look much more relaxed. We need to do this again. Just remember—you'll get to repay the favor with our kids when we have them."

"You bet I will. Auntie Sophy had better be first on your call list."

Sophy hugged them both, and Sean shook hands with Ty. When the door closed behind them, an unnatural quiet fell over the room. She glanced around, then asked, "You want a cup of coffee?"

It took him a long time to answer, as if he was debating the pros and cons. Pro: he did like her, and she always stocked good coffee. It was one of her little luxuries. Con: he did like her, and he liked the kids, and he was afraid of liking any of them too much.

"I don't think so," he said slowly, and she was pretty sure some part of him was disappointed by the answer as much as she was. "It's been a long day, and you get to start all over again in the morning."

"That's the great thing about life, isn't it? No matter how bad today is, you always get another chance tomorrow." And no one needed to give himself another chance as much as Sean did.

Taking her hand, he pulled her to the door with him. "I'll wait while you lock up."

Sophy stepped outside on the landing and folded her arms across her middle. "I'm always careful."

The porch light illuminated his face, showing the half-smile quirk of his mouth, the intensity of his gaze, the strong lines and stark beauty and breath-stealing appeal. "I don't know about that. You're here with me, aren't you?"

Without conscious thought, she moved a few steps closer: one instant there was distance between them, and the next there wasn't. Just a little bit of breathing room, the smell that was him, the strength that was him, the need that was all her. "You're more worried about that than I am."

He raised his left hand, with those scarred, crooked fingers, and brushed her hair back so gently that it felt more like a whisper of a breeze than a touch. "That's because I know what people in this town think about my family and me. I've been on the receiving end of the insults and the snubs and the disdain. And I know that hasn't changed. You, Sophy, you're their princess. They would forgive you anything except getting in bed with the Holigans."

Getting in bed with this particular Holigan…now, there was a thought to make a woman go weak. The air in her lungs heated and made her skin damp, her voice unsteady. "Do you think I care what people think?"

His thumb grazed her cheek, stroking oh, so lightly down to her jaw. "I think you think you don't care."

She laid her hand over his, pressing his callused palm to her face. "I'm a grown woman. If I can handle running a business and taking in two foster daughters, I can handle choosing who I get involved with."

It wasn't much of an argument, and she could tell he thought so, too, from his expression and the tightening of his muscles beneath her hand. It was easy to think she was immune to everyone else's opinion because she'd never gotten the looks, the remarks, the hostile reception. Louise Wetherby's response when she saw Sean in the shop yesterday was typical Louise; she didn't like anyone. But it was the reaction he would get—she would get—from a lot of people.

Was she really certain she wouldn't care? Relatively. Pretty much.

But not 100 percent.

With a regretful squeeze, she released his hand, cleared her throat. "Will you be over to see the girls tomorrow?"

"Yeah. I'll even read Daisy a story if she'll stand on her head." His voice was laced with regret. For the change of subject? For the loss of contact? Was he disappointed that she hadn't shamelessly ignored his warnings and seduced him anyway?

She wasn't shameless, she was sorry to admit. It was kind of nice being on that princess pedestal, forgiven for her smaller failures and presumed to be incapable of bigger ones. She had never really given any thought to climbing off it, but maybe it was time.

"I'll see you tomorrow."

He nodded, went down two steps, then pivoted and came back, nudging her into the doorway with his body, catching her hands, pressing his mouth to hers. Heat and need exploded through her, driving her to maneuver closer to his body. She tried to free her hands so she could hold on to him, never let go, but he held them gently, firmly, at their sides. His head blocked the light, leaving her in dark, toasty shadow, palpable against her skin, and his hips pressed against hers, and his tongue stroked with sensual promise.

She felt as fragile as if a heavy breath might shatter her and, at the same time, strong enough to accomplish anything. She could attract this man, could make his breathing ragged, could make him want her almost as much as she wanted him.

But she couldn't make him stay. Not without morning-after regret, not yet. He ended the kiss, nibbled her lower lip, drew back and placed a final kiss along her jaw. He didn't pull away quickly but stood there, bodies touching, breath mingling, fingers still entwined. His forehead rested against hers, and she could tell his eyes were closed just from the absence of that intense gaze.

Finally he murmured, "I'll see you tomorrow." His fingers flexed, emphasis to accompany the words, then he let go and took the stairs two at a time until he disappeared into darkness.

When the Chevelle started, the vibrations rumbled through the ground and right up the stairs to her stoop. Still a little bemused, she went inside and did up the locks right away, then strode through the house to her bedroom window, easing the glass up, to watch as he drove away.

Too dreamy to jump right into nighttime concerns, she remained at the window, listening until the Chevelle's distinctive engine faded away, until the only noises disrupting the quiet were birds, a squirrel creeping along the River's Edge fence and the yip of a small dog. As she watched, the animal darted out of the shadows fronting Breakfast in Bed, pulling its owner on a leash.

It was Bitsy and her master, Zeke. Sophy's first thought was whether he scooped when Bitsy walked. The second and third came more quickly and were more pertinent: how long had he been over there, and how much had he seen? Her porch light was a beacon; anyone looking would have had a well-lit view. Aw, well, there would probably be no more friendly invitations to a meal from him.

Zeke and Bitsy walked south, then turned left at the next corner. A moment later, a car engine started down there, and seconds after that, a white car turned onto Oglethorpe at the next block down. It was probably a coincidence, a resident leaving his house at the same time Zeke was walking past. Far more likely than him driving the dog downtown to walk past her house. The attack at Christmas had spurred her security kick. Maybe Maggie's house blowing up was going to leave her overly suspicious for a time.

Better to be safe than sorry, the security guy had commented when he installed the alarm the day after Christmas.

Better to be paranoid than dead, Miri had murmured.

Better for her, at this moment, to be in bed, storing energy for tomorrow and having sweet, steamy dreams of Sean.

Chapter 7

Sean came out of the jail Wednesday morning with his head throbbing and a nervous twitch in the corner of his right eye. He'd heard a lot of people complain over the years that dealing with their spouse/children/mother/father made them crazy, but he'd been so far removed from anyone in his own life that he hadn't truly sympathized.

Half an hour with Maggie, and he sympathized. He shoved his sunglasses on, then pressed the tip of his little finger against his eye, stopping the tic as long as he held pressure to it. If he'd sent for her when he could have afforded it, when she was eighteen, nineteen years old, he could see only two outcomes: one of them would have killed the other, or one—likely him—would have sneaked out in the middle of the night and never come back.

He had an appointment in an hour with Masiela Leal, the district attorney married to the chief of police who used to date Sophy. He'd been raised to view prosecutors and cops as the enemy—it was a family joke that every member's first words after *Mama* or *Daddy* were *We don't talk to cops*—but luckily he'd outgrown that. What bothered him about this situation was the dating-Sophy part. She'd begun dating AJ Decker with high hopes that he was the one. If the freaking chief of police didn't qualify, how the hell could someone like Sean?

"You're not applying for the damn position," he reminded himself as he slid behind the wheel. "You're keeping things cool between you."

Yeah, that's why you kissed her last night.

And enjoyed the hell out of it.

He drove the few blocks to the quilt shop, parked in the driveway again and was headed for the stairs when a voice bellowed his name from across the street.

"Don't bother going up and ringing the doorbell 'cause we ain't there." Tugging Sophy's hand, Daisy bounced on the curb, waiting for the okay to cross the street. Her denim overalls ended in the middle of her calves, her top looked like half a swimsuit and her flip-flops were a size too big, giving her more flip than flop. The outfit was capped off by a black cowboy hat.

A grin fought to escape as they crossed the street to meet him on the sidewalk. Sophy held up one finger, her gaze warning him, but she spoke to Daisy, not him. "Don't say *ain't*. We *aren't* there."

"But now we are. Well, mostly. Hey, Uncle Sean,

you know what? We walked Dahlia to school today, and you know what? We saw Maria somebody, and her little girl Gracie and me are gonna have a swimmin' party at her house, and her friend Cary's coming, too."

"Clary," Sophy corrected absently. He would bet she was listening with only half an ear, with the rest of her attention on him.

"Do you know how to swim?" Sean asked.

"Yup. Gavin throwed me in the creek when I was little, and I swum right up to the shore."

Sounded like something Declan's kid would do. In fact, Sean was pretty sure Patrick had done the same to all of them.

"The kids will be wearing life vests as long as they're in sight of the pool," Sophy said. "Anamaria is Robbie Calloway's wife and Nev's sister. He'll be there, too, and Clary's mom, and they live in a gated community. She'll be safe."

Was she reassuring him or herself? "It sounds like fun."

"Yeah." Daisy beamed. "Dahlia has to go to stupid ole school, and I get to go to a swimmin' party. And with hot dogs! I am so cool!"

As Daisy danced along the sidewalk to the porch, Sophy asked, "What brings you downtown this morning?"

Sean fell in step with her. "Killing time before my appointment with the D.A."

She gave him a long look—khaki trousers with a belt, a white shirt with buttons—and smiled an oddly sweet and provocative smile. "You clean up good."

"I even shaved."

"I notice." She brushed the back of her fingers across his jaw. "Looks good. But just for the record, don't ever feel you need to shave on my account. You work the beard-stubble look pretty well."

Damn. His skin was hot now, and not just where she'd touched.

Daisy was waiting impatiently at the door. "Come on, I'm gonna be late when Gracie's mama comes. Hurry up!"

She was so excited and happy. An impromptu pool party shouldn't be such a rare and special thing, and wouldn't be for other kids. *They seldom smile,* Sophy had told him, *and they rarely laugh. They don't have any friends.* No one to invite them to parties. No one to make them feel cool. No one to play with, to count on, but each other.

He could give them that—a house in a neighborhood full of families, close enough to walk to school, put them in activities where they could meet other kids, get invited for sleepovers, have parties. It had never been in his plan, but plans could change.

You can have more than you want, Sophy said last night. Raising two kids wasn't on his agenda, but that didn't mean he couldn't do it and do it well.

Even enjoy it.

As soon as Sophy opened the door, Daisy raced into the bedroom to change. From the kitchen island, Sophy asked, "Coffee?"

"Please." Hands shoved into his hip pockets, he wandered around the room, gazing at photographs, a couple of elaborately pieced and quilted wall hangings, a ragged stuffed bear nestled on a shelf high off the floor. "Your favorite toy?"

She looked up from the coffeemaker and smiled. "That's Boo. Miri held on to him for more than twenty years for me. He's a little threadbare, but I love him."

A little threadbare was being kind. Much more loving and he was going to disintegrate into dust.

"Did you have a favorite toy when you were little?"

Pretending to think about it, he picked up a framed photo from the mantel. He didn't need to ask to know it was her first family. The three sisters were practically identical, and the brother's resemblance was almost as strong. "My favorite toy was Maggie," he said after returning the frame to its place. "My dad used to say they had her so we could torment her instead of them."

As he'd intended, Sophy laughed. "If we'd all been raised together, Oliver would have felt that way, I bet. Miri and Chloe and I can be a little overwhelming at times."

She offered an insulated mug, steam seeping from the small opening on its lid. "One sugar and a little cream."

Nodding his thanks, he slid onto a bar stool while she fixed her own in a matching mug. "You're prettier than your sisters."

Her look was level, though one brow was raised crookedly. "We look alike."

"So do my brothers and I, but I'm still better-looking than they are."

"I won't argue with that." After sipping her coffee, she leaned against the island. "Since Daisy won't be back until school's out, would you like to have lunch?

We could have something delivered, or I could pick it up. Luigi's is still in business and still makes the best pizza anywhere. We've got good Mexican, steak, home cooking, barbecue, soul food…"

Sean's hands tightened around the mug until his left fingers throbbed. So far, the only time they'd been in public alone was last night, driving through town and back again. Was she reluctant to be seen with him but without the girls?

"You don't want to get caught by your friends out alone with me?"

For a long moment, she stared at him, then abruptly laughed before clapping one hand over her mouth. "I'm sorry. Actually, I was thinking that if we ate here, maybe we could pick up last night's kiss where we left off, and somehow I don't think you'd be real enthusiastic about that in the middle of a restaurant."

Slowly his fingers eased and the ache faded— there, at least, but it was growing elsewhere. Damn, but it would have been better if she'd said yes. He could resist a woman who was embarrassed to show her face with him in public. But when Sophy wanted privacy for personal, intimate activities…

Daisy saved him from having to respond right away. She bolted into the room wearing the same out-fit, though she'd traded the cowboy hat for a brown-and-tan visor that had giraffe ears on it. "Are they here yet? Don't worry. I took off my panties and put on my swimmin' suit bottom. Aren't they here?"

Sophy checked her watch. "A couple minutes. Come on, we'll go downstairs and wait on the porch." She gave him a smirk as she passed, knowing he would rather wait there. Hide there.

Picking up his coffee, he followed Daisy out the door and down the stairs.

They'd barely had time to settle in the rockers when a restored 1960 convertible Beetle pulled up to the curb, its Brunswick-blue paint job gleaming, the top down, the engine a perfect hum. A woman was behind the wheel, and a girl not much smaller than Daisy occupied the booster seat in the back.

Though he wasn't a big fan of chick cars, his attention was pulled in two directions—admiring the restoration work on the car and dealing with the surprise Anamaria Calloway presented. She was beautiful, tall, slender, exotic, the kind of woman who made a man look three or four times. But that wasn't the surprise. It was pretty much a given that all the sons from the wealthy, socially prominent family had married beautiful women.

The surprise was that she was black, because like a lot of wealthy, prominent, former slave-holding families, the Calloways embodied the Old South. They married people just like themselves: wealthy, prominent, a long, illustrious history that usually also included plantations and slaves. White people.

Anamaria left the car, her movements graceful and sensual. Oddly, Sean realized, he preferred Sophy's efficient way of doing things. Maybe because she had so much to do, she didn't waste energy.

When Sophy introduced them, Anamaria took his hand in both of hers. "Robbie's been telling me stories about the mischief you and your brothers and he and his brothers got into. I'd like to believe you didn't do half of what he's saying, but I know him too well."

"His mother said our two families were put in this

town to keep the police department on its toes." Sara Calloway had always welcomed him and his brothers into their house. If she'd ever discouraged her kids from hanging out with them or blamed them for getting her boys into trouble, she'd never shown it.

Odd. He'd forgotten that until now.

"How is Robbie?"

"He's wonderful. Handsome, funny, smart. A wonderful husband and father. Though not grown up as much as you would've thought in the years since you've seen him."

"He takes care of his baby," he said with a glance at the car.

Anamaria laughed. "I know better than to think you're referring to my child. Yes, Gracie is his daughter, but the cars are his babies, and he tinkers with them routinely. He's had a '57 Vette for years, but he was so fussy when I drove it that I made him get this one for me."

Sophy snorted. "At least he lets you drive the Vette."

"Having a little car envy, Sophy?" Anamaria asked.

"Just a little."

"Are you ready, Daisy?" Anamaria crouched to her level. "We've got four rules. You have to obey all the adults at the party. You can't push anyone into the pool. You have to wear a life vest. And what's number four?" She tapped one scarlet-colored nail against her lower lip in thought. "Oh, yes, you have to have fun. Can you do all that?"

Daisy's eyes were wide, her anticipation level

close to redlining. All she could do was bob her head up and down, making her giraffe ears bounce.

"Then let's go."

Looking over her shoulder, Daisy called, "G'bye, Sophy. G'bye, Uncle Sean. I gotta go ride in a combirdable now."

A few minutes passed in silence, then Sean said, "They're like little tornadoes. They blow in out of nowhere, stir things up, then blow out even faster."

"And they leave your ears ringing when they're gone, until you realize it's just quiet." Sophy finished the last of her coffee, settled comfortably in the chair, feet tucked under her, and said, "You never answered about lunch. If you're afraid of being alone with me, we could always go to Louise Wetherby's steak house."

After giving her a look that clearly said what he thought of that, he drained his coffee cup. "I'll be back around noon." He passed close enough to touch her shoulder as he set the cup on the railing, then started down the steps. At the bottom, he looked back.

"And I'll bring lunch."

Sophy let herself into the shop and sighed deeply. This peace and welcome and solitude was what it had been like every morning B.C.—before children. With only a few lights on, lots of shadows filled the space that smelled of new fabric. It was the pleasant sit-and-talk-a-few-hours place she'd wanted it to be even before it existed, boosted by lovely quilt projects and the endless rainbow of colors and patterns provided by the fabric. Along with her apartment, it was her refuge, her safe place. Home.

But she could make a refuge and a home anywhere.

If ever came along a reason to do that.

And if ever that reason quit being so stubborn.

With more than an hour before the shop's opening, she wandered along the fabric aisles, her fingers brushing over each sample. These were her most popular fabrics, varying in weight and weave and price, affordable and the basis for a lovely sturdy quilt that would last decades. The ones she ultimately chose, though, came from a rack against the wall, a small collection of hand-dyed fabrics that she'd done herself in a class. She laid six selections on the measuring table in the middle of the room, pieces with subtle patterns in gorgeous deep colors: royal-blue, emerald-green, crimson, chocolate-brown, deep purple, a gold that seemed to change hues depending on the light.

She was laying them out in an overlapping pattern when the bell rang. Accustomed to friends dropping by before opening time, she rarely locked the door when she arrived early, so she glanced up, ready to greet her surprise visitor. The words caught for a moment before she forced them out. "Hey, Zeke."

"I know you're not open yet, but I just wanted to say hello." Sauntering along the center aisle toward her, he grinned. "Hello."

Her smile felt strained as she moved around the table to the other side, facing him. She continued to arrange the bolts, studying one color or pattern beside another before testing it against a third. "Do you work downtown?"

"No, out on East Carolina Avenue."

"What do you do?"

"My ex used to say I was in crisis management. Sounded better to her than 'insurance adjustor.' About the only time she didn't mind my job was when it was her car that had been totaled." He picked up a pattern book and flipped through it, then glanced at the quilts on display around the room. "You make all these?"

"Yeah. I sell quilts. I teach classes. I stock the latest and greatest in tools. For my customers who only want to piece the tops, I do the quilting. I dye fabric. I show in quilt shows. Mostly, though, I give advice."

"Impressive. Though I've always wondered… This looks like a lot of trouble when you can buy one at Walmart or somewhere for, what? Forty or fifty bucks?"

Her father had made that comment when she'd broken the news that she was going into the quilt-shop business. So had her sister, though the opinion hadn't stopped Reba from requesting a free custom-made crib quilt the first time she got pregnant.

"Not one of these. The last king-size quilt I sold went for a thousand dollars. That's not the usual price—it was an award-winner in a large quilt show—but comparing handmade quilts to printed fabric that's machine-stitched is like saying a meticulously restored Chevelle—" *gee, wonder where that came from?* "—and a beat-up station wagon are worth the same because they're both cars."

"My mistake." His charming grin didn't take the

edge off her discomfort. Maybe she was overreacting. Definitely she felt more vulnerable alone in the shop with a stranger. Funny how Daisy, not even forty pounds soaking wet, made her feel safer.

Granted, she'd been in a house that blew up yesterday morning. That was enough to make anyone edgy. Then there'd been that sense that someone was watching her and Sean when they left for dinner last night, and seeing Zeke and his dog lingering in the shadows across the street when Sean had kissed her. She was justified being a little antsy.

"Where are your partners?" Zeke asked, glancing around the shadows, skimming over the worktables usually scattered with the girls' stuff.

Two days ago, even yesterday, she would have answered without thinking. This morning, she shrugged. "They found more interesting things to do today. Who can blame them? For a few more weeks, it's still summertime."

"To be young and carefree at the end of the summer, getting in that last picnic, day at the beach, snow cone, cookout, baseball game, fishing trip…"

His smile was nostalgic, matching his sigh, and she smiled in response.

After a moment, he shifted, then picked up a stack of fat quarters—precut coordinating swatches of fabric—from the display bin beside him. "I didn't want to ask in front of the kids, but…Sunday evening, Dahlia said you aren't their mom. Stepkids?"

"Foster."

One brow raised. "Wow. I'm impressed again. Have you had them long?"

"A few weeks."

"No family around to take them?"

"No."

"Will their mom be getting them back soon?"

"I don't know." The hair on the back of Sophy's neck prickled. Why the questions about the girls? Could he know Maggie or the boyfriend who'd been making meth with her? Work for one of their lawyers or social work? Or was he just making small talk while she was overreacting again?

Then, with a studied casual air, he asked, "Have you and your husband been taking in kids for long?"

Relief washed over her. So that was the point—finding out if there was a husband who might not appreciate his coming around. Smiling faintly, she unrolled a length of the gold fabric, aligned it with the yardstick attached to the edge of the table and used a pair of insanely sharp scissors to cut it. "If you want to know whether I'm married, Zeke, you can ask."

Grinning unabashedly, he tossed the packet back into the bin and took out another, fanning the loose edges. "Not as subtle as I thought, huh? Okay, are you married?"

"No." She wiggled her left hand in the air.

"Yeah, man, I should've looked first. You seem like the kind of woman who would wear a ring."

"I would." For a commitment of that magnitude, absolutely, if for no other reason than to be able to look at it, touch it and be reminded every time that she'd found her very own Mr. Right.

"Are you involved with someone?"

After a hesitation, she nodded. She wasn't sure

exactly what would happen between her and Sean, but she would regret it if she didn't find out.

"I thought so." At her glance, he shrugged. "When Bitsy and I took our walk last night, we decided to see if you were enjoying your porch on another warm evening. Instead we saw…" Raising his eyebrows and tilting his head in the direction of the outside stairs, he slowly grinned. "But you can't blame a man for trying, can you?"

She wasn't sure what to say, but he didn't wait for an answer. Frowning at the material he held, he asked, "Do people really make quilts with this stuff?"

The particular patch that offended him was almost violently vivid: slashes of electric blue, lime-green and orange on a tiny floral background.

"They really do." Walking to the quilt hanging high on the nearest wall, she used the scissors to point to a very small piece in the overall twelve-inch-square pattern. "Sparingly."

With a shake of his head, he tossed that packet back, too, then pushed his hands into his pockets. "I'd better get back to work, or I'll find myself in crisis management for sure. I'd have to move back in with my ex, and it wouldn't be pretty." Before starting toward the door, he grinned and winked at her. "I'll see you around, Miss Sophy."

The wink was charmingly old-fashioned. With a breath, she released the tension humming inside and went back to work.

First, though, she locked the door. She'd had enough surprise visitors for one morning.

* * *

In Sean's experience, district attorneys had always been older men with balding heads, beer guts and pompous attitudes. If they'd had a prosecutor like Masiela Leal back when he was a kid, he would have made a point of getting hauled into court more often.

Her age was tough to peg, somewhere between thirty and forty, he'd guess. She was black-haired, dark-eyed, olive-skinned, and she commanded the space she occupied. Her handshake was firm, her greeting polite. After introductions, she invited him to sit, then took the second chair herself instead of the authoritative spot behind the desk.

Her posture was perfect but not rigid, not something she thought about but came naturally to her. She crossed her legs, clasped her hands and studied him, her head tilted to one side. After a moment, she smiled. "It's nice to meet another Holigan. Your family is legendary around here."

"Don't you mean notorious?"

"Legendary, notorious…" She shrugged. "I hear good things about you from Tommy Maricci and Ty Gadney."

"You know Ty?" Immediately he chided himself. Of course she did. Ty was a detective; she prosecuted his cases.

"He once helped save my life. Got shot for his efforts. I owe him."

Sean's neck and jaw muscles eased a fraction. "He's a good guy."

"He says the same about you." She paused half a second before getting down to business. "You're here about Maggie."

He nodded. "What is she facing?"

"With her record, a conviction on all the charges would likely be twenty-five years or more. She would have to serve ten to fifteen, then the remaining ten to fifteen would probably be on probation."

Twenty-five years. She would be past fifty before she was totally free of this mess, more than half her life gone. And ten to fifteen years on probation, keeping herself clean and staying out of trouble? She hadn't managed that for ten to fifteen minutes.

"She's talked about making a deal."

After a moment, Masiela nodded. "Her attorney's mentioned the possibility. Not knowing what she has to offer, it's hard to say how much dealing we can do."

"If it's worth something?"

"She would probably do some time, maybe three to five years. Again, not knowing what she has to offer, I can only speak in very general terms."

"Is there any chance she could avoid prison completely?"

Masiela shook her head. "I can't imagine the information she could offer that would allow us to make that kind of deal."

He understood that. Maggie was a small-time meth head who talked a lot. Who in their right mind would share anything important—anything that could get them and others sent to prison or killed—with her? Who would trust her to keep her mouth shut?

Though, apparently, her boyfriend, Davey, the meth addict and cook, had done just that.

At least, Maggie and Craig believed so.

"Do you know what she knows?" Masiela asked.

Would it be in Maggie's best interests to tell the D.A. about Craig and the threats against her and the kids? About Davey? Special Agent Baker and the DEA? Of course Masiela would tell the police—with her husband the chief, how could she not?—who would put Maggie in protective custody, which would get back to Craig, who would send another message, maybe more directly this time, maybe against the kids, who were an easier target…

He shook his head, and Masiela smiled faintly. "A word of advice, Sean. When it takes you that long to answer a simple yes-or-no question, you'll have trouble finding someone to believe the answer. Was the explosion at her house part of the case or just coincidence?"

This time he answered immediately—"I don't know"—but she'd already caught him avoiding the truth, so she didn't seem inclined to take him at his word.

"I understand you want to protect your sister, Sean, but she needs to face reality."

"Maggie and reality have never been on very good terms," he murmured.

She shifted in the chair, crossing her legs the other way. She had the muscular calves of a runner, and her skirt was short enough to show a length of thigh that was the same. "You know, prison isn't the end of the world. Maybe she could straighten herself out. Get clean. Get a new perspective on life. Come out a better person. Look at you. Not a single arrest since your one incarceration."

"I did fifteen months, not years." Fifteen months

for being innocent—once in his life. Besides, he'd left Copper Lake for the sole purpose of making a new life. Not partying, not drinking, not committing petty crimes that would have surely led to more serious offenses.

"You got smart quicker than Maggie has. She's been very lucky. In all fairness, she should have gone to prison on her first felony arrest. She would have gotten a light sentence for a first offense, already been out, maybe in a better place, better able to take care of herself and her daughters."

Grimly, quietly, he said, "In ten years, they'll be practically grown."

Masiela's face softened. "I feel bad for Daisy and Dahlia. I'm sorry they're going through this. But the truth is, Sean, everyone's sorry for Daisy and Dahlia except Maggie. For her, it's all about her. They're an afterthought. I hate to sound harsh, but her going to prison is probably the best thing that could happen to them. You know how they were living. They deserve better."

Holigans always stood up for each other. Half the fights Sean had been in had been defending his brothers or sister, or evening the odds when Declan or Ian had been jumped by more than one guy.

But he couldn't summon even one word in defense of Maggie. It was true: the kids would be better off without *this* Maggie, the scheming, stealing, drugusing, self-centered Maggie. They would have better lives with adoptive parents, or with Sophy.

Or with him.

Prison held its risks, but informing on Craig promised only one: death. Having witnessed him putting a bullet in a man's head…

"Tell her that if she wants to cooperate with us, we'll do the best we can. But the odds of her walking away scot-free are very slim."

She rose, discussion over, and so did he. When she offered her hand, he took it, and she held it a moment longer than he expected. "Tell her to cooperate with us, Sean. It really is best for her."

He nodded, thanked her and left the office, having zero intention of doing that. Holigans didn't cooperate with authorities even if it was in their best interests. They were pretty stubborn about ignoring those interests. And this time…

Even with his eyes wide-open and the hot August sun glaring on every shiny surface around, he could see that whole scene in the garage as clearly as if it were yesterday: the shadows, the single bright light beaming on Craig, his guys and the man kneeling on the floor. The echo of the gunshot, the man's body slumping forward, the blood. The paralyzing horror that the man was dead. That his buddy, to whom he owed so much, was a killer.

Prison wasn't the end of the world, Masiela had said.

But death was. And the only way Maggie could avoid that was giving up those ten to fifteen years of her life. It was all on her. Her chance to learn that actions had consequences. But, damn, it felt like his fault. His failure.

He still had time before lunch, so he drove aimlessly around town, or at least that was what he told himself. But after a few turns, he found himself on a familiar old street, approaching a familiar old building. A sign outside proclaimed it the AME Zion church. Years ago he and Ty had dubbed it NOS: Not an Option on Sunday.

He pulled into the gravel lot, empty of vehicles, and stood beside the car for a time. Nothing had changed there in the years he'd been gone, probably not in the one or two hundred years since it had been built. Whether he'd just stayed a night with Ty or had moved in to hide out from one of Patrick's ongoing tempers, he'd spent enough Sunday mornings here to learn the words to the gospel hymns they sang, to identify every member of the small congregation by name, to attend more than a few of their postsermon potluck dinners.

Ty's grandfather had bought him black pants, a white shirt and a tie, because all his kids had to dress with respect in the Lord's house. Sean would bet that was another thing that hadn't changed.

Pushing away from the car, he walked along the drive, footsteps crunching. He bypassed the path that led to the front doors and kept walking, listening to birds and the traffic on River Road. When the big trucks entered town, their squealing brakes could be heard a mile away.

At the back of the white church, tucked into the tall pines fifty feet away, was a cemetery. A picket fence surrounded it, expanded each year as needed to accommodate new graves. Decorating the graves had been the women's job back then, mowing and weeding the men's, and the task of keeping the whitewash on the fence fresh belonged to the boys, one that he'd helped with a time or three.

The gate creaked when he opened it, again when he closed it. He walked along the broad path until he reached two markers in particular and crouched in front of them: Genevieve and Rozene Gadney, Ty's grandmother and his mother. He'd never met either woman, but he'd felt as if he knew them. He'd known they were special because of the way people remembered and loved them long after they were gone.

"Pull up that weed there, would you, son? It'll save me from having to get down on these old arthritic knees of mine."

Sean pulled the weed at the base of Miss Genevieve's stone, then got to his feet. Mr. Obadiah had shrunk over the years, his knuckles swollen, his pants too big to fit his bony frame without a belt and suspenders. Even though it was Wednesday, he wore dark trousers, a white shirt, a tie and a hat to shade his head from the sun, and he was smiling about as happily as Sean had ever seen him.

"Ty told me you was back. I always prayed you'd come back so I could see you one more time. Got to the point that I wasn't sure I had much more waiting in me." Mr. Obadiah stepped forward to close the distance between them. Sean had to stoop for the old man's arms to reach around his neck, and he blinked rapidly as he did so to keep his vision clear. "You sure are a sight for sore eyes," the old man whispered.

After a long hug, no more words, just reassuring pats, Mr. Obadiah finally stepped back, pulled a handkerchief from his pocket and patted his eyes. "You look good, Sean. 'Course, all my boys look good. You get it from me." He chuckled. "All the single women in the church are still trying to marry me. Now that Ty and Nevy have gotten engaged, I just might let one of them catch me. She can take care of things around the house so I can play with my great-grandbaby all the time."

"I think Sophy Marchand might wrestle you for babysitting privileges." Sean's voice had gone husky.

"Aw, that Sophy…she's such a good girl. You tell her we'll compromise. I'll play with the baby, and when he needs changin' or burpin', I'll hand him over to her." His knobby fingers gripping the handle of a cane, he gestured toward a bench a few yards down. "Sit with me, Sean. Tell me what you been up to since the last time I saw you. I know about prison, so you can start after that."

Sean matched his pace to Mr. Obadiah's, gazing at the stones they passed, some as new as a few months, others dating to the Civil War. There were elaborate carvings of crosses and angels alongside simple ones, nothing but names and dates chiseled into chunks of concrete.

After helping the old man sit, he sat down beside him. "I haven't really done much. I moved to Virginia and got a job working on cars. I run the garage now, and I still work on cars." Life in about twenty words. That was pathetic.

"Never fell in love? Have babies?"

He shook his head.

Mr. Obadiah laid one hand over his. "Take it from an older, wiser man. It's never too late. Well, maybe for the babies part, for me, at least, but not for you. And never for the loving and marrying part." After blowing his nose into the handkerchief, he went on. "I hear your sister's probably going to prison and those daughters of hers are gonna need a home. They don't exactly overwhelm you with their sweetness, do they?"

Sean smiled wryly. "Have you met Dahlia and Daisy, or is that based on everyone's horror stories?"

"I met 'em. Once. Briefly. If I was twenty years younger, I'd take 'em in and get them past that anger and fear. Well, maybe thirty years younger." He grinned, but his expression turned sorrowful quickly enough. "I should have taken in their mama the day you left town."

If anyone in this town could have given Maggie a different outlook, it would have been Mr. Obadiah. He'd known too many kids with sad stories. Even now, stoop-shouldered and frail, he could probably earn Daisy's and Dahlia's respect in no time. Kids just automatically knew they could trust him.

"I should have sent for her, like I said I would. If I had…"

"You listen to me, son." Mr. Obadiah shook one unsteady finger his way. "You were a boy. You could barely take care of yourself. You couldn't have handled her, too. It's not your fault. For all her bad upbringing, Maggie still had plenty of chances to change things. She knew right from wrong. She knew she was making bad choices, and she did them anyway. It's a shame, and I feel bad for her, and I pray for her to turn her back on that life. But at the end of the day, she's a grown woman. She's the only one responsible for the mess she's in. Think on that, and tell me I'm not right."

Sean stared across the tombstones. His upbringing had been no better than Maggie's, but his life now was in a whole different universe. While there were plenty of explanations—he'd wanted something better, he'd been tired of the disreputable label he'd been born with, he'd had enough of handcuffs and frisks and jails—at the end of the day, there was only one reason: he'd made different choices.

God, he hoped the ones he was making now didn't come back to haunt him.

Chapter 8

The sound of a ringing bell was supposed to be music to a retail merchant's ears, but Sophy's were starting to ring, too. She'd had more customers this morning than all day yesterday. Good for the bottom line, not so good when she couldn't think about much more than lunch and Sean and that kiss.

Now it was a few minutes to twelve, and she'd had a whole five minutes without interruptions. She'd made little progress on the quilt she'd started before Zeke came in, so she gathered the fabrics and moved them into the storeroom. The bell rang while she was in there, and her stomach knotted in anticipation. She returned to the shop, a smile curving automatically, ready to greet Sean, and found her mother instead.

"Oh. Hey. Hi." The smile slipped, but the knot in her gut remained. Rae Marchand had never picked up a needle in her life, not even to sew on a button, and she only visited the store when she wanted something—usually a little badgering of her daughter. Well-intentioned but badgering all the same.

"Hey, sweetie." Rae was dressed to impress. Like Nev, she believed in looking her best at all times in a dress and heels, perfect hair and makeup. She'd aged gracefully and beautifully, and though she wasn't the visitor Sophy had been hoping for, she was happy to see her.

Mostly.

It took a few minutes to get the small talk out of the way, with Rae wandering the entire time, touching this, studying that. Finally, she faced Sophy. "Where is Daisy?"

"At a swim party at Anamaria's."

"Oh, good for her. Maybe Gracie will be a calming influence on her. How's Dahlia doing at school?"

"She's making friends." Learning, too, but the friendships with the "lee" girls were more important in Sophy's opinion.

"I hear her uncle Sean is back in town."

A muscle twitched in Sophy's little finger, and she folded her hand to hide it. "Yes, he is."

"And he's seen the girls a number of times."

"Yes."

"Which means you've seen him a number of times."

The twitch extended to the next finger. "I have. What would you like to know about him, Mom? He's a respectable, contributing member of society. He earns an honest living, pays his bills and came back as soon as he heard Maggie was in jail. He's good with the kids—"

"Is he still gorgeous as sin and twice as tempting? Even at eighteen, the boy could have graced any romance novel cover or pinup calendar I'd ever seen. 'Hot Hunks of the South' or 'Bad Boys of Georgia.'" She fanned herself with one beringed hand, apparently cooling the flames. "I can only imagine how he's matured."

"Mom! He's young enough to be your son."

Rae gave a negligent shrug. "There's nothing wrong with looking. Getting older has simply increased my appreciation for beautiful things. Flowers. Art. Fine wine. Incredibly sexy men."

Her lips pressed together to contain a smile, Sophy shook her head. "Well, if you stick around long, you'll get to see for yourself. He's coming by soon and bringing lunch." She watched for even the slightest change in her mother's expression that might show disapproval—the lift of an eyebrow, the narrowing of her mouth—but surprisingly found nothing.

"So…is he tempting *you?*"

Her entire right hand was fluttering now, and keeping her fingers folded didn't help. Sophy clasped it with her left hand, took a breath and evenly replied, "Yes. And I'm doing my best to tempt him right back." A pause. "Do you have a problem with that?"

Rae studied her a long time. "You're my baby, Sophy. You always will be. I admit, I'm not always thrilled about your choices, like quitting college, opening this shop, dating Robbie Calloway and Tommy Maricci and Ty Gadney. I wanted you to have that degree, Sophy, to have the fallback of a career that could support you, so that no man could ever leave you in the position your—"

A lump appeared in Sophy's throat, and she swallowed hard. They'd had a lot of arguments about her dropping out of college, with her parents providing a lot of reasons why she shouldn't, but Rae had never brought up this particular one.

"In the position that my birth mother was in," Sophy said quietly. No education beyond high school, no job experience and, worse, no skills—and four children to raise by herself.

"Not being able to feed her babies when they were hungry...I can't imagine what that did to her." Rae shook her head sympathetically, then went on in a more normal tone. "But look at you. You're doing fine. You were right to follow your passion. It's paid off for you, in business, at least. In romance, eh." She did a wigwag with her hand. "But at least you haven't had your heart broken yet."

Fiddling with a display, changing it this way, that way, then back again, Sophy hesitantly asked, "What if Sean is my passion?"

Rae breathed a time or two before forcing a smile that wobbled. "Then Sunday dinner just got a whole lot handsomer."

It cost her mother to say that, to affect the attitude. In her head, she probably really did believe that Sophy was a woman capable of making her own choices, but in her heart she still wanted to protect her little girl from every little thing, and Sean Holigan was a hell of a *thing*.

Closing the distance between them, Sophy hugged

her. "Thanks, Mom. But who knows what will come of it? You know me. I'm the queen of dating men who fall in love with other women." Though she said it lightly, the idea of Sean falling in love with someone else stirred pain around her heart.

After a moment, Rae stepped back, breaking the hug. "Don't think you've softened me up. Now we're going to talk about the real reason I'm here. Why do I have to find out from Zelda at the grocery store that you were actually *in* Maggie's house when it exploded?"

Sophy laughed, both surprised and relieved that Sean wasn't reason enough to bring her mother into the store. He might not be Rae's ideal choice for her younger daughter, but she wasn't violently opposed to him, either. That was good.

"I won't ask how Zelda at the store found out." Though Copper Lake had grown into a small city, it hadn't lost its very efficient grapevine. Gossip spread faster than soft butter on a hot biscuit. "I hadn't figured out the best way to tell you," she said, fingers crossed behind her back to make up for the lie. Truthfully, she hadn't considered telling anyone. She'd been too busy recovering, dealing with the girls and being with Sean.

"How about picking up the phone and saying, 'Hi, Mom, I just almost got blown up, but I'm all right'? You should have seen Zelda, gloating because she knew something about my own daughter that I didn't."

"I'm sorry. Really, I am."

"Hush and just tell me now. All the details. Don't leave a thing out."

Sophy knew it was easier to answer her mother's questions than put her off, so she quickly told the story she'd repeated to firemen and detectives the day before, in just as much detail.

When she was done, Rae hugged her, then held her at arm's length, looking her up and down. "And you're not hurt? Daisy's okay? Sean's all right?"

"We're all fine."

"Thank God. Heavens, I would have had a heart attack if I'd known… And you were so brave, rescuing Sean and Daisy like that."

"Not brave, Mom. Just scared to death. And I don't know that I could have gotten out without his help."

Rae's gesture was dismissive. "I know my little girl. You would have clawed your way through the wall if necessary. You're a tough one." A shudder rocketed through her. "I'd even hug the stuffing out of Daisy if she were here, and no matter how much she dislikes mushy stuff, she would just have to endure it."

"I'd like to see that—"

Sean's arrival interrupted Sophy's answer. Both she and Rae swiveled toward the door, and Rae sighed. "Oh, my. It's true—men improve with age. And when they're already smokin' hot to start…"

Sophy elbowed her gently. "You behave. Don't embarrass or scare him."

Upon recognizing her mother, Sean stopped just inside the door, still holding it open. He hesitated before slowly letting it go and starting toward them.

In a whisper, Rae said, "He gets points for not running out while he had the chance."

Sophy elbowed her again, then smiled brightly. "Hey, Sean. Look who's here."

"Probably one of the last people you wanted to see on this visit." Rae moved forward, her hand extended. "Look at you. You're all grown up."

Still a little uneasy, Sean shifted the bag he carried to his other hand and accepted her handshake. His gaze darted to Sophy, then he quietly, cautiously said, "Mrs. Marchand." It was definitely not the greeting he expected from her. It was pretty surprising to Sophy, too, given the fact that he hadn't been allowed in the house when he was dating Reba.

"Oh, you can call me Rae."

Sophy rubbed her forehead. Yeah, that was likely to happen.

"You look just like those nieces of yours. Any chance you'll be taking them when their mother goes to—" Rae stopped, not soon enough to please Sophy, and kindly said, "I guess you hope for the best and if it doesn't happen, then you plan for the worst. Well, I should hustle. I'm meeting my girls at the country club, and today I've got the juiciest news, so I don't want to be late." She didn't seem to notice that Sean had flushed deep crimson—just released him and stepped past. Abruptly, she backed up a few steps. "Make me a promise, Sean."

Now he looked embarrassed *and* concerned. "What's that?"

She stepped close, right up in his personal space, and said sternly, "Don't take my daughter into any more exploding houses. And if you do get into something exciting or traumatic, make her call me right away." She glanced back at Sophy. "Zelda at the grocery store, for heaven's sake!"

Sean remained still and a bit flustered until Rae was gone. Finally he turned from the door and started toward Sophy.

"Welcome to Hurricane Rae. She's all hot air but rarely does any damage."

"Depends on how you define *damage,*" he muttered, "and how juicy her news is."

The aromas of food reached Sophy first, radiating from the big brown bag he carried and making her stomach growl none too subtly. "I'm sorry to disappoint you, but the juicy news is me. You'll be on the periphery with Daisy, but it's primarily about my near-death experience yesterday. I'm sure in her version, my clothes will be scorched, my hair singed, my face smeared with soot, and I probably will have carried you and Sophy to safety over my shoulder."

"Well, you do swing a mean vacuum."

Watching his cautious expression shift to a grin and a devilish look appear in his eyes was fascinating. If she had a camera, she would record it so she could watch it again and again, but who needed a camera when the real man was right in front of her?

Her stomach growled again, drawing her from her study of him. "You want to eat here or upstairs?"

He shrugged, so she got her purse, locked up and turned over the out-to-lunch sign and led the way upstairs to the apartment. It was so quiet without the girls. Even when they were asleep, they gave off such an energetic vibe that it was impossible to forget they were there.

"Do you know this is the first time I've been up

here without one or both of the girls since they came to stay with me?" she remarked. "Can you feel the difference?"

Sean gazed around and shrugged. "I can hear it. Even when they're being quiet, they're not."

As he began unpacking the bag of food, she got glasses of ice and tea. The savory spices of Mexican food filled the air. Tia Maria's, her favorite place. The only downside of takeout was no frozen margaritas—

Her nose twitched as a new aroma joined the others. Tequila. Turning, she watched as he uncapped a second plastic to-go cup. "You got them to sell you margaritas to go?"

"If you ask nicely, people will do most anything."

"And these people whom you asked nicely were female, young and highly susceptible to dark eyes and a charming smile?"

He gifted her with said smile. "Actually, the one who agreed to let me have the drinks was about your mom's age. Older women like to be charmed, too."

Oh, she knew that. Her mother had been charmed enough that she was willing to give him her daughter.

They settled at the dining table with chips, salsa, margaritas and all the fixings for fajitas. Between bites, Sophy asked, "How did your meeting with Masiela go?"

He shrugged, muscles rippling. When Daisy or Dahlia shrugged in response to a question, she wanted to shake them and demand that they never do it again. When Sean did it, she wanted to rest her chin on her hand, stare googly-eyed and hope that he did it again.

"She didn't tell me anything I didn't already

know," he said. "And she wanted me to persuade Maggie that it would be in her best interests if she cooperates with her office."

"Will you try?"

His long, slender fingers removed another tortilla from the foil wrapper, balancing it while he filled it with toppings. After wrapping it, he met her gaze. "Sometimes what looks like someone's best interests isn't."

She understood that. When social services had taken her, Chloe and Oliver from their mother the last time, Miri had somehow persuaded them to let her stay at home. She'd just been a kid—ten years old—but she'd cared for their mother until her death eight years later. It had been a tough life for her, but even now she was confident it had been the best choice, both for her and their mom. Few people had agreed; social services had come back repeatedly to take custody of her, but she'd kept their mom on the move, evading them until they lost interest in her.

She'd sacrificed a lot, but she'd given her siblings the comfort of knowing that their mother had been loved and protected until she died.

"You think it would be better for Maggie to go to prison for all those years?"

"I think if she doesn't, she won't survive."

That was a grim thought. Of course, out-of-control drug addicts were less likely to see their next birthday. If she made a deal with the D.A. this time, the next time Sean came to Copper Lake could very well be to bury her. As scary as ten or more years in prison sounded—and it would scare the snot out of Sophy— it had the upside of that chance to survive.

She concentrated on her food, thinking how sad for Daisy and Dahlia and Sean, wondering if she had what it took to keep the girls that long. She was already more successful than the previous foster parents had been: they hadn't escaped her, though they'd tried; they hadn't torn up the house, started any fires, kicked, bitten or scratched her; they hadn't thrown a single meal on the floor; they limited their tantrums; and they had pretty much given up their birth lesson about not talking to anyone outside the family.

Really, though, the question wasn't whether Sophy could keep them that long.

It was whether she could give them up.

Giving them back to their mother was one thing. Turning them over to their uncle would be fantastic. But handing them off to strangers… It could be good or a disaster.

"I saw Mr. Obadiah today," Sean said, his tone lighter, the worry lines etched in his face lessening.

A smile blossomed across Sophy's face. "I adore him. How is he?"

"Still old, still patient, still wise. You know, he went through a lot, losing his wife, then his daughter, taking Ty to raise, along with all the other kids he helped out, me included. He had plenty of good reasons to be a bitter old man, but he's not."

"Oh, no. He'll tell anyone, he's a very happy old man. His faith is a large part of it. He fully believes that he's going to be with Genevieve and their daughter and everyone else he's ever loved again in Heaven. But it's also from a lesson his grandmother taught him—that every day came with choices, and it was his job to make the best possible ones. If he made a bad one, the next day it was his job to fix it. If he made the best choices every day, no matter what the outcome, he had the satisfaction of knowing he'd done his best."

She smiled ruefully as she wiped her fingers on a napkin, then pushed her plate aside. "I interviewed him for a project in high school, and that was just a small part of everything he told me. But I always thought it made sense and that it was something I wanted to teach my own children."

Sean was leaning back in his chair, one arm hanging over the back, his free hand holding his drink cup. "You ever make bad choices, Sophy?"

She did her best patronizing smile and tossed her head. "Well, I *am* the princess of Copper Lake, you know." Then, normally, "Of course I make bad choices."

"Is this one of them?"

This. This relationship with him. This yearning for more. This being ready for more, no matter what the future held for them.

"No. It isn't. I don't regret any of the relationships I've had. I gained something from each one. They made me who I am today, just as *this*—" she deliberately used his own word "—will affect who I am next year. So will the girls. So will my family and friends. Like it or not, this will also affect who you are next year."

He drew one fingertip around his cup, sending rivulets of condensation to drip on his hand. "Maggie hasn't made a single good decision in her life. Not even—"

Sophy's breath caught, but she waited for him

to finish the sentence: *not even having the girls.* It would break her heart to hear it, though she'd heard it before from others. Though she'd been guilty of thinking it herself before she'd met Daisy and Dahlia.

His face turned bronze, and his gaze deliberately avoided hers. "Not even... Hell." He couldn't say it. Because it sounded heartless? Or because he didn't believe it?

Restlessly getting to his feet, he cleared the table, found the trash can in the pantry, then came back for the dishes. "A lot of people think Daisy's and Dahlia's lives are terrible, that it was irresponsible and cruel of Maggie to even have them, but the girls don't agree. They don't wish they'd never existed. You and your sisters and brother, with all you went through, are happy to be here. I'm happy to be here. Nothing's been done to them that they can't overcome with time."

"Or to you," she murmured.

He turned from the sink, his features stark. Then slowly the half smirk came. "Yeah, I know. Being back here brings out the worst in me. I hated living here, and I blame myself for Maggie and for the kids, and for breaking my promise to send for her after I left, and for wanting her to go to prison so she can have at least a chance at kicking the drugs and being a decent mother."

Pushing away from the table, Sophy went into the kitchen. She wanted to put her arms around him, to rest her cheek against him and hear his breathing, feel the play of muscle, but she leaned against the counter instead. "That's because you're a decent person. You want a better life for her. You want her to be a good mother and a good woman and a law-abiding citizen and to have friends and family and be happy, and you know she's not going to get that hanging out with dopers and criminals and exposing herself and the kids to danger. But you can't give her the better life, Sean. She's got to earn it for herself. She's got to *want* it for herself." She paused before quietly adding the major obstacle to Maggie's recovery. "She's got to want it enough to give up the drugs."

And they both knew how big a struggle that would be.

It was almost time for Sophy to reopen the shop, and there'd been no kissing, no picking up where they'd left off, yet. After eating, they'd settled on the couch and made conversation—easy, friendly but intimate, the sort of stuff Sean never engaged in. His attitude had always been that the more superficial his relationships with women, the better for him. He'd never shared secrets, fears, childhood memories or wanted to know anyone else's.

Until now.

"I guess I should go downstairs," Sophy said, but she made no move to get up.

"Yeah. I should go see Maggie." He didn't move, either. Correction: his move wasn't to rise from the couch. He closed the distance between them, easily settling in beside her, and she wiggled into the corner enough so that she faced him. "I believe you said something about kissing when you asked me to lunch."

"I did. I was afraid you'd forgotten."

He snorted, wrapping a strand of her hair around

his index finger. It was as soft and straight as Daisy's and Dahlia's, though the sunny golden shade was on the far side of the spectrum from their black. "Men never forget about anything that might lead to sex."

"Neither do women," she countered.

"You know the odds of me staying here are between slim and none."

For a long time, their gazes locked, hers stark, his— He didn't know what was in his besides desire. Need? Fear? After a few slow deep breaths, she nodded, her hair slipping from his fingers, then patted his hand. "Don't worry, Sean. I'm not the clingy type. I don't make demands. I don't ignore warnings. I won't break your heart."

He'd never kidded himself. He'd always known his heart could be broken—his mother had been the first, Maggie the second. That was just one of the reasons he preferred hookups over relationships. He figured by the time things were settled here, there wouldn't be anything left of him but a million pieces that he'd have to put back together somehow if he had a hope in hell of getting custody of Daisy and Dahlia.

Not that he was positive about asking, but at least the idea didn't terrify him the way it first had.

He touched her hair again, sliding his fingers gently across it. "Don't worry about my heart. Take care of your own."

As light as a feather, she laid her palm against his jaw. "I do worry about you, Sean. I worry that you don't see the good in yourself. I worry that you take on far too much responsibility for someone who says he doesn't want any at all. I worry that you mistake safe choices for good ones."

Safe choices. Yeah, that was what he'd been making all these years, and where had it gotten him? He couldn't help but think that taking a few risks couldn't have landed him in any more trouble than he was already in and might have been a hell of a lot more fun, too.

But he didn't want to think about any of that. Time was limited, and he had a beautiful, sexy woman waiting to be kissed in a way he hadn't kissed a woman in a long time. She smelled of tequila, Mexican food and something delicate and expensive, and her shoulders were slender beneath his hands as he leaned closer.

Her mouth met his, their noses bumping. He'd never given much thought to mouths before, but hers was made for kissing and seducing, her lips soft, pliable. When he slid his tongue inside, she tasted sweet and innocent and intoxicating. A man could spend a lot of time just kissing her, getting lost in her, appreciating her hunger, but they didn't have a lot of time. Not now.

It took him a moment to separate the tugging on his shirt from the other feelings building inside him. She pulled it from his pants and slid her hands underneath, stroking restlessly over his middle, up to his chest. Her palms were small and hot, making his muscles tense, sending flames through him, stirring to life an erection that reached painful in intensity within the space of a breath.

In desperate need of air, he ended the kiss, then immediately left a trail of them along her jaw, down her throat, until the fabric of her blouse blocked his way. He undid the first button, the second, the next, revealing creamy golden skin and a pale green bra. Her breasts weren't large, but the curves were perfect, the skin tantalizingly soft, her nipples peaked against the silky garment.

He was nuzzling one nipple when the rasp of his trousers distracted him. He caught her hand before she managed to do more than brush her fingertips across his belly. When her other hand moved in, he grabbed it, too, and forced himself to sit back.

Both breathing heavily, they stared at each other a moment, then her expression shifted into a pout that would have done Daisy proud.

"You're wicked underneath those angelic looks, aren't you?" His voice was unsteady and hard. So was his body.

Slowly she smiled, and he wondered how he had ever thought her innocent. "Just seeing if I could tempt you."

"All you have to do is breathe, sweetheart," he replied. He loosened his grip, hesitated, then let her go. "You've got to get back to work."

"I could close the shop for the afternoon. It's one of the perks of being the owner."

Oh, hell, yeah, she could tempt him. But he wasn't ready for that—no matter what his body thought—and if he was, when he was, he wanted an entire night, and the next one, and the next.

Leaning so close that his mouth brushed hers again, he whispered, "Yeah, a couple hours until the kids get home isn't going to cut it."

She kissed him, nipping his lower lip, then pushed him away. "You're right. Besides, I really can't close today. I've got a class starting in half an hour." Her fingers quickly rebuttoned her blouse, then combed through her hair. Her movements were efficient, her expression as normal as if nothing had ever happened…but her eyes were glazed, and her breathing was still ragged, and the air around her was shimmering with need.

As she stood, so did he, giving her a hand for balance while she put on first one shoe, then the other. Murmuring thanks, she went to the fireplace, picked up a small stone box and opened it, springing a false bottom and retrieving a key. She pressed it into his hand. "Lock up when you leave."

"I don't need—"

She made a show of skimming her gaze over his chest, his rib cage, his abdomen, stopping at his rather obvious erection. "Maybe take a few minutes," she said with a grin.

He swatted her butt as she walked past. "You're supposed to be impressed."

"Oh, I am. I can't wait to see more. You can bring the key back later. Thanks for lunch." Still grinning, she let herself out.

Sean stared at the key. Several ex-girlfriends had wanted to trade keys, but he'd never given one or accepted their own. His apartment was the one place he could count as his and his alone. He didn't want to come home from a long day and find someone had invited herself over, didn't want the hassle of getting the key back when the inevitable end came, didn't want control of his private time taken away by anyone.

But Sophy giving him this key… She was understandably security-conscious, yet she trusted him enough to give him access to her apartment.

Maybe he'd only engaged in hookups to this point. Maybe he'd always aimed for superficial. But like it or not, want it or not, he'd broken that lifelong rule.

He was as involved with Sophy Marchand as any man could be.

And they were about to go even further.

He tucked his shirt, cautiously did up the zipper and fastened his belt again. While his clothes were presentable, he needed a few more minutes of totally non-sexualized thinking before he went outside. He found the distraction when he passed the hallway. All the time he'd been in the apartment, he hadn't crossed the threshold into the corridor— hadn't gotten a tour of the girls' room or made use of the bathroom.

Now he crossed that line, glancing inside the open bathroom door. The colors were clean, a lot of white, enough navy blue to keep the effect from being blinding, the tub and shower an all in one, a single sink, a small closet.

Offset across the hall, another open door led into the girls' room. The trim was white, the walls pale green. The bedding was stripes, the same white and green with a few flowers in the background. Bookcases occupied space on two walls, painted white and filled with books and toys, a wicker dresser separated the twin beds, and a rug bearing a kids'-style rainforest design protected the wooden floor.

One bed was perfectly made except for a missing pillow. The other was unmade, two pillows sharing space along with a stuffed monkey and a third pillow, crudely sewn, not much bigger than Sean's hand. Above and below the small square safety-pinned into the middle was scrawled *Tooth Fairy Pillow*.

He sat down on the neat bed, hands dangling between his knees, staring at it. He'd made that pillow for Maggie when she was about Dahlia's age. *All the girls have one,* she'd said after school one day, using the tip of her tongue to wiggle the tooth on the verge of falling out. He'd cut it from one of their mother's old blouses, a white one that had long ago turned yellow with age. After letting her label it, he'd stuffed it with old socks cut into pieces and pinned it all together. Then it had been his duty to collect the lost teeth and replace them with money he swiped from Patrick's wallet.

The odds of me staying here are between slim and none. If he were on his own, he could handle it. For all the people who cringed at the idea of a grown Holigan living in town, there were some he could count on: Sophy, Ty and Nev, Mr. Obadiah, Robbie and Anamaria Calloway, maybe Tommy Maricci, probably Charlie over at the hot-rod shop. A few good friends were all a man needed.

But with the kids…everyone in town would know where their mother was, what had happened with her. They would know she had never loved them enough to choose the life they needed over the one she wanted. Daisy and Dahlia would have a lot to live down.

Wasn't it better to start off someplace new? The three of them looked so damn much alike that there would be no reason to explain anything about her mother. People would just assume they were his kids. They could start over with any new story they wanted.

But starting over new didn't guarantee success.

Chapter 9

Sean lost track of how long he sat there, staring at that pillow, until a horn on the street out front jarred him from his thoughts. Standing, he smoothed the wrinkles from the bed, then headed for the front door. After letting himself out and locking up, he pocketed the key and took the stairs two at a time before walking to his car across from the shop. As he opened the door, a voice called from the sidewalk, cool enough to form icicles on the wrought-iron fence encircling River's Edge.

"Excuse me. Do you know where to find a decent hotel in this place?"

He glanced up, meeting Special Agent Alexandra Baker's gaze, then resisted looking back toward Hanging by a Thread. He already knew he couldn't see inside the shop from here—he'd checked the last time he'd been across the street—and he didn't want to draw any more of the wrong attention to the shop or Sophy. "Ask at the tourism office. It's halfway down that block." He pointed to the west.

"Where can we talk?"

"How about by phone?"

She showed zero response to his flippancy. "There's a fast-food place across the river called Taquito Taco. Meet me there in five or ten minutes."

He slid into the car as she walked off, cranking down first his window, then the passenger's. Baker hadn't given him any instructions about calling her, so he hadn't. He figured she was keeping track of everything anyway, and obviously she was. He just wished she was keeping track long-distance. Didn't he have enough complications in his life as it was?

She was walking toward the tourism office when he drove past on the opposite side of the square. Any casual observer would have thought he'd given her directions and she was following them. In fact, damn if she didn't go inside the storefront that housed the tourism office.

He turned onto River Road, then west onto Carolina. He hadn't been to the west bank of the Gullah since he'd come back. There had been no reason to cross the river when he'd lived there except to head to the next shabby excuse for a town ten miles away. All the businesses and homes had been on the east side; crossing the bridge was like entering no-man's-land.

Not anymore. Neighborhoods of expensive houses and condos dotted the waterfront both north and south of the bridge. Convenience stores, a dollar store, a few restaurants, a few other businesses and a motel under construction extended almost a mile along both sides of the road.

He parked at Taquito Taco, got a pop and chose an empty section of the restaurant where he could watch both the door and the Chevelle. The air-conditioning hummed loudly but wasn't doing much of a job dispelling the heat. Overhead fans kept the air moving while speakers blared the current popular music. His tastes ran way more toward the classics—rock music, his car, Sophy. A classic beauty.

Given the effect she'd had on him a short time ago, no thinking about her now. He didn't want to give Special Agent Baker the wrong impression. Didn't want to get frostbite on his penis, either.

She drew more than a few looks when she walked into the restaurant, mostly from a pack of teenage saggy-pants gangsta wannabes across the room. She was dressed as casually as he'd ever seen—shorts, a sleeveless shirt, sandals—but there was nothing she could do to dress down her hair, more white than blond, her pale skin or her eyes that reminded him of hard fresh ice. She was a woman people remembered seeing.

He wondered how that worked with her job.

With a soft chicken taco and a bottle of water on a tray, she slid onto the bench across from him and turned her attention to lunch. She poured salsa on the open tortilla, then began scraping off the shreds of lettuce, carefully leaving onion, tomato, cilantro and cheese.

Figuring that could take forever, he asked, "How long have you been in town?"

"Since Monday. I'm staying at The Jasmine."

Fancy place—an antebellum mansion turned into a bed-and-breakfast. He couldn't afford a room there on his own and wouldn't know what to do in such luxury if someone else picked up the tab.

"I get per diem and pay the rest from my own pocket. When I travel, I like to do so in style."

He assumed the explanation was her way of assuring him the deal was legit. He didn't care whether the DEA put her up in the priciest place in the state on the taxpayers' dime. He just wanted her and Craig and the whole mess out of his life.

"What does Maggie know?"

"That Davey is more than just a two-bit meth cook. That he works for a major dealer on the East Coast that the feds have been trying a long time to shut down."

"Is that all?" She took a bite of her taco and chewed it while studying him.

"That's all she's told me. We don't get a lot of privacy when I visit her," he added, sarcasm creeping into his voice. "I suspect she's got names and maybe some details, because she's counting on this to keep her out of jail."

Without the slightest change of expression, Baker said, "Maybe it will."

Masiela Leal had been levelheaded, polite, sympathetic about the kids and adamant about Maggie serving time for this arrest. Would Baker's casual answer be enough to turn her tough, the way Sean knew she could be?

"You would help her avoid prison?"

"If she can help us nail Kolinski, yes."

The good of the many took precedence over the

good of the few, or however the line went. Letting Maggie off, helping her avoid punishment, setting her free… Sure, Craig would be in jail; a major criminal enterprise would be shut down…for the time that it took someone else to restart it. Maggie, in the meantime, would continue using drugs, continue to have no respect for herself or care for her daughters, and one way or another, accidental overdose or murder, she *would* die.

But as long as the DEA could count Craig as another notch in their convictions, it would be a fair trade.

"And what would you do for her? What would you offer to make it worth the risk?"

Baker swallowed another bite, then took a long drink of water. "Relocation, rehab, a new life."

"You know, rehab is never successful unless the person *wants* to get clean. Clean for a while isn't much of an enticement."

"We can only do so much. The rest of it's up to her."

"Does relocation involve a new name?"

"Complete new identity for her and the girls."

He would never have contact with them again. Wouldn't know how Maggie was doing, whether she was taking care of the kids, whether Daisy or Dahlia needed anything. He wouldn't know if they were making the right choices or if they followed their mother's example into drugs and sex and crime.

The knowledge left a hollow place inside him, a worry—an ache—for the kids he hadn't even known existed until the past weekend.

"What if she didn't take the girls?"

"They're kind of growing on you, aren't they? Them and their foster mother." Baker did something then that Sean had never witnessed: she smiled. It was faint, barely formed, a bit rusty, but definitely a smile. When it disappeared, her usual expression looked even more somber in comparison. "You know why guys like Kolinski carry out threats against witnesses or their families even after they've been convicted? As punishment to the witness and as a warning to anyone else who might ever think about ratting them out. If we move Maggie but leave the kids behind, how easy will it be for him to find them? A guy who will kill little kids because their mother informed on him—that's a hell of a powerful warning."

So all three of them would be out of his life. *Be careful what you wish for.*

"Of course, you could go with them."

He stared out the window, toward the river and the town on its other side. Leave Copper Lake and never come back. That had been his goal since he was a kid himself, and he'd taken a pretty good stab at it. But now that he *was* back…

Don't kid yourself, buddy. It's not the town. It's the people. It's Ty and Nev and Mr. Obadiah. Most of all, it's Sophy. To never see them again, never talk to them…how long would it take him to start resenting Maggie for it?

About as long as it would take her to score her first hit of meth.

"I'm not going into hiding."

"You counting on your friendship with Kolinski to keep you safe?"

"I'm counting on convincing Maggie to keep her damn mouth shut."

Baker smiled that cool smile again. "If your sister could be trusted to keep quiet, neither of us would be here, would we?"

She had a point. God, how the hell had he wound up in the middle of such a colossal screwup?

The school bus rumbled to a stop out front, drawing Sophy's attention to the windows. A boy from down the street jumped off and raced toward home, then Dahlia slowly came down the steps. Her head was ducked, and she scuffed her feet across the sidewalk and through the gate. The closer she got to the steps, the slower she moved, but eventually she had no other choice; she had to climb up, cross the porch and come inside.

Had she had a fight with her friends? Gotten in trouble with the teacher? Been teased by kids who'd heard about her mother's problems? Sophy took a deep breath and headed for the refrigerator. Food always made things better.

"Hey, Dahlia," she called. "Come on back and have a snack with me. I've got grapes—" the girls' favorite fruit "—and we can even splurge and share a bottle of pop."

Dahlia shuffled to the back, dropped her backpack on the floor and sank into a chair. "Where's Daisy?"

Inside Sophy winced. After her own bad day, did Dahlia really need to hear that her sister had been at a pool party the entire time?

"She went for a playdate with the daughters of some friends of mine." She twisted open a bottle of pop, poured half of it into a cup, then carried both with the bowl of grapes to the table. "You want the bottle or the cup?"

"Cup." But she didn't take a drink or reach for a grape.

"How was school?"

Dahlia shrugged and grunted.

"What did you learn?"

"'Bout punctuation."

"Good stuff. You can't write without it, though people continue to try." The next moment passed in silence, then she gently asked, "Anything you want to talk about?"

Picking a grape, Dahlia inspected it closely as if a creature might leap out through its pale green skin and devour her headfirst. Apparently satisfied, she popped it in her mouth, chewed and swallowed. "I need to go to see Mama."

"I wish you could." *Liar.* "But the jail doesn't allow kids to visit."

"But I need to tell her something."

"Maybe if you tell me, I can tell her." It would be the quickest prisoner visit on record. In fact, maybe the jailer could be persuaded to just take her back to Maggie's cell to save himself the trouble of getting her out and moving her to the visitors' room.

Dahlia stared at her, somber, her gaze too troubled for a six-year-old. She was so thin, unsettled, her little bony shoulders hunched forward. After a moment, she muttered, "There was a man at school."

The words were so far outside what Sophy expected that her lungs tightened and her stomach tumbled. It took effort to make her voice sound normal. "What man?"

Dahlia shrugged.

"Did he say something to you?" *Please don't make me pull it out of you one question at a time.*

"He said, 'Tell your mama we're watchin' her.' I don't think he was a very nice man. I need to go tell her."

"There's someone else we need to tell first, sweetie." Sophy pulled her cell from her pocket and called Ty. "How's my favorite detective?"

"I'm fine, according to Nev. How about you?"

"I don't know. Maybe I'm overreacting, but…" She told him what Dahlia had said, and all the humor disappeared from his voice. Okay, Ty was an experienced detective. If the incident worried him, she wasn't overreacting.

"I'm at the station. I'll be there in about two minutes. Stay on the phone with me. Had she ever seen the guy before?"

"I don't know." With a smile for Dahlia, she rose from her chair and paced toward the front of the store. "I didn't ask. As soon as she told me that much, I called you. It's creepy."

"Yeah, that's the kind of people Maggie hangs with. Is Sean there?"

"No. I think he'll be back before long." As her gaze scanned the street outside, she dearly wished the Chevelle would pull up, but there was no sign of it. No sign of anything unusual, either. No one watching the shop. No one skulking among the trees or around the buildings across from her. "Why would someone give a message like that to a little girl?"

"To remind Maggie to keep her mouth shut. Whoever this guy is, he knows Dahlia's her daughter. He knows where to find her. He knows how to get to her if it becomes necessary."

Ty came into sight, and Sophy's heart rate settled to merely pounding. When he walked through the gate, she hung up and opened the door to greet him. "She's at the back."

"Where's Daisy?"

"She's over at Robbie and Anamaria's. Anamaria should be dropping her off soon."

Despite the circumstances, he grinned. "Word must be getting out that they're becoming user-friendly."

"I guess so."

At the worktable, Ty settled in across from Dahlia. "I know you hate being asked a lot of questions, but I need you to tell me everything that happened this afternoon." He placed a pen and notebook in front of him. "Had you ever seen this man before?"

She shook her head.

"Where were you when he talked to you?"

"Outside. After school. I was walking to the bus, and he stopped in front of me. He bent down and said, 'Tell your mom we're watchin' her,' and then he did that." She pointed her thumb and index finger in a parody of a gun. "If Miss Jo had seen him, he'd'uh got detention 'cause that's a gun and you can't make gun signs at school."

A stress headache began tapping a complicated rhythm in Sophy's skull. She needed a Taser and a pistol like Ty's, a knife like Miri's and a shotgun like her dad's, plus the ability to handle all four. She was sure the kids' social worker would have a whole lot to say about weapons, lethal or not, but all she cared about at the moment was keeping them safe.

Ty asked more questions: Could she describe him? Did she say anything to him? Did she notice where he came from or where he went? Could she remember what he was wearing? Dahlia's frustration level rose with each answer, her legs swinging under the chair. It was no surprise when her foot hit the underside of the table and her pop tumbled on its side, but she looked stunned and dismayed.

"It's okay, Dahlia. I'll clean it up." Before Sophy made it to the wet wipes and paper towels, Dahlia was already there, scooping them up.

"I'll clean it myself," she announced.

Sophy sank down again at the table. "Do you have any idea who this guy is?" she whispered.

"I can only tell you it's not Davey," Ty whispered back. "She would have recognized him. God knows how many people Maggie knew through the business. It could be a customer who doesn't want her giving up any names, or someone Davey worked for, some friend of his."

Sophy watched the slight movements of Dahlia's head as she worked to clean the puddle on the floor with wads of paper towels. "Where is Davey? Is he still in jail?"

"Aw, hell, no. He bonded out right away. Got permission from the court to go stay with his brother out of town until his hearing. I wouldn't have let him go, but the judge makes a lot of decisions that I wouldn't make."

Dahlia threw away the towels and wipes, came

back and stood with her hands on her hips. "I need to go tell my mama."

"Sweetie, I told you—"

Ty raised one hand. "Maybe she should. I bet we can bend a few rules."

He thought it would have more impact on Maggie coming directly from her daughter. Sophy didn't have a clue whether he was right.

"You want to come with us or wait here?"

"I'll go." Lately, her sense of security inside the shop seemed to come and go.

They made it to the door when they saw Sean and Daisy climbing the steps. From the street, Anamaria tapped the horn and waved before driving off.

"Dahlia, hey, guess what? I went swimmin' in a big pool at a big house and a big yard with grass and flowers and everything, and I made friends, too, named Gracie and Clary, and—" Daisy looked from Dahlia to Sophy to Ty, and the excitement dissipated, rounding her shoulders and bringing a resigned look to her face. "Are you in trouble?"

Sean's gaze bore into Sophy, silently asking the same thing. Since it wasn't a simple yes-or-no question, she shrugged but said nothing.

"Someone was waiting for Dahlia after school," Ty said, making it sound totally innocent. "He had a message for her mom, so we're going to pass it on. Sean, could Daisy stay with you upstairs?"

"I wanna go, too. I wanna see Mama."

"Not this time, kiddo." Sophy mussed her hair. "Get out of the wet bathing suit and take a warm shower." Shifting her gaze to Sean, she added, "You'll have to help with her hair."

Both uncle and niece drew back, giving her identical looks questioning her sanity. After a moment, Sean grimaced and nodded, and Daisy wrinkled up her face. "I been in the water all day. Why do I have to take a shower?"

"Because that's the rule of the house," Sean replied. "Come on, Nemo."

Sophy never tried to hold Dahlia's hand when they were walking except while crossing a street. She was surprised and touched when the girl slid her small hand into hers. Her heart hurting, she gave her a quick squeeze, then acted as if it were no big deal.

Ty glanced at her over Dahlia's head. "I noticed you didn't have to give Sean a key."

"You did, huh?"

"I'm a detective. Not much gets past me. You two getting friendly?"

"I plead the Fifth."

He grinned. "Good. He needs someone like you in his life."

"Thanks." Sophy was casual on the outside, beaming inside. Ty knew Sean better than anyone in town, even Maggie, so his approval meant a lot.

In her entire life, Sophy had never been inside the jail. While Ty made arrangements to get Dahlia in to see Maggie, Sophy and Dahlia stood just inside the door, gripping hands, looking around with a cold chill.

"This is where my mama stays?" Dahlia's whisper was barely audible.

It was just a reception area: desks behind a counter, beige walls, industrial tile floor, wooden benches along one wall. There was little difference between it and the social-services office, no more forbidding than the principal's office at the grade school Sophy had attended. It was just a *feeling* about the place. It had seen a lot of drama, desperation and hopelessness.

She crouched next to Dahlia. "It's not so bad, is it?" Especially considering the dirty chaos that had been the Holigan home.

"The lights make noise."

She was right; the fluorescent lights overhead hummed. And the big heavy door leading to the back was intimidating, to say nothing of the officers' weapons.

Thankfully, Ty returned then and escorted them through the door. He had to leave his weapon in a lockbox and placed her purse with it, then took them into a room marked Visitors.

Dahlia dropped Sophy's hand and raced to Maggie, who was standing at the window, throwing her arms around her middle. "Mama, I've missed you!"

"I've missed you, too, baby. I think about you and your sister every day."

Sophy couldn't tell how much truth was in those statements. Maggie sounded sincere enough, but when her attention shifted immediately to Ty without talking further with Dahlia or even asking about Daisy, Sophy was swayed in the *not much* direction.

"You ought to be ashamed, Ty, coming here when you're the one who put me here."

Not much at all. Wanting to shake sense into Maggie, Sophy crossed her arms over her middle, hands clenched, and stayed near the door.

After sharing Dahlia's story, with occasional input from the girl, Ty asked, "Why would someone send a warning to you through your little girl, Maggie? What do you know?"

A gleam came into Maggie's otherwise dull eyes. "That's between me and my lawyer and the D.A."

Ty leaned toward her, anger simmering all around him. He would have put the fear into Sophy, but Maggie didn't flinch. "If you've got something to deal with, then deal, but don't sit in here playing games that put your daughters in danger. If anything happens to them, you can forget about a deal of any kind, and I promise I'll find a way to make you pay for it."

Maggie calmly stroked Dahlia's hair. "Nothing's gonna happen to them. With what I know, I'm bulletproof."

Just a good hard shaking—that would make Sophy feel better. Getting in Maggie's face and shrieking, *These are your babies! What kind of mother are you?* Maybe a smack or two to knock some reality into her.

"Then tell the D.A." Ty's voice was little more than a menacing growl. "Make your damn deal so we can keep these kids safe."

Keeping them safe… That would likely mean taking them from Copper Lake, from Sophy's care. Putting them in some sort of protective custody. The thought forced her a step back to the wall for support.

She wasn't naive. Before she'd made the decision to become a foster parent, she'd acknowledged that she would likely get emotionally involved with any child placed with her for more than a few days. It was human nature, a mother's nature—Maggie excepted. She'd known there would be some heartache when the child left, whether returned to the parents, adopted or placed in another home. She'd prepared herself for that from the very beginning.

But she hadn't imagined her first foster children would be as needy as Daisy and Dahlia, and she certainly hadn't imagined that they'd be taken away from her because their lives were in danger.

"I've got a call in to my lawyer. Soon as I talk to him, we'll set up a meeting with the D.A." Maggie smirked. "I'll probably be out of this stupid town in no time."

"Out of town?" Dahlia repeated. "Are you going somewhere, Mama? Are Daisy and me going with you?"

"Of course you are, baby. Do you think I'd go off and leave you behind?"

Oh, gee, no, why would she think that? This is only her fourth or fifth time in foster care.

Dahlia's smile was a beautiful thing, transforming her entire face. "Where are we going? Me and Daisy have never been anywhere."

"I'm thinkin' California. Maybe we'll live on the beach and swim in the ocean every day, and we'll learn how to surf. Would you like that?"

Dahlia's nod was excited. Sophy let her head fall back and hit the wall with a soft thud. Ty met her gaze, disapproval for Maggie radiating from him.

"Don't get your hopes too high, Maggie," he said flatly. "And try to remember that you and your deal aren't the most important thing here. Doing what's best for your girls is. Say goodbye, Dahlia. We've got to go."

As they left the jail, Sophy and Ty were somber. Dahlia was dancing. "We're going to California!

Yay!" She peered up at Sophy. "Where is California?"

"It's way off on the other side of the country."

"How long does it take to get there?"

"A few days if you drive. A few hours if you fly."

"On an airplane? We're gonna fly on an airplane? Oh, boy, I can't wait to tell Daisy!"

Sophy had to take her hand to cross the street, then the girl pulled away and skipped ahead. "Maggie just doesn't get it, does she?"

I was scared, Mama, Dahlia had said, wanting to be held closer, but Maggie had already been thinking ahead, too busy scheming for herself to comfort Dahlia.

"No," Ty replied. "You heard what her first words to me were."

You ought to be ashamed, coming here when you're the one who put me here. Poor Maggie, always the victim of someone else's actions, never responsible for anything she did.

When they got to the apartment, Dahlia and the freshly bathed Daisy chattered over each other's voices, sharing their news, swimming and new friends competing with seeing Maggie and moving. The possibility of flying on an airplane stunned Daisy into a rare silence, and Sophy used the opportunity to send the girls to their room.

She, Sean and Ty were gathered at the island. She hadn't had the chance to do more than exchange worried glances with Sean. When she'd seen him a few minutes ago, she'd wanted to run to him the way Dahlia had run to Maggie, to throw her arms around him and lean on him, to draw comfort and support from him.

The difference between him and Maggie: he would have given it.

"Tommy's assigning a couple officers to the school tomorrow," Ty said. "They'll be in civilian clothes, just hanging out. He's also instructed the patrol officers to keep a closer watch around here. Sean, can you—"

"I'm staying here."

Ty nodded, satisfied. "Sophy, I hate to take over your life, but I'm inviting myself and Nev over for dinner this evening. We'll stay here with you while Sean gets whatever he needs from the motel."

Sophy hated that her smile was wobbly. "You can move in, too, if you want. In fact, to make it easier, if you want to just move the three of us into a cell at the jail, we wouldn't argue." As long as she was nowhere near Maggie. Snatching her through the bars sideways sounded way too appealing.

Nev was the only normal one in the apartment that night. She played with the girls, read them stories, answered a hundred questions from them about California and airplanes—though she'd never experienced either one—and gave a sense of rightness to the evening.

Sean had a headache and figured Sophy did, too, from the way she kept touching her right temple. Stress. In a quiet moment alone, she'd thanked him for moving in. *I feel safer with you around.*

Making a woman feel safe was a pretty good feeling in itself.

Now it was after nine. Sean had already made a run to the motel to pick up his things. His suitcase sat unobtrusively against the end of the couch. The girls were in bed, snuggled like spoons in a drawer in the unmade bed. Would they ever feel at home enough here to sleep in separate beds?

Would they even get the chance?

"Maybe Dahlia should stay home from school tomorrow," Sophy ventured.

"She'll have two plainclothes cops watching her and everyone around her all day," Ty reminded her. "They'll follow you when you take her, and they'll follow her bus home. By the way, drive her to school. Don't walk."

"How do you know we usually walk?"

He gave her a chastising look. "Everyone in town knows you like to walk wherever you can. It's your routine. No more routines, other than work, and only because that place is solid. Steel doors, with solid locks, bulletproof glass, panic buttons all over the room and cops just a few blocks away."

But how much did the door locks matter when the front door was unlocked during business hours? Sean thought maybe he'd get a solid length of lead pipe, pull one of the rockers over in front of the door and sit there all day, denying entrance to anyone Sophy didn't approve.

She stared at her hands a long moment, then looked up, her expression troubled. "If Masiela agrees to work with Maggie, she won't actually get custody of the kids wherever they send her, will she?"

The idea of his selfish, fantasy-world sister taking control of her children again roiled Sean's gut. Of all the priorities in her life, she'd made clear Daisy and Dahlia were at the bottom of the list. She wasn't fit to have a visit with them, much less be in control of their lives.

"If Masiela has a say," Ty said, "the kids will be put in some type of protective custody until Maggie testifies. It could be a group home, a government agency, maybe even a foster home near wherever they stash her."

"If Mas doesn't have a say, who would?" Sophy asked.

Sean was lifting his glass for a drink as Ty answered, "Depending on Maggie's info, the feds could come in—the FBI, maybe the DEA. It's hard to say what would happen then."

At mention of the DEA, the ice rattled loudly in his glass, and he set it carefully on the island, then rested his hands flat on the countertop to keep the unsteadiness from showing. He was pretty sure Sophy felt it, though, when she laid her hand on his arm. "You can't let her disappear out there with the kids, Sean. Who knows what would happen to them, what she would do to them?"

The possibility scared the crap out of him, but he kept it tightly controlled. "She's their mother, Sophy, and she likes being a mom when it suits her. She'll tell the D.A., the feds, the court exactly what they want to hear, and she'll even believe it herself for a while. That she's gonna get straight. That this is the start of a wonderful new life. Yeah, the last five or six starts bombed, but this one's different. This is the *real* one. She wants it so much this time she can't possibly fail."

Her brown gaze locked with his, earnest and troubled and damn near pleading. "But if the D.A. and the feds and the judges have an option, if they have a law-abiding, respectable, sober uncle who wants to step up for his nieces, they don't *have* to give them to Maggie."

"Law-abiding and respectable," he repeated. "With a criminal history dating back more than twenty years. The people you're talking about probably wouldn't find me any more fit to take care of Daisy and Dahlia than Maggie is." Though he'd acknowledged the possibility to himself, saying it out loud in front of Sophy, Ty and Nev hurt. It made him feel about as small and disreputable as he ever had.

Her slender fingers tightened around his arm. "But you do want them."

He held her gaze a long time, searching for doubt, both in her and himself. When he didn't find it in either one, he wasn't sure which surprised him more. "Yes," he finally said. More than he did yesterday, probably not as much as he would tomorrow.

Nev had spent most of the conversation simply listening, but now she slid off the bar stool and came around the island to slide her arms around both Sophy and Sean. "I think about all we can do right now is pray that Maggie will look into her heart and do what's right for those girls."

Give up custody. Terminate her parental rights. Would that be enough to remove them from Craig's threat? The argument could be made that hurting Daisy and Dahlia then wouldn't have the expected impact. The kids would already be out of her life; she wouldn't know where they were or who they'd been placed with. She likely wouldn't even hear about anything that happened to them.

Terminate her rights, keep her mouth shut and go to prison—that would be the absolute best thing she could do for them.

But Maggie never had been into doing the best for anyone but herself.

After a few more minutes, Ty and Nev left, and Sophy locked up behind them. With the locks on the door, the bars on the windows and the alarm system, the old house felt pretty secure.

But none of that would protect them against an explosion or a fire. And a hundred-year-old wood-frame house…how easily it would burn.

On her way back from the door, she caught his hand and pulled him over to the couch. As they settled into the cushions, she lightly said, "I've decided that the girls and I are running away. You wanna go with us?"

Stretching his feet out on the coffee table, he tilted his head back and stared at the family pictures on the fireplace mantel. "Where are you going?"

"Anywhere but California."

He laughed with her. Neither Daisy nor Dahlia knew the first thing about the state, probably weren't sure exactly what the ocean was and didn't have a clue about surfing, but they'd talked it to death this evening. He wouldn't mind if he didn't hear the name again for at least a year.

"How about Montana? I hear it's a beautiful place."

"Yeah, but it gets cold there."

She mimicked his position, then slanted a look at him. "You're too delicate for the cold?"

"I like it warm."

"Arizona?"

"Not that warm." He took her hand, twining his fingers with hers. "How long are you running away for?"

"A week, a month, a year. However long it takes for the kids to be safe."

After giving that a moment's consideration, he pressed a kiss to her hand. "You're a good mom."

"I don't feel like it. Standing there in that room at the jail, all I wanted was to wrap my hands around Maggie's neck and throttle her."

"That's all I've wanted every time I've seen her this week." His gaze shifted to the stuffed bear. It was easy to form a picture of a waiflike brown-eyed Sophy, dragging the toy with her everywhere she went, snuggling with it at night in her bed. Just as it was easy to summon an image of Maggie at the same age, just as waiflike, just as innocent, with just as many dreams as Sophy had had.

Two little girls, the same age, both without their mothers. One placed in the foster-care system with its abundant flaws, the other left with her family. Based on nothing more than that, it should have been Sophy who went off track and Maggie who'd succeeded, Sophy who'd wound up in the judicial system.

The fact that it hadn't been said a lot for the abundant flaws of the Holigan family.

"She wasn't a bad kid." It took him a moment, and the weight of Sophy's gaze, to realize he'd spoken out loud. With a self-conscious shrug, he went on, "She had a lot going against her."

"I know."

"Which is no excuse."

"I know." Sophy's voice was quieter this time.

The house wasn't really silent, but with the kids asleep, it felt that way. There were little noises in the background, the kind of things a person usually didn't notice in his own home. A car went past, and the wind scraped a tree branch against the side of the house. Chimes tinkled somewhere, and a few plops on the roof slowly turned into the steady beat of raindrops.

"I hear Florida's nice in winter," Sophy mused. "A million snowbirds can't be wrong."

"Miami Beach."

"I was thinking Orlando. We could get jobs at Disney World. You could be a pirate of the Caribbean, and I could be a pirate's wench."

He gave her a measuring look, from the demure neck of her shirt all the way down to her bare feet, propped beside his. "You could be my wench anytime."

Her smile was sweet and sensuous and made his gut knot. "I was hoping you'd feel that way, 'cause this couch isn't very comfortable for sleeping."

He was sure her bed was comfortable as hell. He would probably get the best sleep ever in it. He would probably learn that all his life, he'd been sleeping— and having sex—totally wrong because he'd been doing it without her.

Or he'd find he couldn't sleep at all because just having Holigans in her house put her in danger.

And what would she think when she found out about him working for Craig?

God help him.

He stood, pulled her to her feet and started toward the hallway. There he stopped, laid his hands on her shoulders and turned her toward the open door at the other end. "I'll test the couch tonight and let you know what I think in the morning."

She gave him a knowing look. "It's a good thing I have a strong ego, or you'd be breaking my heart now."

He brushed her hair back gently. "You know we'll end up in there together, or at least you should after this afternoon."

Her smile was smug. "Oh, honey, I've known it longer than that."

"But not tonight. I need—" To think. To figure out what to tell her about the rest of his life and when and how. That he was an informant against his best friend. That said best friend happened to be a murderer, drug dealer and thief. That the threat against Maggie and the girls came from Craig. That the explosion was thanks to Craig, too.

That Sean wasn't as respectable as she thought he was.

It wasn't fair to have sex with her before dropping that little bombshell, not when it could change everything between them. Wasn't fair to hurt or disappoint her.

She leaned onto her toes, brushing her mouth across his, light strokes, tender and teasing and tempting. "Think of me tonight," she whispered, wearing that smug smile again as she turned and strolled lazily, languidly to the bedroom.

Oh, he'd think about her, all right, and if he managed to sleep, he would probably dream about her. Forever.

Turning into the kitchen, he made a cup of coffee, then sat down in a chair with a view of a tiny pocket of a backyard, and he settled in for a long night of hard thoughts.

Chapter 10

When Sophy woke, rain still pounded the roof and streaked the windows, giving a dim view outside. The leaves on the trees across the street were water-logged, the weight pulling the branches lower than they would normally hang, and narrow streams flowed along the curbs. It would be a great day for walking to school—would have been, if it were a normal morning. She liked splashing through puddles, getting her shoes and clothes and hair soaked, but that fun would have to wait until quiet returned to their lives.

Please, let the kids be here then.

She'd kept the bedroom door open all night but hadn't heard so much as a snore from Sean. Maybe going all statue-still-and-silent was a talent the girls would master as they grew up.

What had he thought about last night? The ramifications of his taking the girls permanently? The fallout of taking on Sophy temporarily? Did he at least allow for the chance that, like the kids, she could become permanent, too? Had he worried what the court and social services would say? Did he realize that even making the request could bring him a boatload of pain and disappointment?

It sucked to have so many questions and no answers.

After a hasty shower, she dressed in cargo shorts and a T-shirt decorated with the shop logo. A check of the clock showed the girls could sleep awhile longer, so she padded into the darkened living room, following her nose to a mug of steaming coffee.

Sean shifted his feet to make room for her on the couch. He'd been in the shower ahead of her—she'd smelled the tang of his shaving cream and the crisp, clean scents of his toiletries—and he was dressed only in snug-fitting jeans. His body was long and lean, not overly bulky like a weight lifter, but the kind of lean strength any woman could appreciate.

"Do you always get up this early?" She settled next to him, feet tucked beneath her, facing him.

"How early is it?"

"I don't know, but the sun hasn't found its way out."

"I usually get to the garage between six and seven. About half our customers are strictly repair work. 'My car vibrates when I go over eighty miles an hour.' Or 'It shimmies at stoplights.' Or, my favorite, 'It's going *thunka-thunka-thunk*.'"

"So those are the ones you want to get in and out quickly."

With a nod, he offered his coffee. Her fingers brushed his when she took it, and for a moment she breathed deeply of the intense, dark aroma. Finally she tested it, found it just hot enough and took a long drink. It warmed her all the way to her toes.

"And the other customers," she said, giving the cup back. "There for the restoration. They buy the old beat-up muscle cars and pay you well to get them into shape."

"Those are my favorites. And the nice thing about these guys is once they get a taste of the first restored car, it's just about a guarantee that they'll come back with another one every couple years."

There was a change in his expression, his voice, when he talked about his work. He liked it, and he was proud of it. She understood exactly how he felt. She would never get rich with the quilt shop, but she made beautiful pieces and had ready buyers for every one of them.

"Will you be able to make enough time for the girls?"

It took him a bit to answer, his gaze directed out the window, where only gray showed where the sun should be starting its morning job of lightening and brightening the sky. "If I had them, I wouldn't go back to Virginia."

She leaned her arm on the back of the sofa, resting her cheek on her fist. "How about Orlando?"

"Is the pirate's wench going?"

Her smile was faint. She'd dressed up as a wench one Halloween but couldn't remember who her pirate was. She would never forget *this* pirate. "What if the wench stays here?"

His features turned distant and troubled. "I don't know. So many things would have to be settled before I could make a decision." To take the sting out of his words, he set his coffee down, then made room for her in his embrace, her head resting on his shoulder, the rest of her body snug and warm against his.

Sophy had loved a dozen men in her life, good men, fun guys who made her laugh, guys she would love forever, but she'd never been in love with one of them. She'd known Sean far less time than she'd dated any of them, but deep in her heart, she knew he was different. It didn't matter that she could count the number of days he'd been in town on one hand with a finger left over. It didn't matter that he'd warned her from the start that he wasn't staying here. She *knew.*

She wasn't talking about love at first sight. She was a bit of a skeptic about that, though she knew several people who claimed to have experienced it. Her own parents loved to share the story of how they'd told their friends, thirty minutes after meeting, that they were going to marry each other. They had, too, less than three months later.

Sophy preferred to think that, with Sean, she'd found potential at first sight. Some little alert had gone off inside her, slyly whispering, *This* could *be the one,* and every minute she spent with him, every conversation she had with him, added weight to that little voice.

But being sure he was *the one* wasn't a guarantee that he felt the same—that he would *allow* himself to feel the same. He'd spent his entire lifetime avoiding commitments. Now he was willing to take custody of his nieces. Was that enough of a commitment to start with? Did he doubt he would have anything left over for a woman?

She glanced at her watch and sighed softly. "Time to rouse the sleeping beauties. It's usually a slow and painful process—for them. I rather enjoy it myself." With a grin, she pushed to her feet and headed for the girls' room. The soft footsteps behind her told her Sean was following.

A night-light cast pale shadows over Daisy and Dahlia, sleeping back-to-back this morning. "The first night they spent here, I put them to bed in separate beds." She kept her voice low, her gaze on the girls with Sean a shadow in her peripheral vision. "The next morning I found them in the same bed. That night I tried the separate beds again and woke up to the same thing. I just let them be now. I figure when they're ready, they'll use both beds. Or when they've gotten so big that one of them falls out."

"They look sweet, don't they?"

His tone—quiet, hoarse, a bit chagrined—made her smile. "They are sweet…in a really vibrant, exuberant, hell-on-wheels sort of way."

She flipped on the light switch, then raised her voice. "Daisy, Dahlia, time to get up, kiddos."

True to form, the girls didn't stir.

Sophy crossed to the bed and bent over, but not too close. "Dahlia, you've got to get up for school."

With a grunt and a swing of her arm, Dahlia snuggled deeper into the covers. Beside her, Daisy mumbled something unintelligible and flopped onto her back. Her hair covered most of her face, the ends fluttering as her mouth sagged open in a steady snore.

"Come on, kids." Sophy grasped two handfuls

of the covers and tugged them away from skinny arms and slack fingers. "Time to get up, get up in the morning," she singsonged.

"Go 'way!"

Dodging Dahlia's flailing arm again, Sophy shook both girls' shoulders at the same time. "Seriously, guys, get up, get dressed and let's eat. Since we have a little extra time today—" thanks to Ty's instruction that she drive Dahlia to school instead of walk "—I might even fix waffles for breakfast."

Daisy shoved her hair back to reveal one narrowed eye. "Is that them bumpy pancakes?"

"Yep."

"Can I have chocolate butter and syrup on 'em?"

"Yep." In an aside to Sean, Sophy explained, "Daisy will do practically anything for Nutella. Daisy, wake up your sister, will you?"

Daisy sat up, stretched, braced herself against the headboard, planted both feet in the middle of her sister's back and shoved her off the bed. The older girl hit the floor with a muffled *thump* and came up growling, hands outstretched. With a giggle, Daisy jumped to her feet and leaped from the bed into Sean's arms, shrieking, "Save me, save me!"

As Sophy walked past them, she leaned close to him, murmuring, "See what fun awaits you?"

As her mom had said during her visit, he got points for not running while he had the chance.

Thursday was, on the surface, as normal a day as Sean had had in a while. Ty gave them regular updates on Dahlia; customers came and went in the store, paying little attention to him and Daisy; the rain kept falling. When the shop door opened, its clean scent rushed inside on the wind, the air fresh and cooled from its usual end-of-summer heat.

None of that normalcy went very deep, though. His muscles were knotted with the need to move, go, do *something*. Every time the door opened, his gaze jerked to the front. Every time the phone rang, he froze, all his focus zeroing in on Sophy's voice, her face, looking for the relief that came across it after an instant.

Dahlia was home from school now, the bus that delivered her trailed by a police car. It was almost time to close and go upstairs, where they'd already decided to order pizza from Luigi's. The thought, Sophy had said, was enough to make anyone feel better, no matter what their troubles. He agreed.

He was lifting Daisy to return a bolt of fabric to an upper shelf when the doorbell announced Ty's arrival. He was accompanied by another detective, his face familiar, his name eluding Sean.

Sophy looked up from the bank deposit and smiled. "Hey, Ty, Pete."

Pete Petrovski. Ski, they'd called him in school. Another of her exes. What a lineup: four cops, a lawyer, a businessman, who knew what else...and an ex-con informant of a mechanic. Damn.

Petrovski responded to her greeting with a somber nod. In fact, both men were somber. Sean lowered Daisy to the floor, sent her off to help Dahlia and joined Sophy at the counter as she asked, "What's up?"

It was Ty who answered. "I told you that the judge

gave Maggie's boyfriend, Davey, permission to stay with his brother over in Martinez."

Sophy nodded.

The town butted right up next to Augusta, so close that it was hard to tell where one ended and the other started.

"We just got a call from the state police." Ty glanced at the girls, then fixed his gaze on Sean. "He was killed in a wreck this morning. His car broke through the railing on the Savannah River bridge at a high rate of speed. They just got it out of the water and ID'd him."

Cold and stiff, Sean walked away, thinking of all the reasons for an accident like that. Falling asleep. A medical condition. Suicide. Alcohol or drug use. Excessive speed. Weather. Vehicle malfunction.

Accident. Murder. Either way, Craig's life just got easier. One less problem to worry about. Now the only thing that tied Copper Lake's routine drug bust to Craig was Maggie. Would this help her see reason? Make her realize she was playing with danger?

He didn't hear Sophy's approach but didn't startle when she touched his arm. "Does Maggie know yet?"

"No. Pete and I were just coming back from court when I got the call."

"Let me tell her," Sean said abruptly. If this didn't get through to her, he had an idea that might. After he'd given her a chance to—how had Nev put it?—look into her heart and do what was right for her daughters.

Ty shrugged. "Go ahead. Pete will give you a ride. I'll stay here until you get back."

Sophy squeezed his arm before letting go, her look

reassuring. He appreciated that she didn't shy away from contact with him in front of her exes, that—limited though their lives were—she wasn't secretive about him.

He and Petrovski ran through the rain to the Charger illegally parked in front of the shop, hazard lights flashing. But then, for a cop, he supposed, there was no such thing as illegal parking.

After a moment's uncomfortable silence while Petrovski pulled away from the curb, the cop spoke. "Sophy's doing a great job with the kids."

Sean grunted in agreement.

"Our neighbor had them for a few days once before. They painted the bathroom walls with her makeup the first day, set a fire in the kitchen sink the second and on the third day, I had to climb onto the roof to untangle Dahlia from a tree branch. They're… active."

Sean snorted. "They're hooligans, and Daisy, at least, is very proud of it."

"Aw, they're not bad kids," Petrovski said as he pulled into the police department parking lot. "They just need stability and a little bit of civilizing."

Sean could give them stability, he acknowledged as he thanked Petrovski for the ride and headed to the jail door. If the courts let him take custody, he would always be there, never leave them, never let them down the way he had their mom. He understood priorities.

And Sophy could do the civilizing. As Petrovski had pointed out, she'd done a great job so far. If she wanted to. If they could work out the logistics of it.

If he could come back to Copper Lake or she could be persuaded to leave.

Disney World and jobs as pirate and wench seemed more likely.

Ty had called ahead to the jail, so Maggie was waiting when Sean walked into the visitors' room. Sitting on a plastic stool, picking at her fingernails, she didn't look particularly happy to see him.

"What is it with you? I don't see you for fourteen years and suddenly you're coming here every day trying to tell me what I should and shouldn't do with my own life? Where was all this brotherly responsibility when I needed it?"

He didn't look for words to soften the blow. "Davey's dead."

For a moment her look remained the same—vacant, bored. Then the news registered, and her expression shifted to dismay and disappointment. "Well, shit. It's just like the bastard to get himself killed when he could finally be some use to me."

Sean stared at her. She'd lived with the man, had sex with him, done drugs with him, *made* drugs with him. She'd put her kids at risk in part because of him, and all she could do upon hearing he was dead was complain? "Yeah, I'm sorry he was so inconsiderate of you in dying when he did."

Her glare came quick and sharp. "You've got no room to judge me, Johnny. You can't even imagine how hard my life has been."

"I don't care how hard your life has been," he lied. "I care about Daisy's and Dahlia's lives, about them being safe and cared for and having a chance like every other kid in the world."

Her eyes, just like the ones he faced in the mirror every day, widened, then she laughed. "You care, huh? Since when? You weren't around to care when I was pregnant or when they were babies crying all night long. You weren't here to help take care of them or support them or—or—"

God, she was such a lousy mother, she didn't even know what mothers were supposed to do. His nieces were lucky to have survived the helpless baby years.

She stood and shuffled toward the door, but he blocked her way. "Go away, Johnny. Go back to Norfolk and—"

"You didn't even ask how he died."

Her shrug was pathetically disinterested. "Overdose, I suppose."

"He drove through a bridge railing at an excessively high speed and ended up at the bottom of the Savannah River. That's not an easy way to go, though I guess maybe it's better than a bullet in your brain."

She plucked at the too-long sleeves of her sweat jacket, pushing them up to her elbows, immediately pulling them down again. "Why would someone put a bullet in his brain?"

"Gee, I don't know. Maybe because he got arrested and knew way too much about his boss's business. Maybe because he talked too much. You and Davey and your meth-making—that's just pissant games compared to what his boss does. His operation crosses six states and brings in millions of dollars every year. How much tolerance do you think he's gonna have for an idiot who gets himself thrown in jail on a meth charge? Or for the idiot who slept with him and thinks that gives her power now?"

Out of that whole scornful speech, she focused on one word, her eyes gleaming, her greed practically a real, touchable thing. "Millions? Every year?"

His eye was going to twitch its way right out of its socket, followed by his head exploding. He couldn't take much more of this and trust himself to keep his hands off her.

Carefully he walked around her, sat down at one of the tables and indicated the stool across from him. After a sullen moment, she plopped down across from him, arms folded over her chest. Waiting mutinously.

"I'm going to ask for custody of the girls."

Again, the bored look filled her eyes for the time it took the words to sink in, and then she smirked. "*You?* You think you're more fit to be a parent than me?"

"I have a job, a stable home. I'm their closest relative. I'm the only relative who isn't a career criminal. Yes, I can be a better parent than you. I can provide them with a better, safer home than you can."

Her head began shaking long before he stopped talking. "I'll tell their social worker no. I'll tell her you're a perv, wanting two little girls you didn't even know a week ago."

Sean pushed away the ache from the lie she threatened. "And being the fine, law-abiding, upstanding citizen you are, the social worker's going to take your word over mine."

The truth of his words sank in more quickly, turning her scorn into a frown. "Bitch always did have it in for me." One foot tapping on the floor, she started picking at her finger again, pulling off a strip of skin, swiping the drop of blood that welled onto her pants. "You can't do that, Johnny. They're *my* kids. I need them. The D.A. can stick a single woman off in some hellhole, but kids need someplace decent."

For just a moment, she had him—the emotion in her voice when she'd laid claim to the girls, the way she'd said she *needed* them. Then the moment passed, the hope that flared inside him died, and he was done. The little girl he'd comforted and cared for, who'd tagged after him every chance she got, who'd begged him to take her away with him—that Maggie was gone. The woman sitting across from him, willing to use her own little girls to bargain for a better life for herself, was a stranger. He didn't know her. Didn't want to know her.

He played his last card. "I'll pay you."

The gleam was back, bringing a flush to her cheeks. "When I asked you to bail me out, you said you didn't have any money."

He didn't deny it. He could have millions of his own, and he wouldn't waste a dime of it on bail for any of his family.

"How much?"

Except for his car, he lived pretty cheaply. Not having a family, a steady girlfriend or a hobby outside of work made it pretty easy. He named a figure that instantly fueled Maggie's distrust.

"Where'd you get that much money?"

"It's called a job. You should try getting one sometime."

She scratched her chin, then stood to pace the room, stopping at the window. "So what would I have to do to get this money?"

"Terminate your parental rights. Let the girls be adopted."

"And what if the court don't let you adopt 'em?"

That was a possibility. Though Sophy and Ty would speak on his behalf, and for what it was worth, he was family. "At least they'll be out of this mess." He tried to believe that was enough, that he wouldn't wonder every day how they were, if they were loved, if they needed anything.

That he wouldn't miss them every single day.

For a long time she stared outside. Imagining her life without Dahlia and Daisy? Hearing them call someone else Mama? Realizing that she'd be giving up the only decent part of her life?

"I'll have to think about it," she said abruptly, then pivoted on her heel and stalked to the door. She banged on it with her fist and swept out as soon as it opened.

Sean left, too, much more slowly, hunching his shoulders as he stepped outside into the rain. It soaked his hair, his clothes, his shoes, dripped off his nose and caught on his eyelashes. The gray and dreariness matched the way he was feeling for giving up on Maggie, appealing to her weakness to buy his nieces' freedom from her, realizing he might have set in motion events that would not only make the girls disappear from their mom but also from him.

So much for a normal day. It couldn't get much worse.

But then he reached the shop, bypassed the double doors and climbed the stairs to the apartment. He let himself in with his key and found Sophy and Ty having coffee at the table, Dahlia and Daisy watching cartoons on TV, and Sophy looked up at him with a serene smile that eased the ache in his chest. The smile was enough to make anyone feel better, no matter what their troubles. Just that smile was enough to bolster his hope that somehow everyone was going to be all right. Daisy and Dahlia. Sophy. Hell, maybe even Maggie.

And most definitely him.

Chapter 11

Sophy loved the middle of the night. The town was quiet, lights glistening on empty streets. Cars were rare on her street, pedestrians even rarer. The neighborhood dogs were settled in for a few hours' sleep, while a light breeze rustled through the trees across the street, setting ghostly tendrils of Spanish moss swaying. Tonight the vista had the added benefit of being washed clean by the daylong rain, reflecting and scattering the light.

Two o'clock and all's well. Or as well as it could be, considering that she was alone in the bedroom, while Sean was stretched out uncomfortably on the couch. But that was okay. He wanted time; she had a lifetime of it to give.

She wasn't sure she'd ever dated a man who hadn't wanted sex from the start. It was part of the getting-

to-know-you, the fun, sweet, breathtaking and sometimes amazing part of it. It wasn't a big step forward
in a relationship; it didn't signal commitment or even
exclusivity, though she had wound up committed to
and exclusive with most of the guys she'd had sex
with.

But to Sean, it was a commitment, a fact that she
found incredibly sweet. The smoldering, intense,
handsome-as-sin, sexy-as-the-devil big bad boy, pos-
sessor of a wicked reputation and a grin to match,
wasn't indulging in casual sex.

Only fair, since there was nothing casual about
her feelings for him. He could break her heart, and
she didn't care. She wanted him and everything that
came with him. If that included sorrow, well, she
would count herself lucky to have known him.

A board creaked in the hallway behind her, but
she didn't shift from her position leaning against the
window frame. It wasn't either of the girls awakened
for a bathroom trip. Their bedroom door squeaked
ferociously when opened more than a few inches, a
handy alert in the first few days when they'd had a
tendency to be furtive in everything they did.

How did he move so quietly? A whisper here, a
shush there, and he was behind her, close enough
for her to feel the heat radiating from his bare chest.
Wishing for enough light to cast a reflection in the
window so she could see him, she smiled. "Did I
wake you?"

"No. Yes." He slid his arm around her waist, pulling her back to lean against him, then secured her
there with his other arm. Now the heat encircled
her, like a blazing fire on a cold night, chasing away

any chill the air-conditioning had brought and turning her skin warm and toasty and well on the way to feverish.

"I used to be afraid of the dark," she murmured, absorbing the feel of him: broad chest, flat abdomen, strong thighs and, cradled snugly against her bottom, the beginning of a promising erection. "It got worse after our mother got sicker and our father left, until one night Miri showed me the magic of the night. She took me outside, and we listened to the birds singing. We watched for shooting stars and left our footprints on the dew-soaked grass. We searched for the owl hooting somewhere in the side yard, and we snuggled together on the glider on the front porch and just concentrated on the—the peace of it. I was never afraid again."

"Sweet memory."

"It's possible to have sweet memories even when it seems the rest of your life was hell." She paused, her hands clasped over his, her fingertips rubbing the crooked joints on his left hand. "Tell me one of yours."

He was quiet a long time, not because good memories were hard to find, she was sure, but to find one that he trusted enough to share. She had no problem with sharing personal stuff, but she'd been raised to be open and forthcoming, to believe that people were trustworthy until they proved they weren't, while he'd been taught not to talk—to cops, strangers or people in general.

"One day Declan and Ian were supposed to be at school, which means they were anywhere besides there, and our old man was at work. Mom put Maggie and me in the car and drove us out to the lake for a picnic. Usually she was too tired or disappointed to talk much, but that day she talked a long time about how things were and how they should be and about taking care of a baby like Maggie and taking care of myself. She said school was important—you needed education to make something of yourself. She made me promise that I would finish school." His chuckle was soft. "I hadn't even started yet, and I was making solemn vows to graduate."

The humor faded slowly. "We ate our sandwiches, and she showed me how to give Maggie a bottle, how to change her diaper, and sometimes her eyes would get wet and she'd stop and close them for a while. When the afternoon was over, we went home, and the next morning she left. We never saw her again."

"She was telling you goodbye." Trying to prepare him to become his baby sister's responsible brother, crying when it got too hard for her. "Do you know where she went?"

He shook his head, the beard on his chin catching fine strands of her hair.

"Do you ever wonder if she's alive and well out there, thinking about the babies she had to leave behind and aching to make the acquaintance of her granddaughters?"

"Mostly I think Maggie had lousy parental role models. Was it any surprise she turned out to be so bad at it herself?"

"There's more to it than just role models. You'll be very good at it." Slowly she turned within the circle of his arms, resting her hands flat on his chest, using what little light made its way into the room to study him. With her hair and white nightgown, she practically gleamed in the dark room, casting even more shadows over him.

Not even the blackest shadow could hide the fact that he was gorgeous or that his muscles rippled beneath her fingers or that his breath had hitched just a bit or that his pulse was throbbing a little more obviously.

"You are so incredible," she murmured. "God was surely having a fine day when He made you."

"In a few years, I'll probably be cross-eyed and half-bald."

Laughing, she lifted her hand to his hair, silky, fine, different from the girls' only in that his was short enough to have a tendency to curl. "I love crossed eyes, and who needs hair?"

His smile lingered a long time while he toyed with the ribbons that served as straps for her gown. All he had to do was untie each one, and with a shimmy, a shake and a tug, she'd be naked. But the smile faded, and the bows were still tied when he drew back. "We need to talk."

"Oh-kay." She'd heard those words before and said them herself a few times, never followed by anything good. But she didn't get the vibe that he was giving up on the idea of something more intimate between them. He seemed troubled, but not about her, at least, not directly.

Letting go of him, she sat on the bed; he pulled the wicker rocker from the corner closer and sat down where their knees bumped.

It was hard for him to start—would have been hard for any man she knew—but he took a breath and haltingly began. "I know you want us to have sex, and I want that, too. But first…I need to tell you…"

"You're not married. You're not in a long-term relationship back in Virginia. Your car is your baby. You really don't want to be a pirate of the Caribbean. What am I missing?"

Another breath. "The truth about why I'm here. The real reason I came."

Sophy hadn't expected that.

"I told you I wound up in Norfolk because that's where the guy I hitched a ride with was going. His name is Craig Kolinski, and his father had a garage, run-down, on the verge of bankruptcy. We both went to work there, doing our best to get it cleaned up and profitable again. We slept on cots in the back room for the first year because neither of us could afford a place to live.

"And things turned around. Craig knew cars in general, and thanks to Charlie, I knew restoration. When his dad died, Craig used his life-insurance money to hire new mechanics, buy new equipment and add more space, and we began focusing on the restorations. There was a lot of business, a lot of money coming in, and eventually Craig turned the garage over to me, and he concentrated on the business end."

So far, so good. Nothing more than she'd assumed. Still, Sophy couldn't shake the tension curling through her like a wisp of smoke.

Sean met her gaze. "Craig was a good guy. He didn't care that I'd been in prison, he understood dysfunctional families, he had the same goals I did. For a lot of years, he was the best friend I'd ever had."

And then... A lead-in like that always had an *and then*.

"I like what I do. I kind of live in my own world at work. That's why it took me a long time to realize that Craig was spending a lot more money than he was bringing in. Then I found out shipments were coming into the garage overnight off the books and disappearing again the next morning. I asked Craig about it, and he finally admitted they were stolen parts he got from Florida, Georgia, Alabama, the Carolinas, and sent up to the New York area. I quit right then, but he convinced me to stay awhile longer, just till he found someone to replace me. He promised the stolen stuff would be kept separate from the rest of the business, that he wouldn't do anything that could come back to bite me on the ass."

Sophy spoke quietly, putting a lot of effort into making her voice even, nonjudgmental. "He put off finding someone to replace you, and before long it was back to business as usual for both of you."

Sean nodded, a strand of hair falling across his forehead. He swiped it back with his left hand, those injured fingers, and she thought briefly of all the ways fingers could get injured in a garage.

"For the most part, I put it out of my mind. Like I said, I worked in my own world. And it was easy to ignore. I mean, life had been good before finding out, and by forgetting about it, it pretty much went back to good. But it changed things between him and me. We stopped hanging out, having dinner, playing poker together. Then..."

The *whick* of tires on wet pavement outside

sounded loud in the quiet. Someone headed home from a late job, or a police officer on routine patrol.

"About a month later, a Friday night, I went out with some buddies and had a little too much to drink. I realized I'd left my cell phone at the garage, so I had them drop me off there. It was only a mile or so to my apartment, and I figured the walk would clear my head. I went inside and had just picked up the phone from my workbench when I heard voices at the other end of the garage. No one was supposed to be there, and I thought maybe Craig had gone back on his word and it was another shipment, so I went to see."

He fell silent, his gaze distant, his brow wrinkled. It took him a long time to pick up the narration again, his voice so low that she instinctively leaned closer to hear.

"It was Craig and a couple of these thugs he calls his associates and another guy, some stranger. I could tell Craig was pissed. He doesn't raise his voice, doesn't swear. He just gets real quiet and intense. I couldn't hear what he was saying, but when he stopped talking, he pulled a gun and shot the guy in the back of the head."

Sophy gasped. "Oh, my God. Sean... Who did you tell?"

His gaze shifted to her, his head tilting to one side. "What makes you think I told anyone?"

"Because that's the man you are." Pretend he didn't know about the stolen car parts? That was one thing. How many people preferred to look the other way when they knew a crime had been committed, especially by someone they cared about and respected? But pretending he didn't see a man murdered before his eyes? He wouldn't do that. He couldn't.

He leaned back, and the chair creaked comfortingly. "I had a customer who's a cop there in Norfolk. I called him, and he hooked me up with a DEA agent. Seems car parts weren't the only thing Craig was shipping from the South to New York. The bulk of his business, in fact, is in drugs. I've been keeping them informed on his activities ever since—what he's doing, when he travels, who he sees." His shoulders lifted and fell in a shrug. "And that's how I wound up coming here."

Sean rubbed his eyes, then dragged his fingers through his hair. At least Sophy had enough faith in him to know he wouldn't let a murder slide. More faith in him than anyone else ever had, except maybe Mr. Obadiah.

"So." She drew her feet onto the bed, sitting cross-legged the way the girls generally did. He'd been awake in the dark long enough to see plenty of details. The somber expression she wore. The hair that was mussed from sleep. The delicate white gown with ribbons and lace that was nothing like he'd expected. The curve of her breasts and that little hollow between. The pale shadow of color on her toenails.

Even when she was just the quiet, studious little sister of the girl he was dating, he'd thought she was beautiful. Tonight, looking so solemn and serious, *beautiful* just didn't say enough.

"Your friend is a drug dealer being investigated by the DEA," she said slowly. "And your sister was just recently arrested on drug charges. Are you saying Maggie works for him?"

"No. But her idiot boyfriend does—did. And Davey had a tendency to talk too much."

"And he told her things about his boss—your boss—and now Craig's worried that she'll sell him out to save herself."

Sean nodded. "He sent me here to make sure that doesn't happen. If Maggie keeps her mouth shut, goes to prison and never mentions his name, he'll leave her and the girls alone. If she doesn't..." The chill that had settled in his gut slowly leached farther, drawing a shudder from him. He knew what Craig was capable of. He'd taken his threat seriously from the moment he'd heard it, but Davey's death this morning made it even more real.

Davey had talked. Now he was dead.

Maggie intended to talk.

"Does Ty know this? Have you told anyone besides me?"

"The DEA knows. My contact—" God, he felt foolish saying that word "—is in town, too. They knew Craig was going to send me here before I did."

"Does Maggie really think she can rat—inform on a murderer and walk away unscathed?"

Rat out. That was what she'd started to say. It was just slang, common enough, but when he was the rat, it didn't feel like just slang. "It's ironic, isn't it? I tell her what a fool she is for thinking that, but it's exactly what I'm doing. So who's the fool?"

"Big difference, Sean—you're not guilty of anything. You're a witness. She's a criminal who's trying to serve up someone more important so she can avoid punishment for her crimes."

You're not a criminal. Not anymore. Not for a long time. That was good enough for her and Ty. When would it be enough for him?

"The fire at Maggie's house? That was Craig?"

He nodded.

"And the man who approached Dahlia?"

"Yeah."

"Is the DEA any closer to catching this guy?"

His smile was crooked. "Special Agent Baker doesn't share that kind of information with me. She's not the confiding type."

"She, huh? Young or old?"

He called up an image of the woman and tried to put years to the face. It was impossible. "Somewhere past twenty-five and not yet close to fifty."

"Pretty?"

Yeah, in the way a marble statue was pretty. Cold, hard, unyielding. "I never noticed."

A smile flashed across Sophy's face. "Good answer." Then she sobered again. "Will you have to testify against him? Will he try to kill you?"

"I don't know. Special Agent Baker seems to think their case will be strong enough without putting me on the stand, but there's no guarantees." Another thing he'd put out of his mind. As long as he didn't dwell on it, he didn't have to consider the worst-case scenario.

And he accused Maggie of living in a fantasy world.

"So to make Craig happy, Maggie needs to commit to spending a huge chunk of her life in prison, and you have to possibly make yourself a target. I haven't met him, and already I don't like him." After a moment, Sophy gracefully unfolded her legs and stood up, walked across the room and closed the door. The lock clicked in the sudden silence before she came back.

She took his hand and tugged forward as she tumbled back onto the bed. Caught off guard, he followed her down, getting one arm out to brace himself a second before landing on top of her. "When you say, 'We need to talk,' you don't skimp on the seriousness, do you?"

Her hair tumbled around her, and her small breasts strained against the fabric of her gown as she gave him the sweetest, naughtiest of smiles. "How about we quit talking at all for a while?"

He rested his forehead against hers, his eyes closed. He'd told her everything, and she still wanted him. Still wanted *this*. He was… Hell, he didn't even know the word to describe how he felt. Lucky. Grateful. Humbled. Aroused. Oh, yeah, nothing to give a guy a hard-on like a woman who deserved so much better but wanted him anyway, with her eyes wide-open.

Her hands were resting on his shoulders, small, delicate, sending heat into his skin, and her body was radiating heat, as well. When he lifted his head to look at her, he found her staring at him with such… tenderness. Had any woman ever felt tenderness for him?

He couldn't recall.

"They say every cloud has a silver lining," she whispered, "and you, Sean Holigan, are mine."

Of course he kissed her. After words like that, how could he not? He took her mouth, searching for some tenderness of his own but finding only need and demand and hunger of a fierceness he'd never known. He explored her mouth and stroked her tongue, swallowing a groan as she slid her hands down his spine, rousing shivers everywhere she touched.

When she reached his jeans, she fitted her hands into the breath of space between them, and he shifted his weight to accommodate them, to give her room to undo the metal button, to slide the zipper tab down, to push at the denim. A middle-of-the-night conversation alone in her bedroom had seemed to require something besides the boxers he'd been wearing, and now the jeans were the best and worst idea he'd had in a long time. Best because her fingers were agile and talented and fumbling and touched everywhere, worst because her fingers were agile and talented and fumbling and touched everywhere. If she brushed his erection one more time, he'd be lucky to make it—

With a grunt that was both pleasure and torment, he pulled her hands away, rolled onto his back and shucked his clothes, then drew her on top of him. Her long blond hair fell around her face, the ends tickling his chest and shoulders and the stubble of his beard, and the soft white gown settled in puffs over his body, brushing, teasing, heating his blood.

He kissed her lips, her jaw, her throat, over skin and bone and muscle, until her gown blocked his access. "How do I get this thing off?" His voice was rough, his breathing barely sufficient, as he tugged at a strap, pushed at a fold of material.

"There are thirty-two itty-bitty buttons down the

front," she said in an air-starved tone, then she braced herself against his chest and sat up—oh, sweet damnation, sat up, her bottom cradling his penis, and shifted sensuously. "Or we can just do this."

Grasping the hem of the gown, she rose onto her knees, pulled it over her head and dangled it to one side of the bed. He didn't see where it fell, didn't care, because now she was naked, and *beautiful* still didn't come close to being adequate, and she was settling her hips over his again.

He stroked her breasts, spanned her waist with his hands, explored the curve of her hips. The catch of her breath told him when she liked something, and a pleading whimper told him when she really liked it. Blood pounded through his body, rushing and throbbing, draining him of thought and worry and concern, filling him with nothing but pure, sweet sensation that had an edge like a razor. It took every bit of his control to not grab her, roll her over and slide inside her, fill her, feel her, but he managed— barely.

Until he didn't. She was leaving hot, wet kisses along his jaw, down his throat, across his chest, and his restraint snapped. He lifted her to the side, grabbed a condom from his jeans pocket, sheathed himself in it, then sank slowly, deeply inside her. Sweat broke out along his forehead, and the razor inside him began to slice, demanding release of the emotions he'd never felt, the intimacy he'd never known, the satisfaction he'd never thought he would have.

It was an easy matter, matching his rhythm to hers, lifting her hips so he could fill her more deeply, touches and kisses that made them both struggle for air, that made their skin quiver and their muscles tighten like a spring. Faster, hotter, harder, sweeter, building the emotional bond that he'd always avoided, the affection need desire longing wanting yearning entreaty hunger breath-stealing soul-stealing vital-as-air hunger.

Sophy came first, small explosions of delight, guttural groans, trembling body, a flash of golden heat that held to him as if he might keep her safe, hold her together, bring her back to her senses when it was time.

His orgasm was a few heartbeats later, throbbing through his body, making his arms and legs weak, leaving him shaking like a small child experiencing the ten best things in life all at once. Slowly he lowered himself to the mattress, arms too tired to hold him, muscles too knotted to relax, and he rested his head on her shoulder.

As his breathing slowed and evened and blood began to flow to his brain again, he recalled when he'd thought that Sophy would teach him that he'd been sleeping and having sex all wrong because he'd been doing it without her. He hadn't been *all* wrong about the sex part. He'd understood the basics of it.

But sex for its own sake with the girl of the moment had nothing on making love to the woman he had somehow gone and fallen in love with. *That* sex was the most incredible best anything ever.

Sophy had known odds were good that she would fall in love with Sean—not at first sight, like her parents, or even third or tenth. Love at first orgasm—

that made her sound like a loose woman, but all that kissing and touching and sweating and sharing had clarified the maybes in her brain. Any man who could make love to her like that was well worth keeping.

If he agreed to be kept.

All the warm, fuzzy feelings were still enveloping her hours later, after waking up with Sean, breakfasting with the kids, taking Dahlia to school, spending the morning together with Daisy-of-the-million-questions between them. There was a bit of a hypervigilant air about them, but frankly, it was hard for Sophy, when everything was so perfectly right in her world, to keep reminding herself that, outside their little cocoon, there were still problems.

After the regular Friday shipment to the shop, Sophy had claimed a little quiet for herself by sending Sean and Daisy into the storeroom to unpack and inventory the order. There were fabrics for Halloween, autumn, Thanksgiving and Christmas, with all the accompanying stuff—matching threads, patterns, accessories to turn little girls into princesses or rock stars, little boys into superheroes and sports stars. It should take them a while, long enough for Sophy to relive last night from every romantic angle possible.

She was working at one of the cutting tables, templates and quilt pieces spread around her. Next week's advanced class was learning a new pattern, one with lots of points, odd angles and circles, one to test their skills and their patience. There were six students in the class, including one lady whose skills weren't nearly as advanced as her ego, but no number of polite suggestions could convince her to move to the intermediate class.

Sophy smiled fondly. That was okay. She had a lot of patience herself. In fact, today she felt as if she could do anything. She'd had the best sex, the best romantic night of her life, and she'd officially Fallen In Love. She was superwoman; hear her roar.

As she noted measurements and yardages and tips on keeping the pieces of fabric in the proper order, she let her mind wander to the Double Wedding Ring quilt hanging above the stairs. It was an old one that Grandma Marchand had received as a wedding gift, well worn and long used, and had inspired the similar quilts Sophy had made for each of her siblings. Only Reba and Miri had received theirs. Chloe's and Oliver's were stored in boxes in back, waiting for their marriages, and Sophy's…well, she hadn't started her own yet. It sounded silly, when she'd made her birth family's quilts not having seen them in twenty years, not knowing if she would ever see them again, but she'd wanted to meet her groom before starting her wedding quilt.

Once she finished Dahlia's coverlet—and Daisy's and Sean's—could she start planning her own? Or would he leave Copper Lake, as he'd warned her from the beginning, and break her heart?

If he left and asked her to go with him, would she?

It was too perfect a day to worry about that. She was still basking in the sensations of last night. No thoughts of heartache allowed.

She was pinning together the pieces that made up one square, studying the lines, determining the quickest, most efficient way of seaming the section, when the storeroom door opened and Daisy raced out. Sean followed at a slower pace, hands behind his back.

"We're finished with the invatory, and guess what?" Daisy climbed onto the tall stool at the end of the table and shoved her hair from her face. "I found some 'terial for a dress, and Uncle Sean said maybe you'd make it for me."

That was scary, coming from a five-year-old who'd just helped unpack Halloween-themed fabric. Sophy gave Sean a raised-brow look, but he merely grinned and kept his hands hidden. "A dress, huh? What kind?"

"A church dress. If I gotta go, I may as well show some—" Daisy's gaze shifted to Sean. "Some what?"

"Style."

"Yeah, that. Will you do it? Make me a dress?"

Her little face was just so appealing, her dark eyes dancing with anticipation, that Sophy couldn't resist giving in. No matter how awful the fabric was for a dress. "Yes, I'll make you a dress. Can I see the material now?"

Sean leaned over Daisy, laying the bolt on the clear space at the end of the table, and Sophy silently groaned. It was black, with giant spooky orange spiders sitting on deep purple webs. She couldn't imagine walking into church with Daisy in that—all the looks they would both get. The snickers, the smiles, the laughter, all of it encouraging Daisy to be as outrageous as she wanted to be. *What were you thinking?* Rae would ask, but Reba wouldn't be so kind. *Have you lost your freaking mind?*

Daisy and Sean were waiting for a response, so she gave one. "Eek! Spiders! Get 'em away!"

"They're not *real* spiders, Sophy," Daisy said with exaggerated patience.

That was the first time she'd called her by name, and it brought a lump to Sophy's throat and dampness to her eyes. She swallowed, sniffled, then pulled a few yards from the bolt and wrapped them around Daisy before stepping back to look. "I think it looks spook-tacular, don't you, Sean?"

"It's boo-tiful."

Daisy collapsed in a fit of giggles. Sophy unwrapped the material and rolled it up again, then watched her slide to the floor and skip down the aisle, chanting, "I'm gonna have a spider dress."

"Nice to see her happy, isn't it?" Sean murmured, wrapping his arms around Sophy from behind.

"Yes. It is." She clasped her hands over his, loving the strength and the calluses from years of hard work. Those calluses made for some interesting sensations when he touched her—gentle touch, rough finger pads, followed by the silky, liquid heat of his tongue… Ah, she would fan herself if it didn't require letting go of him.

"Daisy pointed out that it's been a loooong time since breakfast. You want to close up and get some lunch?"

She'd rather close up and go to bed. Sadly, Daisy didn't take naps, and it would feel just a little weird making love with Sean in her bedroom while Daisy was awake in the living room.

She gave a soft, disappointed sigh, and Sean laughed. "You're thinking what I'm thinking."

Giving him an arch look over her shoulder, she shifted her body against his and found proof that he *was* considering the same thing. "Really? You're thinking that I need to get this class prep finished and start working on the holiday displays, too?"

"Aw, Sophy, you could hurt a man's ego like that." He nuzzled her ear a moment before releasing her. "Since you're more interested in working—"

"And you're more interested in food."

"—how about I go out and get something and bring it back?"

"That would be sweet."

They settled on sandwiches from Ellie's Deli— *Sammiches!* Daisy cheered—and Sophy called in the order. Ten minutes later, Sean left on foot to pick them up.

After a moment, Daisy climbed back onto the stool, sat and started swinging her legs, hitting the cupboards underneath the tabletop with a *thunk*. "Are you really gonna make me a dress with spiders?"

"Do you really want one?"

Daisy slumped in her chair and stared at the ceiling before scratching her nose. "Kind of, but not really. Me and Uncle Sean thought you would say no, so we was joking." A sly gleam came into her eyes. "But one with skeletons would be cool!"

"I'll make you a dress out of whatever material you want, sweetie."

"And Dahlia, too?"

"Sure." Stacking the pieces for the class together, she left everything on the counter near the computer. She would type her notes, print them and put together packets for the students, as well as a selection of fabrics for two of her students. They were skilled piecers and beautiful quilters, but with all their experience, they lacked the confidence to choose their own prints and colors.

She'd just walked back to the worktable when a horn outside drew her attention that way. It was sunny and hot, and everyone was dressed accordingly—light dresses, dress pants and shirts sans suit coats, shorts and sleeveless tops. A group of older women in bright florals and purple hats were strolling through the gardens at River's Edge, and a younger woman in cropped pants pulled a wagon carrying two small kids and a puppy along the sidewalk.

Maybe that was what made the three men outside the gate catch Sophy's attention, because they looked out of place. The tallest of the three wore an elegant pale gray suit, and the other two were dressed in jeans, polo shirts and windbreakers.

Something niggled at the back of Sophy's neck. It wasn't their dark shades; practically everyone wore those. It was just a sense of...*wrongness*. She couldn't identify it any further. When they turned and walked through the gate, she didn't try. She just reacted. "Daisy, come here. Hurry."

The girl slid to the floor and came around the table. Crouching, Sophy opened one of the cupboard doors and gestured. "Listen to me, sweetie," she whispered. "I need you to get in here and be very, very quiet, and don't come out unless Sean or I tell you to. Can you do that?"

Daisy slid inside, wrapped her arms around her knees and grinned. "I'm a good hider. Am I gonna surprise Uncle Sean?"

"Yes, you are. Remember, no noise at all." Sophy grabbed the flashlight she kept on the table to help her locate stuff in the large cabinet, gave it to Daisy, then closed the door and stood just as the bell at the front door rang.

The first one into the store was Zeke, of the auburn hair, blue eyes and big strong muscles. In insurance and crisis control, and full of questions about Daisy and Dahlia and their mom. He could make a woman feel safe, she remembered thinking, but there was nothing that felt *safe* anywhere around here. The man in the suit came next, trailed by a walking mountain of muscles. The third guy stayed by the door while Zeke and the other approached her.

Sophy's smile was bland and steady, though she was shaking inside. "Good morning."

"Hey, Soph." It was Zeke who replied as he swiped at his forehead. "Damn, it feels good in here. You wouldn't believe how hot it is outside."

"Especially when you're wearing a jacket." For what? Concealment? And what might he—they—be concealing? If the tension that had snaked down her spine and into her gut was anything to go by, she'd say weapons. She'd dated a lot of cops who were armed on and off duty. Handguns could be hard to hide completely with just a shirt. "What can I do for you today?"

The man in the suit smiled, but it was too big, too oily, his gaze searching the room too curiously. "We're looking for Sean."

Sophy pressed her hands together out of sight and kept her own gaze from darting anxiously to the door only by pure will. "He's not here. You might try back in a few hours."

The man smiled again, toothy, feral, reminding her of a predator who'd just spotted his prey. "Then you'll do. By the way, my associate failed to introduce us. You're Sophy Marchand. I have to admit, I've been curious about the woman who could capture Sean's attention so thoroughly."

Barely able to breathe, to keep her voice steady, she asked, "Who are you?"

The smile disappeared, giving her a moment to note that he appeared less dangerous without it. Then any question of possible danger disappeared, as well, thanks to his cool reply. "I'm Craig Kolinski."

Sean's neighborhood in Norfolk wasn't really the walking sort. The only restaurants were fast food, the businesses mostly automotive or industrial, with a few bars in between. The closest grocery store was three miles away, the closest restaurant with tables and waiters just past that. He understood why Sophy lived downtown here, why she preferred to walk wherever she could. It was convenient. Homey.

He'd been thinking a lot about homeyness lately, whether here, Norfolk or someplace else. He could live there; he couldn't live here. Truth was, he could live wherever he had reason to live.

The smells coming from the bags he carried were making his mouth water. Sophy's toasted ham-and-cheese and Daisy's grilled-cheese *sammich* brought a growl from his stomach as he turned onto Oglethorpe. Since he hadn't bought drinks—Sophy kept the shop refrigerator stocked—he'd splurged on desserts instead, decadent small pies, maybe four bites each. The girls campaigned regularly for an eat-dessert-first rule, and today he might join them.

He checked cars on the street and traffic around before he went through the gate. His shoes on the steps were probably warning enough to Sophy and Daisy, but the bell added its own alert as he went inside.

There was no sign of Sophy or Daisy. The table where she'd been working was clean now except for the spider fabric and the small pile of stuff she always kept at the other end

Slowly he moved along the aisle to the table, his gaze shifting constantly, his ears straining for some sound. He saw, heard nothing.

Maybe they went upstairs to the apartment. Maybe they were in the storeroom or Daisy had made a mess and they were cleaning it in the bathroom. Reaching the table, he set the bags down, took a step or two toward the back, then picked up the sound of rustling right behind him. It stilled as quickly as it had started. Still, his gaze searched the area of the worktable, then settled on the cabinets underneath.

Standing to one side, he drew a breath, then opened one of the double doors in the middle. A light bounced eerily inside, showing Daisy's sneakers, her legs curled back and her shorts, dusted with dirt, finally rising to dirt stains on her shirt and cheek, tangled hair and eyes double their usually size.

"Uncle Sean?" Her whisper wavered as the water level rose in her eyes. Launching herself at him, she threw her arms around his neck and burst into sobs. "The bad men came and took Sophy away with them.

They said they were looking for you, but she would do, and they didn't get me because she told me to hide in there before they come inside, and I stayed real quiet, just like she said. I did good, didn't I?"

He smoothed her hair down. "You did real good, kiddo." His hand trembled, his gut knotted so tight it hurt, and for a moment he hugged her hard. Craig had gotten Sophy, but she'd saved Daisy. Thank God for that miracle, but he wanted another. He wanted Sophy back, safe and unharmed.

Why the hell had Craig wanted him? And what would Sophy do *for?* He couldn't think, couldn't get his mind to function for anything but fear. If Craig hurt her...

The fear was joined by something primal, need at its basest. If Craig hurt her, he would kill him. Plain and simple.

With Daisy's tears dried to an occasional snuffle, he wondered what to do first. Craig didn't need to say *don't call the police.* People who got on his bad side understood that automatically. Just as Sean automatically understood that he likely couldn't rescue Sophy on his own.

Setting Daisy on the work surface, he grabbed a napkin from the lunch bag and wiped her face. "How many men were there, Daisy?"

"I didn't see 'em."

"Did you hear their voices?"

Her head bobbed. "There was the one that asked about you, and one that sounded like he was far away and Zeke."

Sean's gaze jerked back to her. "Who the hell is Zeke?"

"He's a friend of ours. He walks his fat dog, Bitsy, sometimes. Well, once, and we got to play with her."

Yeah, he'd seen one of Craig's thugs with an ugly little mutt on several occasions.

He dug the grilled-cheese sandwich from one of the bags and unwrapped it for Daisy, then went to the checkout counter. The project Sophy had been working on was neatly stacked over there, and on top of it, weighted by her cell, was a large manila envelope.

All of her projects involved small pieces of plastic, paper and fabric. Maybe this was her filing system to make sure it all stayed together. But in all his time in the shop, he hadn't seen a similar envelope.

It was heavier than he expected, and a glance inside explained why: it was filled with bundles of money. Ten thousand dollars' worth, he counted, along with a business card for Triple A Bonds.

The ugly truth took root in his mind. The money was to bail out Maggie; kidnapping Sophy was Craig's way of making sure Sean complied. Somewhere along the way, he would offer a trade, Sophy for Maggie, and when he got his hands on Maggie, he would kill her. Problem solved.

And then he would kill Sean and Sophy, too, no matter what kind of deal he'd promised. Sean had heard him say it before: the only good witness was a dead witness.

Grimly he put the money back in the envelope, scrolled through Sophy's phone book and called Nev. Her greeting was cheery and affectionate, but he butted in. "I need a favor, Nev. Could you come watch Daisy for a while, and Dahlia when she gets home from school?"

"Sure, I can. You want me to bring them home—"

"Upstairs. In the apartment. We'll be waiting in the shop. Thanks." He hung up, switched to his own phone and dialed Craig's number. His boss answered on the first ring.

"What the hell do you want?"

"I thought the message I left was pretty clear, but Jimmy said you couldn't figure it out on your own. Zeke, pay him."

"You expect me to bail my sister out of jail and trade her to you for Sophy so you can kill her?"

"Aw, not so fast on the money, Jimmy," Craig said, and a background groan carried over the line. "That's exactly what I expect, Sean. Hell, I left you the cash. You're not even out any money. You're as big a winner in this as we are. Maggie'll be out of your life, you'll have her girls with no more hassles, and you'll have this pretty little law-abiding respectable blonde if you want her. It's win-win."

Sean rubbed the throbbing ache in his left temple. He couldn't deny his life was much easier without Maggie around or that he didn't want anything to do with her until she'd cleaned herself up and proved she could stay that way. But God help him, he didn't want her dead. She was a self-centered idiot doper, but she didn't deserve to die.

"Where's Sophy?"

"She's sitting across the table from me. She's fine, I promise." Then, in an aside: "Here, say something to him."

Sophy's voice came from a distance, as if he'd held out the phone but not handed it to her. "Did you find Daisy? Is she okay?"

"Yeah, she's just a little scare—"

"So." It was Craig again. "You go take care of the bond and pick up Maggie, then call me and we'll set up a trade."

"Craig, I can't—" Breaking off, Sean clenched his teeth. "Just give me some time with Maggie. Let me talk to her one more time. Let me try—"

"Sorry, buddy, but her one-more-times ran out when she had her lawyer call me last night. She got to thinking about that offer you made her and figured if she could get that kind of money from her brother the mechanic, how much more could she get from the major drug dealer?" Craig's voice was quiet and flat. "She's trying to blackmail me, Sean. *Nobody* gets away with that. Like I said, I'm sorry, but she had plenty of chances to do what she needed to do. Now she's left me no choice but to do what I need to."

Damn Maggie and her greed and her stupidity. Damn her and Craig and the DEA for putting Sean in this position—and as long as he was damning people, he had to include himself, for dragging Sophy into this mess. He'd had plenty of chances, too, to keep his distance, to make his usual safe decisions, but no, he'd been too drawn to Sophy, too interested in his nieces.

Now everyone was going to suffer.

He swallowed hard. "Craig, I can't—"

His boss's voice was barely audible now, tightly controlled, totally menacing. "You know I'll kill Sophy if you don't." Then he hung up.

Sean returned the phone to his pocket, then picked up the envelope again, staring at the money it held. Craig could have bailed out Maggie himself, but that would have required proof of identification. It would have meant associating himself with her, being the last person to see her alive, being the first suspect when she was found dead.

Plus, it probably gave him some sort of sick pleasure to force Sean to do it himself.

How much did Craig think he could trust Sean? Was there any chance all those years of friendship and working together still meant anything to him? Was there any way Sean could convince the bastard that, unlike Maggie, he and Sophy were smart enough to keep their mouths shut? That their own lives and the girls' meant more to them than money, justice or anything else?

Was there any way in hell he could walk into the meeting place with Maggie, grab Sophy and all three of them walk out alive?

Not without serious help.

"Uncle Sean, are the bad men going to hurt Sophy?"

Daisy's scared little voice sliced through him. He crossed the room to her, pulled her close and lied through his teeth. "No, kiddo. She's gonna be okay. She'll be back here in no time."

Trying to believe his own lies, he took out his phone again and dialed Ty's number.

Chapter 12

Unless Sean worked some magic soon, Sophy was going to die.

Oh, his boss and former friend had insisted she was merely leverage, a pawn to be traded for Maggie, but Sophy knew better. Craig's plan was to silence Maggie, to *kill* her, all because she knew a little something about his drug business. He sure as hell wasn't going to kidnap Sophy, with firsthand knowledge of his crimes, and let her live to testify against him.

Please, Sean. Call Ty, call your special-agent friend, call whoever it takes to save us. And please don't come here alone. She loved him dearly, but he was no match for these guys. He wasn't violent by nature. He didn't seek out confrontation. He cared about people. He didn't have a killer's instinct, a killer's dead soul.

She sat in a wooden chair, her hands zip-tied behind its scrolled back. She'd recognized their destination as soon as they turned off the highway: Fair Winds, a plantation home north of town on the banks of the Gullah River. Though well maintained, the property had sat empty a couple of years, since Mark Howard committed suicide on the front lawn. It belonged now to his daughter Clary, Daisy's little friend, but Clary's family had no interest in living there.

Craig and his men had made themselves at home in the caretaker's cottage across the driveway from the main house. The big guy, Jimmy, was keeping watch at the front door, Zeke doing the same at a side window, and Craig was sitting across the table from her, texting a lot, checking the time a lot more. Funny, he didn't look like a psychopath.

When he caught her watching him, he took it as a cue to start a conversation. "So…you and Sean. You know, I'm not at all surprised that he'd fall for someone like you. All sweet and fresh and innocent."

She stared at him. "I am surprised that he'd be friends with someone like you. All corrupt and cold-hearted and violent." Hey, if the guy was going to kill her, she deserved to tell him what she really thought of him.

He didn't seem insulted in the least. "Don't hold this against him. He doesn't know much about my business outside of the garage. He's a good guy. He keeps the place running, keeps the mechanics in line and keeps bringing in money. It's just his bad luck that Maggie happened to hook up with one of my guys."

"Bad luck?" She snorted. Even if she didn't feel brave or bold, it helped a tiny bit to pretend it. "You didn't just happen to send one of your guys to Copper Lake with instructions to hook up with Maggie?"

Craig smiled. He really was scarier when he smiled—the way his mouth curved up and showed a little bit of teeth, the way his eyes went blank for an instant, as if he needed the time to figure out how they should look when he was smiling. "You can't blame a businessman for expanding into new markets. And, yeah, since Sean found out about my auto-parts sideline, I thought it couldn't hurt to have something to hold over him."

Sophy shifted, the plastic line biting into her wrist. Zeke had done his best to make the position comfortable, but some things just weren't possible. "Instead, you created this mess. If Davey hadn't hooked up with Maggie, he wouldn't have confided in her. He wouldn't have been arrested with her, and she wouldn't have any information to use against you. She wouldn't know Craig Kolinski even existed."

From the doorway came another snort as Jimmy glanced over his shoulder. "She's got you there."

Craig gave him a look that would have turned Sophy to jelly, but the big guy shrugged it off. She wondered what kind of hold Jimmy had over Craig, to be so sure that after today's business was done Craig wouldn't put a bullet in him and Zeke, too.

It seemed everyone was expendable in his world.

Sophy was expendable. In all her life, that thought had never really occurred to her, not even during the incident at Christmas with the men after Miri. Her family and friends loved her, but really there wasn't anything so special about her that would mark her as off-limits from senseless death. Daisy and Dahlia would find someone else to love them. Her family would grieve for her but move on. Someone would keep Hanging by a Thread open, move another business in or let it stand empty.

She would never get married. Have babies of her own to love. Chase them all day and curl all night in Sean's arms. She would never know if he knew she loved him, or if he loved her back. The whole lifetime of experiences she'd been looking forward to, erased in one day by a pathetic egomaniacal excuse for a human being.

"Do you know the history of this plantation?" Craig asked after a while.

She didn't bother answering, since he obviously knew or he wouldn't have brought it up. Besides, the history seriously creeped her out.

"Rumor is, it's haunted. Do you believe in ghosts, Sophy?"

"I believe there are far worse evils in life than the afterlife could ever offer."

He was good at ignoring insults. "The last of the Howards to live on this property were an old couple. Their grandson spent summers here, then moved nearby when he got married. Turned out, he was studying at Grandpa's side, learning to track and hunt and kill people for the pure pleasure of it. Grandpa died, and grandson carried on the family tradition until his own death. They say the front yard out there was a virtual cemetery, filled with old skeletons and newer corpses. How many bodies was it they found?"

Through clenched teeth, Sophy replied, "More than forty."

"A killing grounds. As soon as it became clear I was going to have to take care of Maggie myself, I knew this was the place to do it. Years from now, when they find more remains, maybe they'll think it was some of the family's victims they missed."

DNA, dental records and possibly fingerprints, at least for Sean and Maggie, would prove otherwise. But with an inward cringe, she didn't point that out. Dear God, she didn't want to hear that he intended to cut off their heads and hands and boil their bones clean or something.

He shook his head with enough admiration to turn her stomach. "Not many people get to take care of their problems on an honest-to-God killing grounds."

Fierce cramps made her hope she didn't lose her breakfast. She hadn't even liked being on Fair Winds the few times she'd visited, when the Howards were alive and in residence and the old man's and Mark's secrets were still safely buried. She'd had no problem even then believing the ghosts of long-unhappy residents roamed the house and the grounds.

Thankfully, after that sickening comment, Craig scraped his chair back and went out onto the porch, Jimmy trailing behind. Once the slamming of the screen door settled to silence again, Zeke turned from the window. "Sorry about this."

"Yeah, me, too."

He went into the kitchen and returned with two bottles of water, one with a long paper-wrapped straw. *So thoughtful.* He set the one with the straw in front of her, then took the chair to her right, facing the door.

She could duck her head just enough to take a drink of water without putting too much pressure on her shoulders. It was cold and washed away some of the cotton fear had formed in her mouth. "Do you really have a daughter?"

A faint flush colored his face. "Yeah."

"She must be so proud of her daddy. But, of course, she doesn't know you kill people for a living, does she?"

"She thinks I'm in insurance. It's not so far off."

"What? You ensure your greedy, crazy whack job of a boss doesn't get in trouble for killing everyone who gets on his bad side?"

His head turned away, Zeke muttered something. Sophy couldn't be sure, but it sounded like, *He doesn't have a good side.*

A few silent moments and long, cool drinks later, Zeke asked, "Where'd you hide the girl?"

Because Sean had found Daisy and turned her over to someone who would keep her safe, Sophy didn't mind answering. "In a cabinet."

"You did it pretty quick. What alerted you?"

"Three men in jackets in this heat?"

He chuckled and leaned back in the chair. They'd all shucked their jackets as soon as they'd hustled her into their SUV. The air-conditioning had been blasting so high that she'd started shivering before they'd gone more than a block. Granted, not all her chills had been temperature related.

Outside a breeze blew, earning a sad jingle from a broken set of chimes hanging in the corner of the porch. Ordinarily she found the sound soothing, even when storm-driven winds were jangling them wildly, but this one just sounded lonely. Eerie.

"What do you think Holigan will do?"

Sophy wanted to hug herself tightly to chase away the shiver growing inside, but she had to settle for giving Zeke a level look. "He'll find a way out."

Jimmy, she was pretty sure, would have laughed. Craig would have smiled his ugly threatening psychopath's smile. Zeke returned her look for a long moment before standing up and walking away.

Dear God, please let him find a way out.

"Are we ready?" Ty gazed around the room before looking at Sean and nodding.

Unashamed that his hand trembled, Sean picked up his phone and called Craig. The police department's air-conditioning didn't seem to be working very well. The air in the room was thick, stale and warm enough to make sweat pop out on his forehead.

Pete Petrovski, Tommy Maricci and AJ Decker, the chief of police, sat on the left side of the table; the chief investigator for the sheriff's department, along with three deputies, occupied the right. At the far end was Special Agent Baker, dressed to confuse but cool and controlled as ever.

Each ring of the phone in Sean's ear grated on his already-raw nerves. By the time Craig answered, he needed a drink, a smoke and the ability to reach across the distance and strangle the son of a bitch.

"Hey, bubba, how's it going?"

Grinding his teeth, Sean replied, "I'll have Maggie out of here in a few minutes. Now what?"

"Took you a while."

"Yeah, well, who knew you can't just walk in, pay the bail and walk out with the prisoner?"

"No, you can't. All that paperwork to process, and then they take their own sweet time with the release because they can. Okay. You know where Fair Winds is? Old place out of town where the serial killer lived?"

Some part of his brain registered surprise—Copper Lake had its own serial killer?—but the rest of him didn't give a damn about anything but Sophy. "Fair Winds? Yeah, I know."

Moving silently for big, armed men, everyone except Petrovski and Baker cleared the room, as Ty had told him they would. By the time Sean got out of the station, they would already be making their way through the woods at Fair Winds, setting up position.

"Okay, we left the gate open for you. Come on out, and go past the big house to the little one on the right. Jimmy's on the porch. You can't miss him. He's a big guy. There's plenty of parking—it's a freaking plantation just like in the movies—and we'll trade women." Craig paused, then added, "Don't do anything stupid, Sean. Don't force me to do something stupid."

"Yeah, sure." Hanging up, he repeated the instructions to Petrovski, who passed them on to the others by radio. "Can we go?"

"Not yet," Special Agent Baker replied. She didn't fidget, tap her nails or toy with the big black sunglasses on the table in front of her but simply sat slumped in the chair as if the effort to straighten her spine was beyond her. Not a posture he'd ever seen her in, but until now he'd only seen her as an efficient DEA agent, not a snotty-nosed, meth-head moron. Did she feel anything while waiting to pass herself off as Maggie? Adrenaline? Fear? Nerves?

He felt enough of all three for the whole damn town. So many lives at stake, all because Craig had an unholy fondness for money and power and control. Sean had loved him like a brother—hell, better than a brother. How could he have not seen the evil in him? Had it always been there, hidden, controlled, looking for an outlet, or had something changed him in the past fourteen years?

God, he didn't care. He didn't give a damn about anything at the moment beyond getting Sophy back, telling her he loved her, that he could live anywhere as long as he got to live with her. If she could forgive him for bringing danger into her life, he would spend the rest of his making it up to her.

The minutes ticked by slowly, the silence adding another layer of tension to the air. He stood, paced, stared at the clock. His gut was knotted, the muscles in his neck and shoulders and hands tight enough to hurt, needing release. Decking Craig would be a nice start, and beating him within an inch of his life would be a nice finish.

Something must have been passed over the radio because Petrovski stood up, adjusting his earpiece. "Time to head out."

Baker stood and smoothed out the baggy clothing, not even so much as a twitch of her nose betraying the fact that the clothes Maggie had been wearing when she was arrested stank to high heaven. Together with Petrovski trailing them, they went out to the Chevelle, parked a few yards from the jail entrance. Petrovski went on past to his own vehicle a couple spaces away.

A few turns, and they were headed north on River Road. Sean couldn't remember how far out the Howard place was. They hadn't liked commoners setting foot on their property except for the few they'd employed, and even Declan and Ian had admitted the old man kind of spooked them.

But after a few miles, a small sign announced Fair Winds, and the dirt road showed signs of recent traffic. It ran straight to the river before turning right, where Petrovski pulled to the shoulder and shut off his engine to do his job of managing communications. Another right turn led Sean into the driveway. Elaborate wrought-iron gates stood open, revealing a house right out of *Gone with the Wind* set in the middle of a huge lawn. It should have looked like the last place a serial killer would practice his hobby, but something about it felt right. It was creepy—dark in spite of the sun, chilly despite the heat. Being here made his skin crawl, and he swore Baker felt something similar as she hastily folded her arms across her middle.

"Park beside that damaged tree," she instructed, "with the passenger side angled a bit away from them."

Sean did as she instructed, left the engine running and started to open his door, but her hand on his arm stopped him. Her touch wasn't like ice cubes against his skin, he registered with some surprise.

"I already told the officers—that guy Zeke in there? He's ours. Don't try to take him out."

Sean stared at her. "An informant?"

"No, a special agent. He's been undercover with Kolinski for nearly a year."

"Gee, that would have been nice to know sooner."

She made no apology. "We try to keep that information to ourselves. We don't want a dead agent because someone couldn't keep a secret."

When she removed her hand, he drew a deep breath, got out of the car and walked toward the cottage. As soon as the car door slammed, Baker was supposed to crawl across into the driver's seat, just in case "Maggie" needed to make an escape.

Jimmy the goon watched from the porch before saying something to the people inside, then he came down the steps, a shotgun resting comfortably in his arms. He wasn't actually pointing the gun at Sean, but it wouldn't take him more than a few seconds to rectify that.

"Why'd you park down there?"

"Where's Sophy?"

"Where's Maggie?"

"In the car." He gestured as Jimmy stared hard that way. At that distance, with the tinting on the Chevelle windows, it was just possible to see someone moving in the front seat, fiddling with the stereo would be his bet.

Sean stood in the feeble shade of a sugar pine, sweat collecting in the hollow of his spine and trickling down to soak into his waistband. His arms hung limply, just a little away from his sides. When he dared move his gaze, he caught glimpses of outbuildings, more manicured lawn, the straight rows of pines that had survived Fair Wind's timber operation and the tangled woods. Ty and the others were out there somewhere, but where?

Well hidden but close enough, he hoped to God, to do their job.

The bang of the screen door jerked Sean's attention to the cottage. Craig stood on the porch, jacket off, sleeves rolled up, the other guy—Zeke, the DEA agent—a step behind him. Craig wore the pistol in the shoulder holster easily, as if it were as much a part of his outfit as the tie. He stepped down, hands on his hips. "Can you believe this place, bubba? Isn't it freaking incredible? I might have to buy it for myself. I hear the owner's three or four years old. A few toys for her, a few mil for her mom, and I'll own a piece of history."

"Yeah, what if her mom doesn't want to sell?" Sean asked sourly because he still couldn't see it. Couldn't see the greed and the evil in Craig. He could remember all the help Craig had given him. All the hard work they'd done together. All the good times and bad times they'd shared. But knowing what he knew, looking at him now, there should be *something*. Some warning. Some feeling. But mostly all Sean felt was anger and sadness and disappointment.

"You give up too easily, bub. There's *always* some way to get what you want if you want it bad enough. If she doesn't want to sell, then she needs to be persuaded that it's in her and her kid's best interests."

Sean's gut twisted tighter. Do anything, hurt anyone—Craig didn't care as long as he got whatever his latest whim was. "I want to see Sophy."

Craig came a few feet closer. "I want to see Maggie."

Sean filled his lungs with searing-hot air. None of the men knew Maggie, and according to Ty, her appearance could go through some amazing transformations depending on the status of her drug use. A few weeks clean could change *haggard and bone-thin* to *well rested and well fed*. Her skin cleared up, her hair lost its greasy lank look, and her nervous habits went away. Hopefully, they'd think the time in jail had straightened her out some.

He waved, and slowly the car door opened. Special Agent Baker pushed herself out, tugged at her clothes and shoved one hand through the silky black wig she wore, a perfect imitation of all three Holigan girls. With the sunglasses covering half her face, even Sean could have mistaken her for his sister on first glance.

She walked haltingly, unsteadily, veering to one side, overcorrecting to the other. If Sean didn't know better, he would think she was the most awkward person alive or was under the influence of her favorite illegal substances.

When she got to the halfway point, Sean called, "Stop there, Maggie."

She obeyed, her feet kicking up puffs of dust, her body swaying slightly until she corrected her balance. Keeping her head ducked, she folded her arms over her stomach, her left hand tucked underneath her right elbow, right on the spot where she'd clipped her weapon onto the jeans.

Sean looked at the men, searching for any sign that they suspected it wasn't Maggie. Even Zeke, the DEA agent, either didn't recognize his fellow special agent or was way too slick to let even a hint of surprise show.

"Why'd you stop her?" Craig demanded.

"I want Sophy. You bring her out, she goes to the car. When she's there, Maggie will come over here."

Craig's look was chastising. "I can't let people dictate terms, Sean. You've worked with me long enough to know that."

Long-ago advice from his grandfather popped into Sean's head. He'd been having trouble with some kids at school, foul, loudmouthed boys who'd kicked his ass repeatedly when he hadn't taken their insults in silence. *Don't say nothin',* his grandfather had told him. *Don't argue, don't stoop to their level, just don't say nothin'. Trust me, it drives people crazy.*

And so he said nothing, just stood there and waited. Jimmy brushed away a fly buzzing around his head, then looked from Sean to Craig and back again. Craig stared, waiting for him to flinch, and Sean stared back, determined not to flinch.

"Remember what I said about not being stupid?"

Sean said nothing.

Insects hummed. The sun's heat intensified. A boat chugged past on the river. Sean's heart was pounding in his chest, every beat louder, harder, faster, until finally Craig swore, swiping his forehead with his sleeve. "Jeez, man, you can be so damn hardheaded. Zeke, bring her out."

The DEA guy went into the house while Sean and Craig continued their staring contest. An ache throbbed in Sean's temple, the kind that sent a wave of nausea through him and made just holding his eyes open hurt. She was all right; she had to be. God couldn't make him come back here, deal with his family and fall in love for the first time in his whole damn life, then take her away from him.

Zeke reappeared in the doorway, holding the screen open with his foot, his expression stark. "She's not here, boss."

Craig spun around, drawing his pistol in one easy motion. "What the hell do you mean, she's not here? We left her tied to the freaking chair!"

Zeke made a helpless gesture. "The back window is open, and she's gone."

Craig cursed again, the first time Sean had ever heard his voice raised in anger. That couldn't be a good sign. "Find her, damn it! Maggie, get your ass over here!"

Sean looked over his shoulder, wondering what Baker would do. When she shuffled toward them, he turned back to Craig and found he'd moved. His old friend, his best buddy, had his arm outstretched, the muzzle of his pistol maybe two inches from the sweet spot between Sean's eyes.

"If he doesn't find her, Sean," he said quietly, "you're dead."

Sophy leaned against the back of the house, bent at the waist, trying to fill her lungs with air, trying not to empty her stomach on the pine needles. Sweat beaded on her face, burned her eyes, and shudders vibrated through her from head to toe. She was safe, thank God, but Sean wasn't. Maggie wasn't.

When she'd heard Sean's voice outside, she'd felt the most incredible relief and the most painful regret, so grateful that he'd come for her and so sad that he'd had to experience this—his sister threatened, his friend betraying him, facing death when he'd finally discovered life. She hadn't known what his plan was, but she knew he had one. She'd known he would do his damnedest to save her, and he had. He'd brought the cavalry.

Damn it, it couldn't mean sacrificing himself.

Beside her, intimidating in tactical gear and apparently not even noticing the heat, Ty held his weapon as if it were an extension of himself. She knew nothing about guns and didn't want to, but she was thankful he and the others did.

"You okay?" he whispered.

She lifted her head to nod and caught a glimpse of movement behind him. It was Zeke, pressed tight against the building, easing around the corner of the house not fifteen feet from where they stood. Clamping her hand over her mouth to keep from shrieking, she raised one shaky hand and pointed. Ty whirled around, the gun ready to shoot, then relaxed. "It's okay, Sophy. He's one of the good guys," he said, and Zeke flashed a friendly smile.

A *good* guy? How smart was Craig that two of his close employees were both working against him? But it wasn't smart that mattered, she grimly reminded herself. Craig was vicious and manipulative and murderous—enough to kidnap her, to kill people who threatened him, even to kill people who didn't threaten him.

"I need to take her out front." Zeke's tone was as normal as when they'd met, when they'd discussed ice cream instead of handing her over to a killer.

"Just for a minute. A distraction. Defuse the situation and give the rest of the team a chance to move in."

Ty started shaking his head before Zeke finished speaking, but Sophy didn't give him a chance to argue. "Will it help Sean?" At Zeke's nod, she nodded, too. "I'll do it."

"Sophy—"

She waved Ty off. "What do I have to do?"

"Look scared."

Her smile was wry. "I'm very good at that."

Laying his hand on her arm, Ty said intently, "Be careful. And you—you protect her."

"With my life," Zeke answered with an easy grin.

Sophy couldn't find anything amusing in his words.

"Put your hands behind your back," Zeke said as they walked toward the front of the house. "Pretend they're still zip-tied. Otherwise, they'll know someone helped you escape." In a louder voice, he called, "I found her!"

As they reached the front corner of the house, he moved to her right side, unholstered his gun, took hold of her upper arm with his free hand and murmured, barely moving his lips, "That isn't Maggie out here. It's my boss. Don't give her away."

Sophy got a glance at the scene and stumbled, her brain too frozen to even think about Maggie. Sean stood motionless, tension radiating off him in thick, suffocating waves, with Craig's gun so close to his head that the steel almost touched his skin. Craig was statue-still, too, his arm never wavering, his aim as steady as a rock. Nothing on his face to suggest he even knew the man he was about to kill. *Oh, dear God.*

"She was hiding out back," Zeke said as he half nudged, half dragged Sophy a few yards closer. She wasn't trying to put on an act or be obstructive. Her brain just wasn't functioning. She couldn't get beyond the gun pointed at Sean, the look on his face, the terror that robbed her of breath. She would never forget this moment, this one horrible ugly terrifying moment, as long as she lived.

"Nice of you to join us again, Sophy."

She tore her gaze from Sean long enough to see that some of the tension had eased in Craig. He cocked his head to one side, studying Sean, then slowly lowered his arm and widened the space between them again until he stood even with Jimmy. Things were back to normal, back to the way he'd expected them to go this morning, and that calmed his ire.

"I'm sorry, buddy." The expression on his face really seemed regretful, but his voice didn't. It was the quiet, deadly cold Sean had described to her. "You really have been the best friend I've ever had, but I know you, man. You're too honest. You won't stay quiet about a murder, especially your sister's or your girlfriend's. You've got a conscience, and I can't afford that."

"Now the team has some room to work with," Zeke whispered. "When I give you the sign, duck around to the back of the house and get down." He released her arm and shifted his body forward to help block the men's view of her.

"You can't afford—" Sean's voice was husky,

thick with bitterness. "How many millions have you made, Craig?"

"Not enough."

"Remember when all you wanted was to clear enough to rent an apartment? Then enough to buy that motorcycle, then to party a little? What happened?"

"I realized I lacked ambition. The money's there to be made, Sean. Why shouldn't I be the one to make it? Why shouldn't you?"

Sean sadly shook his head without offering an answer. Sophy knew him well enough to know this was the end of the conversation for him. Presumably so did Craig, because he gestured with his pistol. "All three of you, on your knees."

The fake Maggie swayed on her feet, looking too tired, drunk or high to hold her position. Sean caught her, holding her until she was steady, then helped her to the ground. Sophy was pretty sure the unsteadiness was a ploy on her part to tell Sean something. Was she giving him a signal, like Zeke, to run like hell?

Unsure what to do, Sophy dropped to her knees, tightly clenching her hands behind her back. A dozen feet separated her from Sean, less than that from Zeke, whose left hand was behind his back. He surreptitiously flashed three fingers, then two, then one, and AJ's voice boomed across the clearing from an electronic bullhorn, "This is the police. Lower your weapons."

She didn't need to see Zeke vigorously waving her on. She dived from where she knelt, then belly-crawled like a snake on hot steel to the cover of the house. She was struggling to her feet when footsteps thudded behind her. Sean grabbed her arm, hauling her with him so that her feet only touched the ground every few steps. The fake Maggie was with him, her own weapon in hand. As soon as they turned the corner to the back, she yanked off the black wig and glasses and fluffed her sweat-soaked pale blond hair.

Shouts came from the front, the loudest, most enraged ones from Craig. His ranting was mostly unintelligible and punctuated with rapid-fire shooting. Sophy sank to the ground, Sean with her, his arms tight around her, her head against his chest, and she focused hard on not hearing the sounds of the battle: Craig's screaming, gunshots from a half dozen different weapons, a grunt and a thud from the roof above them, a new barrage of shots. She covered her eyes with her hands and silently chanted, *Sean's okay. Daisy's okay. Dahlia's okay. I'm okay. Sean's okay. Daisy's okay—*

Abruptly the shooting stopped. The air seemed to simmer, the echo of each shot vibrating across her skin, and the scent of fresh-spent ammunition drifted as lazily as the scent of the flowers that grew across the driveway.

Special Agent Baker crouched, taking Sophy's and Sean's hands into hers. "Are you two all right?"

Sean nodded.

"Stay here until one of us comes to get you. You don't want to see…" Breaking off, she quickly straightened and strode off.

You don't want to see… Anyone dead? That grunt and thud from the roof above them—had one of their rescuers been injured or killed? Ty or Tommy or one of the others? And Craig... All his screaming and shooting... They'd likely had no choice but to kill him.

"I hope he's dead." Sean tilted his head back against the wall, sorrow etched into his face, shadowed in his eyes. "I know it sounds awful, but..."

"So many people would be safer with him gone. Including us." She snuggled closer. "I'm sorry, Sean. For so long you saw only the best in him, but the worst had overtaken the good. I don't think he was salvageable."

A crooked smile touched his mouth. "Mr. Obadiah said that about me once—that I was salvageable. What do you think? Was he right?"

"He must have been because you're pretty near perfect."

His smile slowly faded. "Who got you out?"

"Ty." He'd whispered her name from the shadows of the bedroom, sliced the plastic cables with a wicked-sharp knife, then dragged her across the room and out the window, all in a matter of seconds.

"I owe him." Sean ducked his head to watch her. "I owe you, too. All the time I was waiting, all I could think was how desperately I needed you—"

He stopped abruptly, somberly, leaving her to wonder how he'd meant to finish it. *I needed you to survive. To be safe. To know that I'm sorry. To forgive me.*

But he finished simply. "I needed you. I didn't even know you a week ago, and now I don't know how I could live a week without you. Am I crazy?"

It felt so good to smile, warming the cold places inside her, banishing the fear, giving her hope and strength. "If you are, I am, too. I'm crazy in love with you."

"Crazy in love..." His voice was barely audible, as if he was talking more to himself than her. "Yeah. Last night in bed you drove me mad with wanting and having. Waking up this morning with you beside me seemed like the craziest, best thing in the world. Finding you gone today made me insane with fear. Yeah, I've been crazy since I met you."

Footsteps sounded a moment before Ty rounded the corner. Like Special Agent Baker, he crouched in front of them. "You guys okay?"

Sean exchanged a look with Sophy, then said, "Yeah. We are."

Ty studied them both a long time before taking his word. "You heard Kolinski's meltdown. He shot Jimmy by accident and wounded one of the deputies, nothing major. We had to take him out before he killed anyone else. He's dead, Sean. I'm sorry."

Sean stared into the woods for a time before replying. "He wanted me to make Maggie understand the consequences of her actions, but the funny thing is, he never got the consequences of his own actions. He didn't want to kill her—she forced him into a corner. He didn't want to kill me—I gave him no other choice. Things didn't go his way, it was never his fault." He sighed and confessed, "I'm glad he's dead."

"Some people deserve to die." Ty stood, extended his hand and pulled Sean to his feet. Still holding on to Sophy, Sean pulled her up, too. "There's a lot of people on their way out here—medical examiner's office, crime-scene techs, reporters. We know where to find you. Go home, clean up and cuddle up with the kids. We can wait until tomorrow to talk to you."

"Thanks, Ty." Sean's voice was husky, his eyes bright, his movements jerky as he hugged his friend, then just as quickly let go. Holding tightly to Sophy, he set off toward the Chevelle, careful, she noticed, not to look back.

She didn't bother to herself. As of the moment he died, Craig Kolinski and all his problems became part of the past, and she fully believed that the past was best left behind. All the shadows, the fears, the worries, the mistakes… In the eternal scheme of things, Craig had to answer for his actions, but she and Sean could concentrate on the future.

And what a happy, bright, sunny one they faced.

Sean was in one of the places he liked best in the world—the garage at Charlie's Custom Rods— finishing up for the day when he heard the voices he loved best approaching the open bay door. Doing up the last buttons on the clean shirt he'd changed into, he walked toward the front as Daisy and Dahlia skipped inside.

Daisy stiffened her left leg, hunched her back and dragged herself to him, making a menacing face along with a growl that dissolved into a giggle. "Did I scare you, Uncle Sean?"

It was Halloween, and she'd ignored all the girlie options in favor of a custom-made zombie costume. If not for her sweet little face underneath all the makeup, it would be a little on the disgusting side. When he'd said as much in the planning stages, all three of his girls had given him *duh* looks. *It's Hal-*

loween, Sophy had said, as if that explained everything.

He shrank back and made his voice squeaky. "Oh, no, it's a zombie! Everyone, run for your lives!"

Daisy *whooped* and continued to limp around the space, trying different growls.

"What about me, Uncle Sean? How do I look?" Dahlia's dress was pale blue and white, reaching to her toes, and her hair hung in long curls, held back from her face with a sparkly tiara. She'd been practicing wearing it—and correcting him every time he called it a crown—for the past few days.

"You're beautiful, doll. You're gonna capture all the boys' hearts." A few months ago, he would have said *break* instead of *capture.* But a few months ago, he hadn't known Sophy.

His gaze shifted to her, wearing jeans and a sweater, her hair pulled back in some fancy braid. He loved that style, mostly because it was so much fun to take it down. "That goes for you, too."

Her smile turned smug. "I've already got the only boy's heart I care about. Are you ready to go trick-or-treating?"

"Yep." He closed the door, set the alarm, then followed them outside before locking the front entrance behind him.

"First we go downtown," Dahlia said.

"Because the places down there have candy," Daisy added.

"Then we go to the houses nearby—"

"Because they have candy, too."

"And then we get to go to the haunted house at River's Edge—"

"Because they have ghosts and coffins and screamy things *and* candy!"

As the girls picked up their pace, Sean took Sophy's hand. "Their first Halloween."

"I bet you were more of a trickster than a treater when you were a kid."

"Aw, we never did anything worse than toilet-papering a house or putting shaving cream on a car. No real damage. I bet you were always a princess."

She smiled, and everything in his world felt exactly right. "So often that Mom bought me a real tiara. That's what Dahlia's wearing."

They turned at the corner to head downtown. It wasn't dark yet, and the evening was just cool enough to make zombie outfits and princess dresses comfortable. A few yards ahead of them, two pint-size superheroes walked with their mom; across the street was a vampire with a fairy and a monkey trailing behind holding their parents' hands. It was the kind of scene Sean had never imagined himself in— homey, small-town, bordering on saccharine.

He'd never known he had a need for those things hiding inside him.

He'd had a lot of anger at Maggie for getting herself in trouble and making him come home, but he owed her a lot. If not for her, he never would have set foot in Copper Lake again, fallen in love with Sophy and his nieces, and had a family who meant everything to him.

Things hadn't turned out so well for his sister. Sophy's kidnapping and Craig's and Jimmy's deaths had finally made her see reality. She'd pleaded guilty and terminated her parental rights to the girls. Sean was in the process of adopting them, and Maggie was learning a tough lesson in prison. It would be years before she got out, but the last time he'd seen her, she'd remarked that she might be better for it.

With Craig dead, Sean's involvement with the DEA had ended. There had been no one in his former boss's organization who cared enough to avenge his death. The DEA had made a lot of arrests and closed down his operations, but someone else was just waiting to take them over, Special Agent Baker had told Sean. Still, she and Zeke would stop them, too.

There was a crowd on the streets that bordered the square. Traffic had been blocked off so the kids could roam freely, lining up to get candy, running across the grass with capes flowing behind them. Sophy gave the girls their bags, then slid her arm around his waist, smiling up at him. "Too bad we couldn't leave the kids with someone else and do a little trick-or-treating of our own."

"I know some tricks."

"And I have some treats." Her look was bold and wicked and roused an immediate response in him, and the mischief dancing in her eyes told him she knew it.

He pulled her close and nuzzled her ear. "Halloween's not over until midnight, princess, and I know for a fact you don't turn into a pumpkin at the stroke of twelve."

"I think you're mixing your holidays with the fairy tales you've been reading the girls." Her voice was breathless, and she became more so when he kissed her.

A call from a few yards away forced an end to

the kiss. "Uncle Sean, Aunt Sophy, come on!" Daisy shouted while Dahlia held her back from heading on to the next storefront.

"We're coming." Arms still around each other, he and Sophy followed the girls.

Fairy tales. He'd never believed in them, not as a kid, not as a grown-up. But he knew now: wishes were granted; dreams did come true; princesses could fall in love with commoners.

And Holigans could live happily ever after.

* * * * *

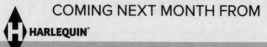

REQUEST YOUR FREE BOOKS!
2 FREE NOVELS PLUS 2 FREE GIFTS!

ROMANTIC suspense

Sparked by danger, fueled by passion

YES! Please send me 2 FREE Harlequin® Romantic Suspense novels and my 2 FREE gifts (gifts are worth about $10). After receiving them, if I don't wish to receive any more books, I can return the shipping statement marked "cancel." If I don't cancel, I will receive 4 brand-new novels every month and be billed just $4.74 per book in the U.S. or $5.24 per book in Canada. That's a savings of at least 14% off the cover price! It's quite a bargain! Shipping and handling is just 50¢ per book in the U.S. and 75¢ per book in Canada.* I understand that accepting the 2 free books and gifts places me under no obligation to buy anything. I can always return a shipment and cancel at any time. Even if I never buy another book, the two free books and gifts are mine to keep forever.

240/340 HDN F45N

Name	(PLEASE PRINT)

Address		Apt. #

City	State/Prov.	Zip/Postal Code

Signature (if under 18, a parent or guardian must sign)

Mail to the **Harlequin® Reader Service:**
IN U.S.A.: P.O. Box 1867, Buffalo, NY 14240-1867
IN CANADA: P.O. Box 609, Fort Erie, Ontario L2A 5X3

Want to try two free books from another line?
Call 1-800-873-8635 or visit www.ReaderService.com.

* Terms and prices subject to change without notice. Prices do not include applicable taxes. Sales tax applicable in N.Y. Canadian residents will be charged applicable taxes. Offer not valid in Quebec. This offer is limited to one order per household. Not valid for current subscribers to Harlequin Romantic Suspense books. All orders subject to credit approval. Credit or debit balances in a customer's account(s) may be offset by any other outstanding balance owed by or to the customer. Please allow 4 to 6 weeks for delivery. Offer available while quantities last.

Your Privacy—The Harlequin® Reader Service is committed to protecting your privacy. Our Privacy Policy is available online at www.ReaderService.com or upon request from the Harlequin Reader Service.

We make a portion of our mailing list available to reputable third parties that offer products we believe may interest you. If you prefer that we not exchange your name with third parties, or if you wish to clarify or modify your communication preferences, please visit us at www.ReaderService.com/consumerschoice or write to us at Harlequin Reader Service Preference Service, P.O. Box 9062, Buffalo, NY 14269. Include your complete name and address.

HRS13R

SPECIAL EXCERPT FROM

H **HARLEQUIN**®

TM

ROMANTIC suspense

Discovering he's a father of a newborn, rodeo cowboy
Theo Colton turns to his new cook, Ellie, to help out as
nanny. But when Ellie's past returns to haunt her,
Theo's determined to protect her and the baby…
but who will protect his heart?

Read on for a sneak peek at

A SECRET COLTON BABY

by Karen Whiddon, the first novel in
The Coltons: Return to Wyoming miniseries.

"A man," Ellie gasped, pointing past where he stood, his
broad-shouldered body filling the doorway. "Dressed in
black, wearing a ski mask. He was trying to hurt Amelia."

And then the trembling started. She couldn't help it, despite the tiny infant she clutched close to her chest. Somehow, Theo seemed to sense this, as he gently took her arm
and steered her toward her bed.

"Sit," he ordered, taking the baby from her.

Reluctantly releasing Amelia, Ellie covered her face with
her hands. It had been a strange day, ever since the baby's
mother—a beautiful, elegant woman named Mimi Rand—
had shown up that morning insisting Theo was the father
and then collapsing. Mimi had been taken to the Dead River
clinic with a high fever and flulike symptoms. Theo had Ellie
looking after Amelia until everything could be sorted out.

But Theo had no way of knowing about Ellie's past, or the danger that seemed to follow her like a malicious shadow. "I need to leave," she told him. "Right now, for Amelia's sake."

Theo stared at her, holding Amelia to his shoulder and bouncing her gently, so that her sobs died away to whimpers and then silence. The sight of the big cowboy and the tiny baby struck a kernel of warmth in Ellie's frozen heart.

"Leave?" Theo asked. "You just started work here a week ago. If it's because I asked you to take care of this baby until her mama recovers, I'll double your pay."

"It's not about the money." Though she could certainly use every penny she could earn. "I...I thought I was safe here. Clearly, that's not the case."

He frowned. "I can assure you..." Stopping, he handed her back the baby, holding her as gingerly as fragile china. "How about I check everything out? Is anything missing?"

And then Theo went into her bathroom. He cursed, and she knew. Her stalker had somehow found her.

Don't miss
A SECRET COLTON BABY
by Karen Whiddon,
available October 2014.

Available wherever

HARLEQUIN®

ROMANTIC suspense
books and ebooks are sold.

Heart-racing romance, high-stakes suspense!

HRSEXPO914

ROMANTIC suspense

THE AGENT'S SURRENDER
by **Kimberly Van Meter**

Rival agents uncover a monstrous conspiracy

From the moment they met, sparks had flown...and not the good kind. Agent Jane Fallon would rather chew nails than work with arrogant—and much too good-looking—Holden Archangelo. But, convinced his brother was no traitor, Holden had Jane's investigation reopened. And now Jane is forced to partner with him.

As new leads come to light, Jane's certainty about the case is shaken. But the assassin's bullet whizzing past her head convinces her they are onto something. Jane's determined to keep things professional, but as the danger around them intensifies, so does the fierce attraction they try so hard to deny....

Look for *THE AGENT'S SURRENDER*
by Kimberly Van Meter
in October 2014.

HRS27891

ROMANTIC suspense

Heart-racing romance, high-stakes suspense!

SNOWSTORM CONFESSIONS
by *New York Times* bestselling author
Rachel Lee

Available October 2014

Return to Conard County...where reunited spouses face a dangerous obsession

The last man that Nurse Brianna Cole expects to bring home is the one she remembers all too well—her ex-husband, Luke Masters. But when he needs to recuperate from serious injury, her Wyoming cabin becomes his refuge. Though concussed and hazy, Luke is convinced someone pushed him off the snowy mountain he was evaluating for a ski resort. And though he can't remember why, he knows Bri is next.

Snowed in with her ex, Bri is blinded by old feelings, an attraction that never died. But the closer she gets to Luke, the closer she gets to murder. Because someone is watching her...stalking her...and if he can't have her, *no one* can!

Available wherever books and ebooks are sold.

HARLEQUIN®

A *Romance* FOR EVERY MOOD™

Love the Harlequin book
you just read?

Your opinion matters.

Review this book on your favorite
book site, review site, blog or your own
social media properties and share
your opinion with other readers!

Be sure to connect with us at:
Harlequin.com/Newsletters
Facebook.com/HarlequinBooks
Twitter.com/HarlequinBooks